Contract for Chaos

Kelly O'Connell Mysteries, Number Eight

By

Judy Alter

Alter Ego Press
Fort Worth, TX 76110

ISBN 978-0-9969935-1-7 (digital)
ISBN 978-0-9960035-0-0 (trade paperback)

Editor: Lourdes Venard, Comma Sense Editing
Cover Art Design: Sherry Wachter
Release Date: October 2018

In memory of my father, R. N. MacBain,

who taught me, a child of the South Side of Chicago,

about equality and respect for all

Chapter One

"We got to get outta property management, Kelly, or else I'm gonna blow my stack at someone." Keisha sipped at her wine, put the glass on the coffee table, and sank back into the couch.

Keisha is my office manager, confidante, trouble-shooter, and general all-around angel. She came to my office through a work-study program at an alternative high school, and I've blessed the day ever since. Big and black, Keisha is a style show unto herself, specializing in colorful, loose, flowing outfits, spike heels, and equally spiky hair, often tinted to match the outfit of the day. She and her new husband, José, are in their late twenties, whereas Mike and I are pushing uncomfortably close to forty. The age gap makes not one whit of difference in the closeness of our families.

I had taken a day out of the office, even though nowadays I was mostly back there, taking twelve-month-old Gracie with me. She had her own Pack 'n Play and almost a complete nursery in one corner of the office. After the kidnapping scare when she as an infant, I still couldn't bring myself to trust anyone else with her care, except occasionally Keisha and her husband, José. I've never left my baby with my mom, who lives just blocks away. That, as you can imagine, is the source of some bitter comments.

Today, I just wanted to stay home with my baby. I knew the baby days would pass too quickly. Keisha was reporting on a young man who wanted to rent a house. It was property we managed for a client, not something I would have ever added to our company holdings.

"He came in, took one look at me, and asked, 'Where's the boss?' Polite as I could, I said you were out for the day, but I could help him. He looked real displeased, but he told me he and three other 'men' wanted to rent that house on Alston. Saw our sign."

I knew the house only too well. It was a square box, two-story, four bedrooms upstairs, living, dining, and kitchen down. The owner was a good client, who had bought and sold much more costly residences through our office, and I didn't want to alienate her. My suggestion that she sell this property fell on deaf ears, but she did paint and update the kitchen and bathrooms. Still it wasn't charming or old or Craftsman, not one of the houses that distinguished our historic neighborhood.

"I whipped out the form, asked him to fill it out, told him we'd check his references and get back to him, and that we also needed references for his roommates. All this time he stood in front of me like a statue, no smile, no introduction. I indicated the chair by my desk, but he stayed standing. When I said we'd need to meet the other tenants, he looked disdainful.

"'I'm sure that won't be necessary,' he said. 'I'll discuss it with the realtor when he returns to the office.' I told him the owner was Ms. Kelly O'Connell, and he got that sour look on his face again."

"I wonder what his problem is," I said idly. Honest, I was more interested in watching Gracie's efforts, so far unsuccessful, to pull herself up. It wouldn't be long, and she'd be standing . . . and then walking. I sort of hated to see my baby grow up.

Keisha's next words pushed Gracie and kidnapping right out of my mind.

"Kelly, you know what his problem was. It was me. I'm black. I bet he's one of those supremacist folks or something. I got a bad feeling about this."

"We don't have any supremacist organizations in Fort Worth," I protested. "I'm sure, but I'll check with Mike when he comes home." Mike Shandy, my husband and Gracie's father, is the division head of the downtown Fort Worth police district. He's wary of my inquiries and worse into police business, but sometimes I can't help myself. At least this would be an innocent question, just to prove Keisha wrong.

7

And I made a note to call the young man. "What's the tenant's name?"

She giggled. "Whitehead. Tom Whitehead. Fits, don't it?"

* * * *

Me? I'm Kelly O'Connell, proud mom of Maggie, who turned seventeen just before this school year started and is, gulp, a junior in high school. She's a star on the basketball court and a good student, a bit shy around the boys, which is why that evening was a big occasion. She was bringing a boyfriend for supper, a new experience for all of us. Maggie's popularity had grown exponentially when Mike and I gave her a used Honda for her birthday. It wasn't smart, showy, or any of those things, but it was reliable, safe, and low maintenance. She was thrilled.

Then there's Em, thirteen, and in her first year of high school. Em is a sweet, protective child—and I use that word advisedly. While Maggie shot into high school and its supposed sophistication, Em remained the child who loved to be home. Now she dotes on her baby sister. I dread the day she'll discover the outside world.

Maggie and Em are the children of my first marriage, which I would write off as a total disaster, except that it gave me these two amazing daughters. Their biological father no longer walks this earth, and I am sorry for him that he is missing seeing the girls grow. My husband, the wonderful Mike

Shandy, adopted the girls with love in his heart, and he is the only father they know.

Baby Gracie got off to a rough start in this world, though she'd never know it. Someone who I'd crossed in my sometimes-misguided efforts to protect others and defend my neighborhood decided to take revenge by threatening to kidnap Gracie. Of course, we didn't know who it was at first, and for agonizing weeks we lived in a cloud of fear. Mike increased the security system at home, doubled the bolts on the doors, and even asked occasionally for police surveillance. José brought a guard dog, and we prayed a lot. We are out from under that threat now, but it had been a rough patch for me as a mother and for us as a family. It taught us the color of fear, the fact that fear can make the closest families turn on each other. I bless Keisha for holding us together and upright during that ordeal.

We are recovering and trying hard to once again be the happy, cohesive family we had been before fear took over our lives. We still occasionally snap at each other, and I'm not sure when I will ever feel safe with Gracie out of my sight, but little by little we are clawing our way back to normality. That bit of history is one reason I was overly cautious about Maggie's new boyfriend.

Those three girls sound like enough to keep me busy every day, but I am also the owner of Spencer & O'Connell Real Estate. The Spencer was my late husband, proud of what he claimed were aristocratic English ancestors and always a bit scornful of my Irish roots. We specialize in renovating Craftsman houses—I use that pronoun proudly, but it's just Keisha and me, and we both like it that way. Of course, there's also my construction manager, designer, and carpenter extraordinaire, Anthony. The three of us focus on the Fairmount Historic District in Fort Worth, Texas and we've done enough houses to leave our mark on the neighborhood, in a positive way. But there are plenty of houses left that need our attention—some classic beauties suffering from deferred maintenance, some that have been "updated" in a way that hid or distorted the wonderful features of Craftsman homes. You might call me a lady on a mission.

We also buy and sell other properties that come our way in Fairmount and surrounding neighborhoods, and we do property management for a few select clients. That's how Tom Whitehead landed in our laps.

As I watched Gracie and listened to Keisha, a part of my mind was even then on supper. Cooking is not my forte but I'm getting better, and I wanted to fix a special meal. Maggie asked for Doris' casserole, a dish Keisha had taught us that was meat and tomato sauce, and noodles with sour cream, cream cheese, and green onions, all topped with grated cheddar. One friend calls it American lasagna.

By the time Keisha arrived with her tale of woe, the casserole was ready to go in the oven, the salad crisping in the fridge, and bread ready to broil at the last minute. Em had set the table, so I was ready and more than willing to sit for a quiet glass of wine.

Keisha declined to stay for supper, though I knew she was busting out of her panties to see the boy Maggie had invited to meet the family. "That's a big deal," she said, "when you bring a guy home for dinner. I don't want to intrude, but you tell me every detail, don't forget nothing."

"I don't want to think about a big deal, Keisha. She's only seventeen."

"Oh, she won't marry him. Don't worry."

"You're welcome to stay for supper, since José is working. You know that." José is the night patrol officer in our neighborhood, commonly called the NPO for Neighborhood Police Officer. He usually works from three to eleven or thereabouts.

She laughed, that deep, hearty laugh. "Baby girl would think I'm spying on her. Naw, I won't ruin your dinner party."

Before I could ask if her sixth sense had kicked in or not, she turned serious. "And, Kelly, let me handle Mr. Tom Whitehead. You don't be running interference."

My mouth was still open when she waltzed out the door.

* * * *

Dave Tucker was, at best, a nice looking but unremarkable young man, and I couldn't understand why Maggie chose him. But then I remembered some of the boys I'd subjected my folks to and the fact that I chose from a limited field—boys were much more interested in cheerleaders and party girls than in the shy bookworm that was me. Of course, I saw Maggie as neither shy nor overly studious, but who knew how she came across at school. Besides, who can understand teenage attractions? Not me.

Maggie buys her clothes, with my approval, mostly from online boutiques these days. Dave's shirt and jeans looked like they'd come from J. C. Penney or Sears, and while they were clean, they were rumpled and wrinkled. His hair was just a bit too long, but his face was scrubbed and his fingernails clean. Yeah, I notice details. If he'd worn glasses I would definitely have classified him as nerdy. Maggie was wearing glasses these days, because she finally confessed she had a hard time seeing the blackboard at school. She wore what she called her "geek glasses."

When Maggie and Dave came in after school, I gave them lemonade and sent them out to the yard to play with Clyde, our dog. It was a smart move, because they were still outside when Mike came home. Em and Gracie were in the living room, so I corralled Mike in the kitchen.

"Remember, Maggie brought a friend home for supper tonight."

He rubbed the top of his head, a gesture that meant he was thinking. "Oh, yeah, the new boyfriend." He reached in the fridge for a beer.

"That's right, and you are not to cross-examine him." I used my sternest tone of voice.

"Me? I just take an interest in what these kids are like. You know, what they like to do, how they feel about school."

"And what their fathers do for a living. Back off, Mike."

"Al right, all right."

Dinner was okay but strained. Em was actually the one who asked "the" question, "What does your dad do, Dave?"

"He works construction."

"Oh!" Em brightened. "Like Anthony, who works for Mom and makes houses look great again."

"I guess." He pushed his food around on his plate and looked down.

Maggie seemed to know more about Dave's dad. "He works for a company that builds brand new houses, Em, not like the old ones Anthony works on."

Even I was tempted to rise to the bait, but I took another bite of casserole and let it go. Our conversation was punctuated by occasional screams and outbursts from Gracie, who sat in her high

13

chair, happily banging her plastic sippy cup and nibbling at the bit of casserole I'd spread out for her.

After a moment of silence, Mike asked the other question I should have remembered to forbid. "So how was everyone's day? Em, you start."

She folded her hands in her lap and sat up a bit straighter, clearly happy with what she could report. "I gave a book report today. Teacher said it was good, and I didn't get too nervous, but I really didn't like the book." They talked a bit back and forth about *A Tale of Two Cities.* I remembered hating it, but again I kept quiet.

Mike went around the table. Maggie was a bit subdued, just mentioning basketball and driving to pick Dave up. He apparently lived on the other side of the freeway. I tried hard not to be a neighborhood snob, but I wouldn't want Maggie driving him home after dark.

Dave must have sensed that because he was quick to say, "My dad's gonna pick me up tonight. And the best thing about my day was that Maggie brought me here for supper."

A diplomat. Mike turned to me, and I reported that I'd stayed home with Gracie and had a pleasant day. "The only remarkable thing was that Keisha came by after she closed the office. Some young man had come in to ask about Arlene Tuttle's house on Alston. You know, that plain one. A guy named Tom Whitehead. Keisha said he was kind of rude, kept asking for the owner, didn't want to do business with her. She got the impression it was a racist thing."

Too late, I noticed Dave's head pop up. Mike didn't notice at all and said, "Keisha's usually right about such things."

Dave was a bit bold. "Is she a colored woman?"

Both Maggie and I nearly choked, and Em stared at him as if he were a creature from another planet. Mike said gently, "I think the appropriate term is 'black,' son."

"Black, colored, it's all the same," Dave muttered. "I know Tom Whitehead. He grew up a couple blocks from me. 'Course he's a lot older than me."

I should have just walked away from the conversation right then, but I didn't. "Mike, have you heard any reports of supremacists in our neighborhood?"

He shook his head and sent me a look that I knew well enough. It was a warning. We did walk away from the conversation then, and Dave was the one who changed the subject.

"I've asked Maggie if she'll go to the homecoming dance with me. If that's all right with you, of course."

Mike's face froze for just a moment. Finally, slowly, he asked, "You drive yet?"

The answer was quick and polite. "Oh, no, sir. My dad would have to drive us."

I knew my husband well enough to know that he silently let out a smile. "Let me talk to your dad when he comes to pick you up." Then he turned to Maggie. "I assume this is all right with you?"

She nodded, struck slightly dumb by the conversation. Finally, she said, "I was going to ask Keisha if she'd drive us, since José probably has to work."

And that's when Dave stepped in it. "The colored woman?"

Maggie was immediately defensive. "She's my friend. She's practically raised me."

I was proud of Maggie for standing up for Keisha, but I thought asking Keisha to chauffeur them was probably the world's worst idea. Keisha might love it, because she'd loved the girls and wanted to be as involved in their lives as she could, but Maggie's friends would see a black woman driving them as a servant.

Maggie wasn't through. "Dave, I don't think I can go to the dance with you."

Dave looked crestfallen but was game enough and smart enough to say, "It was what I said, wasn't it?"

She nodded.

"I'm sorry. I guess I don't learn quick. I better call my dad now."

He called, and then he thanked me most properly for dinner. Maggie said a stiff goodbye, but Mike volunteered to wait on the porch with him for his father. I'll never know what Mike said to that boy, but when he came in, he said, "Maggie, if you change your mind, Dave's father will drive you to the dance, and I'll pick you both up. He's a good boy, Mag, just needs a little polish."

She gave him a long look, turned, and went silently to her bedroom. We heard the door close. I wondered what my daughter would do. How would she balance the values she'd heard all her life against the happiness of finally having a boyfriend—at seventeen, Dave was really her first.

Em didn't help clarify my thinking when she popped up with, "I saw them kissing when you sent them out to the back yard."

Teenage hormones, out of control. As I feared.

Later and privately, Mike told me Dave's father was just like his son, basically a good guy but a little rough around the edges. "I liked him, though," Mike said. "I think he's honest, and he's trying hard to raise a good boy." He paused a minute. "I don't think we can steer Maggie on this one. She's got to find her own way. We can only be encouraging, whatever she decides."

That was one conversation I wouldn't be repeating to Keisha.

Chapter Two

Keisha asked, of course, and I borrowed Mike's words. "Dave is a nice boy, just needs a little polish." I wanted to add an iron for his clothes, a brush for his hair, and an attitude adjustment but kept silent. I didn't like that, didn't like not sharing with Keisha.

"You think he'll be around? Like, her first real boyfriend?"

"I sort of doubt it," I said. "What's on your calendar today? I have to play catch-up."

She laughed. "Not much worrying me. I gave that fellow—what's his name? White something—our standard questionnaire to fill out, and I imagine he'll come in this morning, hoping you'll be here. But I'll deal with him, if you don't mind."

I shrugged. I'd sit and watch how this one played out. I had great confidence in Keisha's ability to handle a sticky situation. I did notice that, for her, she was dressed conservatively this morning. Dark jeans, a medium blue sweater that

19

hung loosely from her shoulders, and flats on her feet instead of her usual spiky heels. Even her hair seemed tame and was its normal color this morning.

It turned out Tom Whitehead did not grace either of us with his presence. He sent an emissary, a young man named Robert Dawson. He was a ginger, one of those rare true redheads whose hair had not dimmed with age, not that he was that old. Twenty-two or so, I'd have said. He wore preppy slacks and a starched shirt open at the collar, sleeves rolled back.

When Keisha asked his business, he said, "My buddy told me I should ask for Ms. O'Connell. Is that you?"

Keisha raised an eyebrow, then nodded at me, "That's Ms. O'Connell, but she's busy right now. I can help you." Staring at the papers in his hand, she held out her own hand to received them.

Robert handed them over reluctantly. "That's Tom's application and mine. We got two more guys going to live with us, and I can take their applications to them." He stood uncomfortably but like his friend ignored Keisha's flick of her hand toward the empty chair by her desk.

"Each of y'all have to come in, in person, and sign the rental agreement. I got to notarize it. That goes for *Mister* Whitehead too."

I swore she was deliberately slipping into dialect, but either Robert didn't notice or it didn't bother him. Neither did he notice her sarcastic emphasis on *Mister*.

"I'll get 'em all in here," he promised, "but Tom's the one you'll deal with. He's sort of house supervisor or whatever."

Another eyebrow raise, but Keisha said nothing. After studying the papers, she said, "Will he be bringing the deposit and first month's rent?"

"Yeah, he will. I think he also wants Ms. O'Connell to walk through the house with him. Sort of an inspection tour so we don't get blamed for something that was already wrong."

"Standard operating procedure," Keisha said in a clipped manner. "We insist on it, but either our contractor, Anthony, or I will be handling it. Ms. O'Connell is very busy these days."

And there I sat, watching them and doing nothing. What was up with Keisha?

The minute Robert had signed his application and she notarized it, he left, and I immediately jumped right in. "What's got you uptight?"

"Nothin'." She turned to her computer.

Now was not the time for confrontation, so I bit my tongue and asked a casual question. "What did their applications say those two young men do for a living?"

She gave me an angry look but shuffled through her stack of papers. "Whiteface is director of shipping at a box factory." She put that paper down and picked up another. "Robert is a graduate student. Physics."

I didn't mention her distortion of Tom Whitehead's name. "A graduate student and a blue-collar worker. Don't you think that's odd?"

She shrugged. "The whole thing's odd. I told you, I got a bad feeling about it."

The day passed uneventfully and without the casual conversation we usually enjoyed. Gracie mostly played and slept, happy in her little corner, but Keisha didn't spend as much time as usual fussing over her. At noon, I gathered her up, grabbed a few toys, and went home for lunch, a bit relieved to be out of the tense atmosphere, though I'd never admit that to anyone, not even Mike. After lunch, Gracie and I were back in the office, and I read and sang to her a bit to get her to take a long afternoon nap. She obliged.

Tom Whitehead called in midafternoon and asked for me. Keisha forwarded the call with a dark look in my direction. I was surprised she didn't tell him I was busy.

Over the phone he was polite. "Ms. O'Connell? I'm wondering when you can do a walk-through for the house on Alston with me. I'm anxious to sign the contract and get into the house."

"Our leases usually begin the first of the month," I told him. "Since today is only the twenty-fourth, let's schedule the walk-through for tomorrow. That way, if anything needs repair, Anthony, my contractor, can work on it in the next few days. After you sign your application and pay the deposit and first month, I can fudge a couple of days and let you move in early."

When he said, "Fair enough," I sensed disappointment in his voice, but he didn't argue or protest. We agreed to meet at ten the next morning, after I checked with Keisha that she could stay in the office with Gracie.

Three thirty is my witching hour to get home in time to greet the girls, though these days Maggie takes a big task off my shoulders—she usually brings Em home from middle school.

"Keisha? Drop by for a glass of wine tonight? I've got something on my mind."

"I bet you do," she said. "Yeah, I'll come by. I guess we got to talk."

On that cheery note, I swooped up Gracie and headed home.

* * * *

Keisha often stops for a glass of wine on her way home from the office. Since José is usually on duty, she has no need to rush home and fix supper, and I sometimes think she stops by as a way of putting off going home to an empty house for the evening. But I also know she stops to see the girls. She is the closest thing to an indulgent aunt my older girls will ever have, and she has formed a special bond with little Gracie, after living through the agony of the kidnap threat.

Usually Keisha makes herself at home in the kitchen, pouring her own wine. But this night inspiration struck me, and I cobbled together a blue cheese/sour cream/mayonnaise dip. Keisha adores blue cheese, a taste she'd never met until she started to work for me. Okay, it was a bit of overkill. I was buttering Keisha up because I wanted to have an honest, face-to-face discussion. As I mixed up the dip, I rehearsed various opening lines in my head. What I really wanted to ask was, "Why are you being so stubborn and difficult about this Tom Whitehead?" Part of me was impatient, even angry with her, but another part wanted to say that if he would cause a rift between us, we just wouldn't rent to him.

Maggie and Em were each in their own rooms, having sworn to me they were doing homework and would not be on the phone. Gracie was sorting plastic blocks while sitting on her blanket on the floor. Clyde, ever watchful, lay nearby. Gracie was his special responsibility.

The minute Keisha hit the kitchen and saw my "arrangement" on the table—two wineglasses, a chilled bottle of chardonnay, the dip with a small tray of crackers—she threw her hands up in the air and then plonked herself down on a chair.

"You don't have to say it, Kelly. I'm being a jackass, and I know it."

I stared at her as I eased into the other chair.

"I'm super-sensitive about the race thing right now," she said, drawing a deep breath. And then came the truth. "A woman called me the n-word last weekend, in public, in the grocery store."

"What happened?"

She answered wearily, as though it were a subject she was tired of thinking about, let alone giving voice to. "I was in line with, oh, a medium grocery cart—maybe fifteen items. This woman came up behind me, and she only had two items. If she'd asked nicely or even if I'd turned and seen that, I'd have offered to let her go first. But it didn't happen that way. I'm standing there, minding my own business, when this really harsh voice says, 'I'm going ahead of you,' and that's when she said it, called me the n-word."

She let the words drop in the air, and my first thought was that I was glad the girls didn't hear that. After a moment, I asked the question that was the second thing that came to my mind. "What did you do?"

"I let her go ahead, didn't say a thing, didn't even give her a dirty look. Well, maybe not much of a one. But my mama taught me it don't do any good to reply to people like that. What was I gonna do? Start a scene in the checkout line? Nope. I just swallowed my anger and waited, and maybe that's what's wrong."

Intuitively, I asked, "That swallowed anger is eating at you?"

"Yeah. You know that saying you sometimes see on Facebook—holding onto anger is like drinking poison and expecting the other person to die? That's what I think is happening with me. That bitch probably doesn't even remember the moment."

"But you do," I said, and it was not a question. I thought for a moment. "She called youf an old term, outmoded, definitely not acceptable these days. But what does it imply to you?"

"Lazy, no education, no manners, probably all the things that were true of that woman. I won't call her a lady again."

"You're so right. She's probably all those things, and you are none of them. You demonstrated that in the store. So get a piece of paper and a pen. No, wait. I'll get them." I fished in the kitchen drawer, drew out pen and paper, and handed it to her. Write this twenty times, 'I am proud of who I am.' You can nibble on the dip while you write, and I'll refill your wineglass." I got up from the table.

Keisha's laughter echoed so loudly through the house that Gracie cried out, momentarily frightened, and both Maggie and Em came running. Em, who had appointed herself her sister's keeper, stopped to pick up Gracie, and the three landed in

26

the kitchen all at once, demanding to know what was the matter.

"Ask your mom," Keisha said, wiping tears of laughter off her face. "Kelly, you're one smart woman."

She stayed for supper—meatloaf, oven-braised potatoes, and salad, and we were back on our usual footing. I was curious what tomorrow would bring, with my walk-through with Tom Whitehead, so far, the villain in our story.

I slept soundly at first that night, but when I woke at three o'clock in the morning, I couldn't banish thoughts about Keisha and her new nemesis, Tom Whitehead. It came to me that the whole country was rocked by racism. It wasn't just our little corner of Fort Worth. Bigotry was once again becoming the prevailing attitude of the land, with harsh immigration laws, riots that pitted people with Nazi sympathies against a group with the strange name of Antifa, and a national fervor to tear down statues of Confederate heroes. Somehow, the country had become racially polarized instead of embracing diversity, which I always thought was the goal.

And now, Keisha was caught right in the middle of it. I didn't know what to do about it, but I sensed that Keisha felt this was her moment to take one small step for diversity. And that scared the you-know-what out of me. I felt we were changing roles—she had always been the one with the sixth sense, the one who saw trouble coming, and got me out of it. And now I saw trouble headed her way, and I didn't know what to do about it.

Chapter Three

I approached my walk-through appointment that next morning with more than a little trepidation. What would this now-legendary Tom Whitehead be like? I didn't have to wait long. He was pacing in front of the house when I pulled up. Of medium build, he had brown hair cut so short it was almost a buzz. His face was marred by heavy eyebrows and some pockmarks, and I bet he'd taken some bullying. He wore clean, stiffly starched blue pants that looked to be part of a uniform and a light blue denim shirt with the logo "Central Box Company" on the flap. He was maybe twenty-five, if you stretched it a bit.

And he was polite, if distant. "Thanks for meeting me, Ms. O'Connell. I'm so anxious to get into this house that I took the morning off work so we could walk through."

I wondered where he'd been living that he was that anxious to be away from it, so I asked. I remembered Dave said he lived within a few blocks of Whitehead.

He waved off the question quickly. "With my folks. But we don't see eye to eye any more, and it's pretty confining for me."

Will Maggie feel that way one day? A moment of sadness came over me, but I told myself to focus on business. Still, I wondered what he and his parents disagreed about. "My assistant could have gone through the house with you in the evening if that was more convenient," I offered.

He stiffened a bit. "I prefer not to do business with people like her."

He didn't elaborate, but he didn't need to. I knew then Keisha was right, and I was sorry I misjudged her. "Let's go," I said briskly.

The house was no charmer, but it was solid and spacious, and as property managers we'd kept it in good shape. The hardwood floors were old and a bit scuffed, but they fit the house. New wood might be out of place. The brick fireplace, painted off-white like the walls, worked and boasted a gas starter.

"Okay if I put gas logs in?" he asked. "I hate cleaning fireplaces. Done enough of that in my life."

Well, that was one problem at home with his folks, but it wasn't enough to move out over I didn't think.

The kitchen had been updated in the last five years. Faux granite counters gleamed—no more

Formica—and the gas range was new and clean. The side-by-side refrigerator was maybe five years old, not the biggest one I'd ever seen but how much cooking would four boys do?

"I wish it had a built-in oven and microwave," Tom ventured, and I replied that he was welcome to bring a microwave.

He thought it looked like the dishwasher, also fairly new, leaked a bit, but I told him neither of us had time to run it on its full cycle. If he found it leaked after he moved in, Anthony would fix it promptly.

"Anthony?" he asked in hesitant tones, and I knew immediately what his problem was. He thought if I had a black assistant, I probably had a black contractor.

"Anthony Dimitrios is my contractor," I said curtly. "He takes care of all maintenance on rental properties."

That mollified Tom a bit. "So if a commode stops up, I should call Anthony rather than try to fix it myself?"

"Depends on how much you know about plumbing," I answered enigmatically. After that, we sparred with each other all the way through the upstairs and out to the patio. There was little he could find wrong with four large bedrooms, a small sitting room upstairs, and a bathroom. He turned water on to check the temperature; he smelled the drain; he tried the disposal in the kitchen; he turned on the automatic oven to be sure it worked. In short, he was just looking for something wrong, but he couldn't find it.

He was displeased that the small patio off the kitchen had no gas hookup. "Okay, if I tap into the gas line to hook up a grill?"

"Not at all." I flared in anger. "That's against the law and dangerous. You'll have to call a licensed plumber, and we will not foot the bill."

Things got a little frostier after that, but in the long run neither of us found any major problems with the house. I told him he could move in as soon as he had Keisha notarize his application—no, I couldn't do that—paid the deposit and rent, and signed a year-long rental contract. I stressed that the two remaining renters had to come into the office. What I didn't say was that I wanted to be sure no piercings and swastika tattoos came in. As I left, I was only a small bit ashamed I'd told a white lie: I could have notarized his application on the spot, but he was eventually going to have to deal with Keisha, and he might as well do it now.

When I got back to the office, Keisha didn't ask, but when I took her and little Gracie to Lili's for lunch, she knew I was apologizing. Lili's is sort of an upscale, business-lunch place to take a baby but the wait staff handled it easily and Gracie behaved…well, gracefully. The only thing I said was, "Tom will be in for you to notarize his application. I told him he can move in after that and after he pays the deposit and first month. The other two can't move in until they come in to the office."

She nodded.

* * * *

I made soup for dinner. That means I cleaned all those bit and scraps out of the freezer and fridge, dumped them in a pot, added broth and canned tomatoes, and called it Soup of the Week. We could never tell how it would come out, except that it was usually brown. The girls loved it, and this night for the first time I spoon-fed a bit to Gracie, fishing out anything that might choke her.

"You know," Em said philosophically after she blew on a spoonful of soup, "we haven't had Sunday dinner—a really big one with everybody— since before Gracie was born."

"We had everyone here for a buffet after she was christened," Mike said. "It was a houseful, and it nearly sent your mother to bed for a week."

"It's not the same as dinner," Em protested.

"I'll tell you what," Mike said. "If your mom agrees, let's start small and have your grandmother and Otto for supper this Sunday. I'll marinate some pork chops and grill them."

Maggie decided to be part of the project. "I'll make scalloped potatoes," she volunteered.

That was a fairly ambitious project for her. "You sure? For six people?"

"Seven," Maggie said. "I'll invite Dave. And Gracie can eat a little bit of potatoes."

"I'll do the salad, and Nana can bring one of her fancy desserts," Em said happily.

And that's how seven of us sat around the Sunday dinner table, with Gracie banging in her high chair.

My mother, Cynthia, is known to the girls as Nana and to Keisha as Miss Cynthia. She moved to what she considered the dangerous community of Fairmount from the oh-so-safe city of Chicago, after much pleading. And, somehow, she found herself new youth and energy. After a disastrous romance, which nearly cost her life and mine, she settled on Otto Martin, a clockmaker who looks and acts like a character out of Germany's Black Forest in the last century. Otto is short, round, usually but not always cheerful, and always content to let Mom spoil him.

Sunday evening was no exception. Nana led the way in, and Otto followed, dutifully carrying a chocolate cake that made both older girls squeal with anticipation.

"You have to eat every bite of your dinner first," she cautioned them as she took the cake from Otto and headed for the kitchen.

Knowing she would return immediately with a cold stein of beer for him—no drinking out of the bottle for Otto—he settled himself in the easy chair with his feet on the hassock. He actually folded his hands over his stomach in contentment, and the result was a sort of complacent German Buddha.

Maggie left to get Dave, and Nana played with little Gracie. I swear the child has the makings of an actress. She knew exactly how to make her grandmother laugh and clap her hands—and then Gracie would mimic her. Otto smiled benevolently at this little charade, and Mike's attempts to start any kind of meaningful discussion fell on deaf ears. Otto did not discuss politics, either of the national or neighborhood variety. Mike left to grill his pork chops.

Maggie came back shortly with Dave in tow, and Nana had someone new to interrogate. Maggie managed to keep Nana from grilling Dave by recounting her high school adventures and urging Em to tell all about her school, but eventually both girls ran out of steam.

By then we were at the dinner table. Mike asked a short blessing, and then served up plates. As soon as Dave got one mouthful, Nana asked, "So tell me about yourself, Dave."

He blushed, stammered, and nearly chocked. Finally, he managed, "I'm seventeen, and I go to school with Maggie. We're . . . we're good friends."

That wasn't the meaty stuff Nana wanted. "Tell me about your family. Brothers? Sisters? Where do you live?"

Dave dutifully reported that he had an older stepsister, with whom he did not get along, and told her where the family lived.

Nana immediately knew it was a less-desirable neighborhood and asked what his father did. Before Dave could swallow the bite of food he'd managed to sneak in, Mike jumped into the fray.

"I've met Dave's dad. He's in construction."

Then it was Maggie's turn, as she seriously said, "Nana, Dave and I are only seventeen. I seriously doubt that we'll marry each other, so please don't ask him about his future prospects."

Em giggled, Mike grinned, and Nana had the grace to blush. Before she could say something, anything to extricate herself, Dave spoke.

"It's all right. I know Mrs. O'Connell is only asking out of interest. Tell me, what do you do?"

Nana's turn to stammer. "Well, I'm retired."

"And what did you do?"

Nana looked down at her plate and mumbled, "I was a housewife."

I was left wondering how one retired from being a housewife, and I bit my tongue to keep from suggesting that now being Otto's full-time maidservant was her occupation.

Even Otto apparently thought this conversation had gone too far. "I'm a clockmaker," he announced. "I'd be glad to show you some old-fashioned chime clocks and how I make them work."

I didn't know if Dave was seriously interested or just glad to see the conversation turn in another direction, but he said, "I'd like that, sir. I really would."

"Maggie, you'll have to take Dave to Otto's store sometime," I said.

And the conversation turned to other matters. The cake was every bit as moist and rich and wonderful as it looked. Nana had even brought Gracie a white cupcake, no doubt store-bought, because who bakes one cupcake? "Chocolate is not good for babies," she announced.

"I thought it was dogs that can't eat it," Em said in all seriousness, but we all laughed and assured her Clyde could not have cake. I snuck a tiny piece to Gracie, who loved it.

Soon after supper, Dave's father came to pick him up but, wise man, declined to come in. As he excused himself, Dave said, "School tomorrow, you know." His manners were perfection as he told Nana and Otto how pleased he was to meet them and how he hoped he'd see them again soon.

After he was out of earshot, Nana said, "Nice young man, Maggie."

She smiled. "He's taking me to the homecoming dance."

"You've decided to go with Dave?" I asked.

Looking mischievous, Em said, "Of course, she has. No one else has asked her." She ducked the blow that Maggie tried to aim her way, and Nana frowned.

"I talked to him a long time, and he saw why we were all surprised at what he said. No one's ever told him any better, Mom. Yes, I'd like to go to the dance with him."

Nana asked what on earth the boy had said, but I quickly changed the subject and urged a second piece of cake on Otto, who accepted graciously. Nana still had a frown on her face, but the conversation went on.

* * * *

Tom Whitehead came in the next day, apparently on his lunch hour, to pay and sign the contract. Keisha told him frostily that his application had been approved, but he never said thank you or anything. He just bent over the contract to sign where she indicated with an x. Since he refused to sit in her visitor's chair, it was an awkward stance. Maybe it was that awkwardness or maybe it was his general unpleasantness, but I watched with fascination as he signed.

"Ms. O'Connell will countersign, and we'll send a copy to you," Keisha said most properly.

He looked at me. "She's just sitting there watching us. Why can't she sign now?"

Keisha looked at me, and when I nodded she brought the contract to me. As I signed it, I looked at his handwriting—cramped, childish, self-conscious. What did that mean?

I had no idea I had just signed a contract for chaos.

Whitehead's two roommates came in separately the next day. The first was Jim Johnson. Like Tom, he looked to be in warehouse work of some kind, with khaki pants and shirt and the monogram Whistler's over the shirt pocket. It meant nothing to me, and when I asked what kind of company it was, he answered with one brief word, "Candy." I vowed to look for Whistler's at the grocery store on my next trip.

Johnson was polite but not talkative. He dutifully filled out and signed his application, watched while Keisha notarized it, and left when she said she'd check his references and let him know if there was a problem. "Shouldn't be," he said softly as if surprised at the possibility, and I didn't know if he was threatening us or the references he'd listed. As if sensing my concern, he explained, "My uncle is one of my references. He's a police officer."

I brightened. "So is my husband. I bet they know each other."

He didn't look enchanted with this idea. As he left, over his shoulder, he said, "Morty'll be in this afternoon."

Morton Berman was an unlikely match for his roommates. Tall and thin, he looked more sophisticated than his roommates, a look his language confirmed. But he was also more cheerful than the others. His whole air set him apart from the others, and I wondered why on earth he was living with them.

He was, he said, delighted to meet us ladies, looking forward to living with "the guys."

"They keep me around 'cause I'm the only one that can cook." He laughed as he said it. "So my joke on them is they get a lot of Jewish food and don't know it. They do love my brisket, and they think I invented the noodle dish I serve them. Oy vey! It's my grandmother's recipe for noodle kugel."

Pretty soon, Keisha was chuckling and talking cooking with him. For every Jewish dish he mentioned, she had a Southern equivalent, and they both had a great time.

In another breath, he assured us, "They're great guys. Always trying to fix me up with some girl. I tell them I'm not interested. They do have some strange ideas, though. I just ignore them."

That last statement puzzled me, and after he left I asked what his application listed for employment.

"Jewelry store. Berman Jewelry on the East Side. Must be a family business. Beats all, don't it? Tom Whitehead doesn't like blacks, but I guess he doesn't mind other minorities. He's got himself a gay Jewish cook."

My smile was tinged with foreboding. We had ourselves a full house on Alston Avenue, but was it a loaded deck?

Chapter Four

All thoughts of dances and Dave and troublesome young men vanished in the dark hours that night when Mike's phone pulled me out of a deep sleep. Gracie was still in a crib in our room because of my admitted overprotectiveness after the kidnapping threat. Mike told me repeatedly that I was spoiling her and ruining both my sleep and our privacy. I knew the day would come when I'd have to put her in her own room downstairs, but I wasn't quite ready for that yet.

When she woke with a scream because of the phone, I thought maybe I was closer to ready. I heard Mike mutter, "Shandy" and then, after a too-quick pause, "I'll be right there."

Gracie began to fuss noisily, and I picked her up and put her in bed with me, reasoning it was okay because Mike was obviously leaving. He frowned on me, a message clearly sent and received, but I ignored it.

"What is it?" I asked, whispering as though that would soothe the child.

He pulled on clothes so hastily that he had trouble getting one leg in his pants and cursed softly under his breath. Finally dressed, he bent to give me a quick kiss and whisper, "Don't worry. I'm just going to headquarters. I'll be back soon." I was relieved he wouldn't be charging off to the scene of a violent crime, but little did either of us know it would be twenty-four hours before I saw him again.

Gracie fell back asleep, but I never really did. It's always hard for me to sleep when Mike is called out in the night, and I was too conscious of not disturbing the baby in the bed with me. Far too early, I put a sleeping Gracie back in her own bed and stumbled downstairs.

While the coffee perked, I turned on the TV and stared at it. Suddenly Mike's face appeared before me. He was standing at a mic, dressed in civilian clothes but flanked by two uniformed officers.

"Ladies and gentlemen, I regret to inform you we've had an officer-involved shooting early this morning."

My heart fell to my stomach. All law enforcement lives in dread of an officer down.

Mike cleared his throat and went on. "A law enforcement officer shot and severely wounded a suspect. We are investigating the incident thoroughly, the officer is off street duty and on paid leave for the time being. Officers are guarding the wounded man at the hospital. We will keep you informed of developments."

The room exploded with questions, and Mike tried to answer them patiently.

"Was the suspect armed?" shouted a voice.

"No, he was not, but he was committing a crime. It is not necessary to be armed to commit a crime," Mike added wryly.

Someone asked if the suspect was African American, and Mike answered negatively. More questions drew out the fact that the officer was indeed black. The reverse of the officer shootings we've all heard so much about. That brought me some relief, because the thought had occurred to me that Keisha's husband, José, could have been the shooter, though it sounded like the incident took place out of his territory and out of our neighborhood.

Information came out in bits and pieces. The suspect's condition was listed as serious, but he was expected to survive. Officers had been called to a jewelry store on the East Side. The suspect had not acknowledged nor responded to repeat requests to halt and put his hands in the air. When he made a gesture that the officer interpreted as threatening, the officer shot once, wounding the man. Apparently, the suspect was alone.

Mike looked tired, and I knew he was frustrated and worried. Where was Buck Conroy, Mike's former boss who had been appointed police chief? Buck wasn't my favorite person for a lot of reasons, so I was probably too quick to criticize, but it seemed to me Conroy should be fielding those questions and not Mike.

Finally, after two cups of coffee, it was time to wake the girls, and I could hear Gracie cooing on the monitor. Besides, Clyde had barked to let me know his charge needed attention. I didn't tell the older girls what had happened, only that Mike was called out in the night. We reconvened in the kitchen, Gracie diapered and ready for her day, the girls sleepy and a bit grumpy. With the extra time I'd had because of getting up early, I had fried some bacon and had everything ready to scramble eggs when they sat down to the table. I knew I'd be ready for a nap as soon as they were off to school.

What I hadn't remembered to do was turn off the TV.

"Mike's on TV," Em screamed so loudly that it alarmed Gracie, who began to cry. Maggie comforted her, while I put an arm around Em and reminded her about inside voices. When quiet once again reigned, I told them briefly what had happened.

"Will the officer get in trouble?" I could tell Em was already worrying about both victim and shooter.

"It depends on whether or not they find he was wrong for shooting."

"What will happen to him?"

I was busy scrambling those eggs, but Maggie answered impatiently. "Mom doesn't know, Em. That depends in part if the victim lives."

"He's supposedly out of surgery," I said.

They left for school, and I piddled, half deciding to work at home since I'd never gotten a TV for the office. I worked steadily but kept one eye on the muted TV while Gracie and Clyde played on the floor by my feet. There were no special reports breaking into the regular program, but the incident led off the noon news. By that time, Keisha had come for lunch, and we both hung on every word.

An even more haggard Mike announced solemnly that the shooting victim had died. He refused to go into details but merely said the deceased was an eighteen-year-old male. Keisha and I exchanged long and anxious looks. It was one of those moments that seems to call for action, but you can do nothing. A helpless feeling settled over me as I prepared to wait out a long day.

Mike called about five to say the city was about to explode. "We've already had protestors downtime."

"Protestors?"

"That White Lives Matter Too crowd—tiki torches and all. And they're laying flowers by the jewelry store. The owners are barricaded inside, afraid to come out."

A stray thought went through my mind. "Is it a big jewelry chain?"

"Nope. Mom-and-pop operation called Berman's. Owners are Jewish, and they're rightfully afraid of the White Lives Matter crowd. They usually don't like Jews either."

I wondered where our new renters were—protesting downtown, persecuting their cook, or rescuing him? There was no way I could ask. And I wasn't going to tell Keisha about the tiki torches. I worried about Mike and the black officer, whoever he was, and even though I'd barely met him, I worried about Morty Berman.

Keisha stayed the afternoon, periodically checking the office phone to see what if anything she had missed. Not much. We kept the TV on while we tried, distractedly, to work both on our own paper load and on plans for the office. None of it amounted to a hill of beans.

Gracie played at our feet, delighted to have Keisha to pay extra attention to her, and she napped. Clyde slept next to her, one eye always open on "his" baby, and only asked to go out twice.

About three, well before the girls would get home from school, Mike appeared on the TV again, this time introducing a statement from the deceased's family. I watched in spellbound horror as a family took their places in front of the microphones: a middle-aged man, nondescript, brown hair, full face, swollen eyes, but wearing a suit, dressed for the occasion as it were; his wife, a woman who could not stop weeping. On other days, she would have been attractive—not thin but not overweight a lot either, blonde hair, obviously not natural but with natural-looking highlights and a good cut, a sensible dark dress, and a face swollen from crying, eyes that begged you to tell her this wasn't happening; and, finally, two bewildered, weeping teenage daughters.

Mike explained, if that can be the right word, that one Douglas Hardin, eighteen years old, had been shot while burglarizing Berman's Jewelry. Apparently, he was alone. The officer who confronted him ordered him six times to raise his hands and throw down any weapons; when Hardin did not comply and finally reached into a pocket as though going for a gun, the officer shot him with one effective bullet. He died in the surgical recovery room. The bad news was that the officer had not called for backup and had no one to corroborate his story.

Hardin's father could barely get through the prepared statement he read. The family, he said, was lost in grief, but they had known that Doug had a problem, a strong addiction to drugs that had been prescribed to treat depression. Haltingly, the bereaved father said that Doug had suffered from depression so severe they had sought medical relief—the drugs were prescribed, though more recently the family had been desperate to get their son off the drugs. Prescriptions had been decreased, and the boy had turned to theft and street drugs.

"We knew Doug was a disaster waiting to happen, but we were powerless to stop it. Nothing we did worked." The father stumbled through this painful confession.

"Last night," he said, "was the realization of our greatest fears. We feel a failure as a family, and our grief is beyond measure, but we do not blame the police. The officer did what he was trained to do. We offer to him our heartfelt sympathy."

By this time, his wife and daughters were openly sobbing, and Mr. Hardin turned from the mic to hide his own sobs.

Without realizing it, Keisha and I were holding hands—not just holding but clutching. I looked at her, and her eyes were moist. "No matter," she said, her voice strong as her hands, "that policeman is in a world of trouble now. What that father says ain't gonna stop the trouble, but God bless him for trying. Young people got to start thinking about the effect of their actions on others, not just themselves."

When the girls came in from school, they wanted to know why we were staring at the TV.

"Is it that the burglar shot by a policeman?" Em asked. "Are they both all right?"

Bless her heart. All Em ever wanted was for everyone to be all right. Maggie's reaction was different.

"He was my age," she said in wonder. "How does that happen to kids my age?"

We talked about it, and I asked straight out if she knew any kids who were doing drugs.

She shrugged and shook her head. "Not even pot," she said. "I think that's kind of yesterday. And I don't know any kids that do the hard stuff, though I know they're at the school. It just really scares me that this kid was my age, and his life is over."

I murmured about the choices we make, but I couldn't lecture. She'd just had a good object lesson.

I made a pot of chili, and Keisha went home to see José off to work but returned for supper. We were a solemn group, though I thought the chili was pretty good.

There were no more bulletins, and by nine o'clock, Keisha was long gone to her own home, and the girls and I were tucked into our beds, emotionally exhausted, if not physically. I had not heard a word from Mike again.

* * * *

Mike crept into our bedroom about three in the morning, silently shedding his clothes, but not silently enough that I didn't wake and know he was home. This time, Gracie slept through any noise he made. Undressed, he slipped under the covers and wrapped his arms around me, murmuring, "I am so glad to be home, and I am so exhausted."

I had no words, so I just clung to him. Little by little, the details of his day came out. Pickets had found the home of the officer involved in the shooting, and Mike had to arrange to spirit him and his family away—a wife and two very young children. They were now in an undisclosed location. "He's a pariah for doing what he was trained to do."

At the Hardin family home, in an upscale neighborhood not far from where we lived, tributes of flowers and teddy bears and who knows what were piling up, and people gathered with vigil candles, song, and prayer.

"The world's upside down, Kelly. They should be singing praise at that officer's home, not the home of this kid who had every chance and mucked it up. He went to private school, he had his own car, his own phone, anything he wanted, a whole wonderful life in front of him, and he blew it. No, doctors blew it. How does a kid that age get addicted to Valium?"

"That's what it was? I guess he had everything he wanted, except drugs," I suggested.

Mike deflated, as though someone had let all the air out of him. "Yeah, and I don't know how we fight that problem. I felt so damn sorry for that family, and yet at the same time I was so angry at them, at their son. None of it makes any sense to me."

"Go to sleep," I said. "You need sleep more than you need to figure it out."

Mike slept until ten o'clock the next morning, unheard of for him. I called to tell Keisha I was staying home to be there when he woke.

"Tell me anything you find out," she commanded, and I promised.

Mike stumbled into the kitchen, drawn I hoped by the smell of the fresh pot of coffee I'd perked. I poured it for him and sat across the table, waiting until he'd had a few sips and wakened enough to be coherent and pleasant.

"Mike, what about the officer who did the shooting? Do I know him?" That had been worrying me all night.

Mike shook his head, and I noticed that his hand trembled a bit when he raised his coffee cup. "I don't think you know him. Seven-year veteran, name's Jason Pickard. He's safe."

That wasn't enough of an answer for me. "Where is he?"

Mike ran his hand across the top of his buzz haircut, his familiar gesture of concentration. "Undisclosed location. We pulled those kids out of school and pulled the family out of their house, which is fairly new to them and they love. Someone even painted an obscenity on their garage door. One of my chores today is to get that erased."

I waited, and after a minute, he said more.

"They're in a safe place and being guarded. He'll have to go through a lot. Extensive questioning, a battery of psych tests. We'll talk to witnesses, except I don't think there are any. Whole process will take a while, and meantime Jason's off the streets, on inactive duty."

"With pay?" It seemed an important question to me.

"Yeah, Kelly. With pay. We're not heartless."

I got up. "Scrambled eggs?"

"I couldn't. How about some instant oatmeal, with brown sugar and cinnamon?"

"Comfort food. Coming right up." As I fixed his oatmeal, I kept up my questions. "What can we do to help? Can I take them food? Invite them to dinner to get out of their prison?"

Mike stirred the oatmeal I'd put in front of him and got very serious. "Kelly, as upset as I am about how we've had to upset their family life, I still do not want them anywhere near this house. I will not put you and our girls, our three girls, in danger."

That reminded me that Gracie was napping in her playpen in the living room. A quick check assured me she was still asleep.

When I came back in the kitchen, Mike said, "You might bake some cookies for the kids. But you'll have to give them to me. You can't deliver in person." He shook his head. "I hope this dies down quickly."

"Mike, where's Buck? Why did this land in your lap?"

"Buck and Joanie are, as we speak, on their way back from a Caribbean cruise. We had to pluck them off their ship. But Pickard's in my division, so it fell to me in Buck's absence. He'll be on board in time for the Hardin boy's funeral."

Contract for Chaos

Chapter Five

Mike didn't get his wish about things settling down quickly. The whole city had to go through Douglas Hardin's funeral. One would have hoped—well, let's say Mike hoped—that the Hardin family, given the circumstances, would have held a small, private memorial service. Not so. They were members of the large downtown Methodist church, and they held the funeral in the main sanctuary. The services were listed in the obituary and in at least two of the many newspaper articles that blazoned some form of the headline, "Cop shoots unarmed teenager." It was probably Mike's worst nightmare come true.

"Mom, are you going to that funeral?" Em asked. "The kids at school are talking about it."

I had no need to ask, "What funeral?" I knew. "No, Em, Mike has asked me not to. He'll go with a group of police officers to show their respect."

"Will there be trouble?" she asked. "That's what everyone at school says."

Blast the school grapevine. I had always believed it was important for young people to be up to date on current events, and I worked to make sure my girls knew about everything from national elections to local school board issues, but there were times I wanted to put them in a protective bubble.

"I hope not, Em. But the police will be prepared. There will be extra men and women there to make sure this is a peaceful, respectful ceremony. I'd be much more worried if a white policeman had shot a black kid." *Ah, the words of the naïve.*

"That's happening a lot," my little wise one said sagely. "I know the Black Lives Matter people come out when a black kid is killed. We've even read about that in school. But this is different."

Loyal police wife forever, I lunged on. "This will probably be proven to be an officer responding as he was trained, but we must never forget that it's a real tragedy for that boy's family."

"Will the officer who shot him be there?"

I told her no, that he was at an undisclosed location for his protection.

"Good. I can see how some bad people might try to hurt him." Then she nodded solemnly, and announced, "I'd like to go to the funeral."

I don't think Em had ever been to a funeral in her life. Certainly, the girls didn't go when their father was murdered. They were too young, and the ceremony was in Arkansas, a long way from Texas. "I'm quite sure Mike will forbid that." Mike rarely forbad, so Em knew this was serious.

"That's the trouble with being a kid," she said dejectedly and headed for her bedroom and homework.

Truth be told, I was relieved that Mike had issued that order. I felt an obligation to go to support him and to support his department, but I couldn't imagine the horror. What could a minister say in praise of this young life so wasted? I supposed he'd dwell on the family's love for their black sheep and, I hoped, God's love for all of us. Methodists didn't tend toward judgmental these days as much as they once did.

The day of the funeral I fixed Mike a good breakfast, which he ignored. "I couldn't eat," he said. "Too much to do and feeling too tense. I'll grab a cup of coffee at headquarters."

I bit off a couple of preachy comments about tense times were when you need good honest food and how bad the coffee at headquarters would be. Just gave him a quick kiss and an extra-tight hug. Both girls stopped mid-breakfast to give him silent hugs, and little Gracie seemed to be screeching her best wishes.

I couldn't help myself. I stayed home to see if the funeral, scheduled for ten o'clock, would be on television. Flipping the local channels, I found live coverage on one I didn't usually watch, a conservative station, and my fears materialized in front of me. Shots of the family arriving in a long, black funeral home limousine angered me. Couldn't they give those poor people any distance? Instead, one cameraman tried his darnedest for a close-up shot of Mrs. Hardin, but her face was protected by a heavy black veil.

Her daughters were not similarly protected, however. True to teen style, they wore skirts that were short enough that they barely skimmed the upside of respectability. That their outfits were black did little to compensate, nor did the fact that they were both bare-headed, with long, blonde locks blowing about their faces in the slight wind that had come up. The wind occasionally pushed their hair off their faces just enough that I could see the pain and confusion, and a couple of tears slid down my face as I pictured my girls in that situation—God forbid.

Mike, on the other hand, did me proud. In full uniform, followed by a small phalanx of his officers, he stood straight and tall and looked neither to the left nor the right as he marched into the sanctuary. What he deliberately avoided looking at was a group of protestors, held back by barricades across the street from the church. Their banners read, "White men, Take back your country" and other similar outrageous sentiments. One even read, "No black policemen."

I pounded my fist on the kitchen table, waking Gracie, who'd been peacefully napping. I got an early lunch ready for her, watching the television with one eye. The cameras could not follow mourners into the church, and pretty soon the channel returned to regular daytime programming. I turned it off and focused my attention on cleaning up Gracie and getting on with my workday. I didn't expect Mike home for lunch and wasn't surprised when I didn't hear from him.

* * * *

I was completely unprepared for what I heard when the phone rang a little after eleven. Keisha was hysterical, and I'd never heard or known her in that state ever before.

"Kelly, oh my God…What if…oh, Kelly, help me." She struggled to talk and seemed to be gasping for air.

I clutched the phone so hard my knuckles hurt. "Keisha, what's the matter? Have you been hurt?"

"No…I'm okay…it's just…oh, Lord, I can't even say it…what if…." Her voice trailed off into sobs.

"Keisha, I'll be right there. Stay. Wait for me."

"I can't do nothin' else," she managed, now whispering.

Heart pounding, I grabbed Gracie so quickly I scared her and ran to the car, without taking any of the necessary things for a baby. She'd survive, and I'd worry about it when I was sure Keisha was okay. I'd known for years how important Keisha was in my life, both work and family, but this distress call, no matter what triggered it, brought that home to me.

I drove almost blindly but paying extra attention to stops signs and the like, partly because of the baby and partly because I was so excruciatingly aware of my tendency at the moment to swing completely out of control. Tires squealing, I wheeled into our parking lot, yanked a screaming Gracie out of her car seat—didn't Keisha once say Gracie was the most placid baby she'd ever known? What was she thinking? What was I doing? Dimly, I realized way in the back of my mind that my own fright and haste were terrifying the child.

Now out of breath myself, I pounded down the hall and slammed into our office with no idea of what I'd find.

What I found was an empty office, except for Keisha, sitting calmly at her desk amid the evidence of her earlier panic. Tears streamed down her face, her clothes were twisted, her shoes kicked across the floor, her wastebasket overturned, and the contents apparently thrown about the room, the phone ringing like crazy. As a first step, I picked up the phone and slammed it back down, effectively disconnecting whoever was on the other end.

"Keisha, talk to me. Did someone attack you?"

She shook her head and reached for Gracie, who went to her willingly with a glance cast back at me. If that child thought Keisha was any calmer than I was, she was mistaken. Keisha buried her face in Gracie's little jacket. Finally, she raised her head and said the words none of us want to hear.

"Officer down. I was listening to the radio on my phone. I went a little crazy, Kelly. Thought I was dying from fear. I still don't know…it's not Mike, I'm sure of that, but it could be José. I'm terrified, but not out of control like I was. Nothin' like that ever happened to me. It was like someone else took over my body."

I desperately wished I'd bought that TV for the office as I'd threatened many times. I couldn't believe that no adjacent offices had one either—what would an accounting company do with a television to distract them from their tiny numbers? I powered up my computer and began clicking around it frantically, finding nothing.

Okay, Kelly. Stop, be quiet, think logically. Start with a deep breath. I couldn't call Mike—that was obvious. "Did you call José?"

She nodded. "He's at the funeral too. Mike wanted as many officers as possible."

Plan B. I called the dispatcher at Mike's headquarters. "Mae, Kelly O'Connell. We heard there's a man down. No TV in the office. What's going on?"

Mae was almost as incoherent as Keisha had been. "Shot," she struggled to say. "Critical. In ambulance right now."

Get to the point, Mae! "Who is it?" My voice trembled, and I heard a sharp intake of breath from Keisha.

"Chief Conroy." Mae stumbled over the words. "I guess it must have just missed Mike, 'cause they'd have been together. Coming out of the church apparently."

"They get the shooter?" How could they not, with that crowd of officers I'd seen earlier.

Still stumbling, still halting in speech, Mae said, "No. It was a rifle shot from high in an office building. Nothing there by the time officers got there."

I let that sink in, vowing to think of the ramifications later. Meantime, my thoughts whirled between wanting to get home and worrying about my once-BFF Joanie, who was now married to Buck Conroy. Since Mike and I married, Conroy had been alternately my enemy and my support. Most times, he thought I was too pushy for a female, too involved in police matters, and I thought his department didn't act quickly or efficiently enough. I also thought he was crude, with his cigar stubs clenched in his teeth, his addiction to beer, his tendency to put his feet on my furniture. He thought I was too strict. Worse of all, in the early days of our marriage, Buck had made insinuations about our personal life that I considered really out of line.

Joanie met Buck when my ex-husband was murdered, and what I considered an unlikely romance had blossomed. For one thing, Joanie was then pregnant with a baby that might possibly have been the result of a one-night stand with my ex, but that aside I thought Joanie had better taste in men. Then again, maybe not if she hooked up with Tim Spencer, even for one night.

All this kind of whirled in my mind as I told Mae to please take care of herself and if she saw Mike to ask him to call me if he had a chance.

"I imagine he'll be staked out at the hospital," she said. "But I'll try. Tell Keisha far as I know José's fine. I'll ask him to call her if I see him."

I thanked her and told Keisha we were going home to watch the noon news. She carried Gracie, who was now clinging to her, while I flipped the "Closed" sign out on the street side door and then locked us out the back door.

In the car, Keisha, now calm but seemingly out of the trance-like state in which I'd found her, talked a bit about what happened to her when she heard the words, "Officer down." From what I could gather and the little I knew, she'd had a classic panic attack—racing heart, shortness of breath, cold sweat, blurred vision. She thought she was having a heart attack. I assured her she wasn't.

And so we went home to wait once again.

Chapter Six

No wonder Gracie was fussy, the way she'd been yanked around this morning by the madwoman who was her mother during that scare. I put her in her crib upstairs and turned on the monitor—no sleeping on the floor for her this time. Clyde obediently went to sleep right next to her crib.

When I got back downstairs, Keisha took one look at me and announced, "It's too early to start on wine."

Indignant, I replied that I wasn't going to suggest that. I was going to brew a pot of tea. So we sipped tea, kept the television on mute with one eye on it watching for breaking news. Keisha called the office three times, but there were no messages. I got my laptop, turned it on, and didn't have the heart to reply to emails. We talked from time to time, tried unsuccessfully to read, and stared at each other a lot. Nothing happened.

Both of us knew better than to call either Mike or José, and I was a bit afraid Mike would scold me if I called Mae, the dispatcher, again. So we waited.

The girls came home from school, and Maggie made an unfortunate joke, asking, "Who died?"

When I reprimanded her much more sharply than the occasion called for, she said, "Well, you're both sitting here like you've just been to a funeral. What happened?"

"Buck Conroy got shot," Keisha said, not sugarcoating the facts at all.

That got Em's attention, just as she was unloading her backpack. "Buck Conroy? I don't like him," she said, "but I hate for anyone to get shot. Is he okay?"

Maggie, meanwhile, was demanding, "When? Why?"

And the story tumbled out from Keisha, while the girls listened in horrified fascination. Em had to be reassured three times that Mike and José were both all right.

"I imagine they're at the hospital," I told them, "or out searching for the shooter." *Please, God, let them be at the hospital, where they're safe.*

Hands on her hips, Em demanded, "Will Mr. Conroy be all right?"

"We don't know. That's why we're keeping the television on." I looked at my watch. "News

68

will be on in another hour. Maybe they'll have something."

Just then, Gracie cried, signaling that she was awake, and Maggie went to get her. She came back downstairs carrying a tousled, sleepy infant still rubbing her eyes. I went through the motions—fixing snacks, pouring drinks, putting milk in a sippy cup. I had to lecture myself about the pause—taking that moment before you give in to anger or frustration—when Gracie turned her sippy cup upside down on the floor. Fortunately, she was on wood floor, not carpet, and Em cleaned it up while I stood there counting to ten. All three girls sensed the tension in the air and were subdued.

The five o'clock news finally came on, and we waited again—through the weather, through national headlines, until finally, the broadcaster told an audience what we already knew: the police chief was the victim of a random shooting while coming out of the funeral for the young boy killed by a police officer. He said police believed the shooting was retribution for the death of the young boy and did not believe it was racially motivated. I buried a few choice words in the back of my throat at that.

"As of this hour, Chief Conroy is still in surgery. It's been a long afternoon, folks." And he signed off.

"Do you believe that?" Keisha demanded. "Telling us it's been a long afternoon. I guess José's back on duty, with no sleep. I hope the streets are quiet tonight."

I rummaged in the freezer for supper and finally shut it when nothing leapt out at me.

"I'll go to the Grill for burgers," Keisha volunteered.

I was so undisciplined myself by this time that I let the girls order cheeseburgers, instead of turkey, and let them have curly fries. Then I threw caution to the winds and ordered a burger myself.

By the time Keisha got back, I had the wine poured, and she brought lemonade for the girls. I did not go so far as to allow Coke.

We settled around the kitchen table, and Em asked to say grace. "Please, God, fix Mr. Conroy. He means to be a good man, and he's important to our city and to my dad." Then she lapsed into the conventional and said, "Bless this food to our use and us to thy service, Amen."

We echoed "Amen" and dug in. I'd kept my phone right by me at the table, something I usually refused to let the girls do. When it rang, we all jumped, and I was forced to answer with a mouth full of hamburger. The two older girls stared at me in amazement.

I managed a mumbled "Hello" and then I listened, my eyes growing wide with horror. I hung up, choked down the last of that bite of food, and told the spellbound faces staring at me, "Buck Conroy just died."

Silence fell over the table, until Em said, "God must not have heard me. Maybe my prayer hadn't had time to get to him."

I almost laughed, laughter born out of hysteria. "Mike said he'll call back with details in a few minutes." Food didn't taste good to any of us, and the homeless would have had a feast on what we left behind.

When Mike called back, he was still terse, but details came out. Buck had survived the surgery but went into cardiac arrest in the recovery area, and efforts to revive him were useless. Yes, Joanie was there, but she wasn't at his side when he died. She'd seen him before he went into surgery, though, and he'd been conscious enough to recognize her and tell her thank you. Thank you, I suppose, for giving him a regular home and a family.

I worried about Joanie. When I'd known her well, she wasn't the most stable of people, and I wondered how she'd do as the single mom of two toddlers. I told Mike I'd go to her tonight and get some food together tomorrow to take to the house. He told me she'd be home in half an hour. Just enough time for me.

When I hung up, Keisha asked, "Now what?" but I don't think she expected an answer. I was suddenly thrown from a stupor into action, however, and started issuing orders. "I'll make out a grocery list. You and the girls go to the store. I have to go to Joanie."

The girls protested they had homework, and I relented if Maggie promised to lock the doors and keep her phone at hand. Keisha would take Gracie to the store, and then Maggie would put her down for the night. I had no idea when I'd be home.

* * * *

Joanie was a mess, and so was her house.

For years, Buck Conroy had been rough as the proverbial cob, divorced, footloose. He drank too much beer and chased too many skirts. But Joanie, whom he met at my house, bewitched him, and he married her even though she carried another man's baby. Then they had their own baby, and Buck saw himself as a family man and provider. He lost weight, straightened up both his wardrobe and posture, and walked the earth like a proud and happy man.

And he bought the house of his dreams, an upscale house in an upscale, brand new gated community. Never mind that it looked like every third house on the block. It was at least four thousand square feet, with family rooms upstairs and down, four bedrooms and four baths plus a powder room, and a huge kitchen complete with every built-in known to man.

That night the kitchen, like every room in the house, looked like it hadn't been cleaned in weeks. Dirty dishes were piled in the sink and stacked on counters. A banana peel sat next to a half-empty bowl of cereal on the built-in cutting board; kitchen towels were wadded up on counters, and one had apparently been used to mop up a floor spill.

In the family room, a grandmotherly neighbor sat in a rocking chair, staring at a talent show on the television, with two-year-old Nicolas on her lap—at least I thought he was two. It had been so long since I'd seen Joanie that I'd lost track. Five-year-old McKenzie played on the floor, occupied with a small dollhouse. Children's toys were scattered all over the room. Residue in a coffee cup had been there so long it was growing mold. This wasn't disorder that resulted from Buck's injury—it was apparently a way of life.

Joanie wasn't there yet, so I introduced myself to the neighbor, who immediately asked if she could leave. I asked her to stay since the kids didn't know me, and I had a few quick chores in mind. Quick as I could I scraped and emptied dirty dishes and put them to soak in a sink of soapy water; I whisked up garbage and stuffed it into an already-full garbage can, and I put away little bits of salvageable food.

In the family room, I made a game of picking up toys and putting them in a plastic laundry basket that apparently served as a toy chest. It was apparently a new game to McKenzie, and she played willingly—that said something about Joanie's parenting. At that age, my girls would have protested and delayed until I got firm. Nicolas simply carried toys around aimlessly, and the neighbor looked on without moving from her chair.

Just as we dumped the last toy into the basket, Joanie blew in the front door, with Mike right behind her. I worried for a nanosecond about the other rooms in the house, particularly unmade beds, but Joanie needed my attention.

Her once blonde and bouncy hair hung about her face, looking stringy as though it hadn't been shampooed in days, and her makeup had run down her face with tears, causing black streaks. Her clothes were wrinkled, but I attributed that to a rough day of waiting at the hospital. She'd gained weight since I last saw her.

I held out my arms, and with a cry of "Oh, Kelly," she fell into them so hard that we both nearly went over backward. For a long moment, she buried her face on my chest, while I worried about mascara stains on my clean shirt and Mike stood by looking uncomfortable.

The children stared at her, and McKenzie finally walked over and tugged at her skirt. "Mama?"

Joanie suddenly went from being a limp lump in my arms to standing on her own two feet and bending to hug her child, in a sweet motherly gesture that made me choke back all the negative thoughts I'd had about her parenting skills. She truly loved these children, even if she let them run wild.

Wordlessly she scooped up Nicolas in one arm, took McKenzie's hand, and led both children to the couch. She sat down, with Nicolas on her lap and McKenzie cuddled as close as could be next to her. And she uttered the words I dreaded, "Daddy's not coming home. He's gone to be with God."

I inched over to Mike, who put a comforting arm around me, and we both stood spellbound. The neighbor had slipped into the kitchen, I noticed, and I heard the back door close softly.

McKenzie fixed her mother with a direct look and asked clearly, "Did he die? Did that bad man kill him?"

Tears ran down Joanie's cheeks as she whispered, "Yes." Then she raised her face toward us. "And I'll find out who did this if it's the last thing I do. Buck Conroy was a good man, and he didn't deserve to die like this, not now, not ever." Anger suddenly flashed in those eyes, and I found it scarier than the vacant grief.

Chapter Seven

Mike went home to be with our girls, and I borrowed sweats from Joanie and spent the night. Together, we bathed the children, answered their endless questions about Buck, and got them settled. Joanie coached them to call me Aunt Kelly. Since I had no nieces or nephews, that was kind of sweet. When, at last, their fears were at least temporarily banished, the two little ones slept. Joanie and I settled down with glasses of wine. In some ways, it was like the old days, but in others it wasn't at all the same.

I saw a side of Joanie I'd never seen before or possibly one that hadn't existed before.

"I'm going to dedicate my life to taking care of those two," she said fiercely, "the best care ever. I've been lazy about it, saving all my attention for Buck to keep him happy. From now on, it's those kids. Our kids. It's what I can do for Buck to repay him for his goodness to me."

I wondered if this meant a change in housekeeping habits.

"I'll have to go back to work, but first I'll have to get myself in shape. It's been too long. And we'll move, probably back to Fairmount. Can't afford this place, don't need all the space."

Wow! For a widow of less than six hours, Joanie had really been thinking. I didn't remind her about the perils of decisions made in haste. Maybe getting herself in shape would give her time for reflection.

One glass of wine each. Gone were the days of finishing the bottle and maybe more. There were children to consider and a house to clean.

* * * *

There was a time when Joanie often slept on my couch, and this night as I tossed and turned, caught in twisted sheets with plastic toys creeping up through the cushions to poke me, I had a better appreciation of what she endured in the name of friendship. Still, I slept because I was decidedly groggy when I heard her banging in the kitchen. With gratitude, I smelled brewing coffee and stumbled my way into the kitchen, still wrapped in a blanket.

Joanie was loading those dishes I'd put to soak into the dishwasher and muttering to herself, "Got to get this house cleaned up. Ashamed of the way I've let it go."

"Can I help?" I let the blanket slip down onto a chair and then promptly sat on it, just not quite ready for the day.

"You know everyone and their oxen will be here today. I've got to clean this house, especially the kitchen. Officers and their wives will be bringing enough food for Coxey's Army. And they'll all be curious. I can't let Buck down."

Coxey's Army I understood, but everyone and their oxen? "I'll help. Give me a minute with a cup of coffee, and I'll be ready to go." She poured me coffee, and I took that minute to call home. Mike had the girls started on their day. Keisha would come get Gracie and take her to the office, so all was well. He'd see me shortly at Joanie's, felt he should spend the day supporting her and reassuring those who came to call. I meant it when I said I'd be glad to see him. I somehow had to reassure myself that he was whole and upright and okay.

My next call was to Keisha, with a shopping list. She'd just have to take Gracie to the store again, but of course I triple-cautioned her about watching the baby, not turning her back on her for a minute.

Keisha, who'd lived through the kidnapping threat with us, knew my anxiety and knew that catering to it was eventually the way to cure it. But she couldn't resist asking, "You do all right away from her last night?"

Only then did it dawn on me I'd spent the night away from my baby. Fortunately, I didn't have time to nurture that thought. My thoughts were focused on food, and I asked her to get a ham, some dip and chips, maybe a veggie platter—enough to get us started until the hordes descended with food. I also asked her to get paper plates, napkins, cups, and plastic flatware. Our material footprint on the environment was necessarily going to be large today.

We cleaned. Oh my, did we clean. Joanie took McKenzie to school—she was in kindergarten—and persuaded the grandmotherly neighbor to come back and keep Nicolas in the upstairs playroom, so we could concentrate on the downstairs, the public area of the house that would be on view. I saw Joanie slip the old lady some money and figured out why the neighbor was so neighborly.

While Joanie was backing out of the garage at the rear of the property, there was a knock on the front door. I opened the door expecting an early sympathy caller, but it was a reporter, little notebook and identification in hand. Behind him, I saw two television trucks and a gaggle of cars. The press had hit.

But so had the police. Several squad cars had beaten the press to the driveway, and officers on alert were checking the bushes and backyard. Were they simply protecting Joanie from the press or could they possibly expect trouble here? A shiver ran down my spine.

"Mrs. Conroy is not at home and will not be giving interviews," I said briskly and closed the door with enough force to move the foot he had stuck in it.

The unused living and dining areas had a thick coat of dust, so I dusted and polished until the surfaces gleamed, ran the vacuum on the rugs, and swept the areas of bare wood floor. That sounds easier and quicker than it really was, and it was ten before I was satisfied with the area. Joanie was still working on the kitchen, now unloading the dishwasher.

"Had to clean the refrigerator," she said. "You know some nosy woman will put her food right in it. If she saw all those bit and jars of leftovers I'd shoved in there or all the beer I kept for Buck or the spot where McKenzie spilled something really sticky, it would be all over the city by tomorrow."

Taking a break, we both sat at the table and sipped coffee. I realized I had to get home and change if we were expecting company, but I figured I had until about noon before they descended.

Joanie was still muttering, still working out in her head this catastrophe that had befallen her. "What I don't understand is why anyone would shoot Buck. I could see if Jason Pickard had been in that group. Some alt-right person might take it upon himself—must have been a man—to punish the officer who shot the boy, but Buck? He was investigating the shooting, and one of the last things he told me was that he knew he was going to have to discipline Pickard one way or the other, and it made him mad."

"Maybe some nut case just wanted to shoot an officer, any officer, and what bigger target than the chief?" I shuddered as I said that, thinking of Mike as a target, but I knew my words were true. "The race issue just complicates it. Maybe some alt-right person thinks police are too soft on blacks, though usually you hear the opposite. Who knows?"

"I know," Joanie said, "that I will not rest until the shooter is found. I'll do everything I can—*anything*—to see him brought to justice." She paused only a moment and then said, "I'm going to take a course and get myself a gun."

My shiver of fear was very real this time, but who was I to talk her out of that. A couple of years ago, after too many misadventures, I'd given in to Mike's wishes and taken the course, gotten the gun. It had saved my life twice, though the fact that I'd taken a life would haunt me forever. I couldn't tell that to Joanie.

Keisha's arrival distracted us. "Well, that's some welcome committee you got out there, Miss Joanie," she said. "'Bout wouldn't let me in, 'cept I was carrying this child and one guy recognized me as José's wife. I think they deliberately don't have any black cops out there today. Mike told me this morning there's tension in the city. Real tension."

Busy loving on Gracie, I barely let that statement register, but when it did, it packed a wallop. I was now officially afraid for my husband, my daughters, my city—and for Joanie and her kids.

We unpacked groceries, and Keisha stayed to help Joanie lay things out. They decided on the dining room table rather than the kitchen island, so they could keep the island as sort of a prep area. I left with Gracie, headed for a shower, clean clothes—and a much-needed nap for a fussy baby. As I carried her to the car, I realized again that I hadn't worried about her, even though she wasn't under my direct care.

"Someday, I may even have to let you go to school by yourself," I said as I strapped her in the car and gave her a big, wet kiss. She just rubbed her eyes.

* * * *

Once home, I had time to think and collect myself while Gracie and I both nibbled on peanut butter sandwiches, hers dripping with jelly. I saw a bath in her immediate future. Keisha had been as busy as I had all morning, so I checked the office phone and found only one message: from Tom Whitehead.

"Dishwasher leaking. Please get that Greek man over here ASAP to fix it. You can call my cell, and I'll meet him here. After five is best."

Terse and to the point. Did he really think Anthony was on twenty-four-hour call? I called Anthony, who said he knew they'd have a problem with that dishwasher. It had a tendency to walk away from its connection, just enough to show a slow leak on the floor in front of the machine. He'd have to disconnect it, pull it out, and reconnect it, plus he'd try to brace it somehow so that didn't keep happening. An hour's work, and yes, he'd do it at five.

"You okay, Miss Kelly? I heard about Mr. Conroy getting shot. Too bad. Terrible times we live in. I thank God my Teresa is married to that nice boy, and my own boys are doing well in school. Stefan, he's a junior now at the state university here, and Emil's going to the county college this fall. And that new granddaughter of mine, she's a beauty. You must see."

I told Anthony we'd do a big Sunday supper soon, and Teresa and Joe could bring Elise to meet all our friends. But back to business, I told him I'd call Tom Whitehead and arrange for him to be at the house at five o'clock.

I was hoping Whitehead wouldn't answer and I could leave a message, but no such luck "I said *after* five," he said, anger in his voice. "I don't get off work until five. Now I'll have to get off at four thirty, and I'll be docked for a half an hour."

"Perhaps Mr. Berman would be there in your place. He says he does most of the cooking, so I presume…."

"Morty won't do. I have to be there myself to be sure it's done right." He had cut me off in midsentence. "Just make sure that Anthony fellow is on time."

I seethed but bit my tongue and said calmly, "Anthony doesn't usually work after four, because he starts his day early. He's making an exception for you."

"Well, I hope it doesn't take him all evening. I've got things to do."

I gently clicked "End" and went back to my sandwich.

While Gracie played with her food, I did some serious thinking, wondering how, if at all, Tom Whitehead and his group played into this? Did he know the Hardin boy, even though there was a considerable age difference and probably economic status? How would Whitehead react to the shooting? I didn't want to find out. And what would he say about Buck Conroy's tragic and unaccounted for death? All those threads swirled together in my mind, making one big whirlpool that seemed about to suck me in. I needed a nap.

Gracie and I showered together, with me grateful that she was now old enough to do that, and I confess that when she napped so did I. By the time the girls got home, I was dressed and ready to go to Joanie's.

"Maggie and Em, this is a first, and I'm sorry to spring it on you at the last minute. But I'm leaving Gracie in your care. I have to be at Joanie's when people come to pay their respects, and I'm late now. Just waiting for you. Maggie, there are leftovers in the refrigerator, and you can pick and choose. Just scramble an egg for Gracie and give her a piece of toast, maybe a banana. I'll keep in touch by phone." *Boy oh boy, would I!*

Em squealed with delight. "I'll get to change her and everything?"

I nodded.

Maggie, however, started to protest. "I was hoping Dave could come over."

"Not when Mike and I are both gone. I'm giving you a big responsibility here, and I'm putting a lot of trust in you." To myself, I was thinking, *Why does she make things so difficult sometimes?* Now that I was rested and dressed, I itched to be by Mike's side. But then I softened, "Tomorrow night, you and Dave can go for pizza, my treat."

She brightened at that and threw her arms around me. "Thanks, Mom. You're the best. Come on, Em, let's play with Gracie. You change her, and I'll feed her. Sounds like a deal to me."

Em didn't even think of complaining.

* * * *

Unfortunately, the crowd beat me to Joanie's. The house seemed to bulge with people, most of them gathered in the family room and, despite our best planning, in the kitchen. Many wandered around with plates in their hands, and I saw beer, wine, and soft drinks and wondered where they'd come from.

Mike stood near the entry hall so that he could greet people as they arrived, and I joined him. I knew many of the law enforcement officers, especially those from Mike's district, and I chatted with them and their wives. Uniformly the message was one of grief, tinged by anxiety.

"If it could happen to the chief, it could happen to anyone," one wife muttered to me. "I'm trying to get himself to retire." She was older, and I imagined "himself" was near retirement. I also picked up on her Irish background—she was probably at least third-generation and yet the speech patterns hadn't disappeared.

"I know how you feel," I said, grasping her hand, "but we need good men like your husband now more than ever." *Help! Who was her husband?*

"I just hope they catch the shooter this weekend," she said fervently and moved on.

And so it went for a couple of hours, after which my feet and back gave out. I whispered to Mike, who seemed tireless, that I'd be in the kitchen.

As I passed through the family room, I looked for dishes that needed to be bussed. The room was crowded with men and women, mostly older than me, the women seemingly dressed for church, some men in uniform, others in suits. A man in a clerical collar stood in one corner watching. It was crowded, noisy, almost claustrophobic, and I couldn't wait to get out of there. I headed for the kitchen to find Joanie.

I was almost to the kitchen when a white-haired gentleman reached out a hand to stop me. "Good to see you, Kelly. Terrible times. But my old mother used to say all things work to some good end. I think I'm in line for a promotion now, with Buck gone. Him and me didn't gee and haw. I'm going to see the mayor Monday, I think."

Speechless I moved on but felt the man pat my butt as I passed him. It would do no good to make a scene here and probably some harm, but I was indignant. I knew too well who he was—Al Johnson. Mike had been complaining about him for some time now, claiming he needed to retire.

He called after me, "Ask Joanie's girl to bring me another drink, would you, sweetie?"

The "sweetie" was bad enough, but I knew he had taken Keisha for the maid when she was in reality the wife of one of his fellow officers. Another conversation I wouldn't be repeating to her. I wondered if that status occurred to her as she worked in the kitchen alongside the other wives out there.

Joanie was surrounded by women, most looking appropriately sad, one with a consoling arm around Joanie's shoulders, another speaking earnestly in her face. Joanie had donned widow's weeds, a straight black, loose dress, the kind that looks so simple but is deceptive—in cost among other things. I wondered if Buck had mortgaged the farm to keep Joanie happy. She seemed to be bearing up well under her grief. In fact, as I looked at her, I thought she was enjoying being the center of attention. It's a place mothers of young children often don't get to occupy.

Her face did light up when she saw me, and she said, "Kelly!" Disengaging herself from the knot of women, she came over to hug me and whisper, "Mike and I talked this afternoon. The funeral will be next Friday, a week from today. Mayor has called for an honor escort and everything." She looked pleased.

And every policeman's wife will be holding her breath. I couldn't expect Joanie to understand that.

Was Buck's death going to start a promotion competition? We needed everyone to work together, not against each other.

For the next three or four hours, I snatched opportunities to sit down as I could, sometimes in the relative quiet of the formal living room. Keisha had gone home to be with José, who was off tonight and announced he was going to sleep the clock around. I took her place, putting out fresh food, collecting dishes and cups. The mountain of trash by the back door grew.

It was nearly ten o'clock before the sympathizers had all gone and the food was put away. Joanie looked exhausted, the exhilaration of being front and center gone, and I knew I was beyond tired.

"You be all right?" I asked.

She nodded. "I need some solitude and quiet. Buck's aunt said she'd keep McKenzie and

Nicolas overnight. I'm almost never away from them at night, but tonight I'm ready."

"I'll call in the morning," I said.

Gratefully I accepted Mike's suggestion that I leave my car at Joanie's and ride home with him. "There'll be an officer on duty all night," he told me.

In the car, I finally switched my phone back to on. One message, from Anthony. "Miss Kelly, I got to talk to you." Urgency tinged his voice, but whatever it was could wait. I'd call him tomorrow.

Chapter Eight

Mike and I came home to a quiet and dark house. I checked on the girls immediately and was not at all surprised to find all three on a pallet on Maggie's bedroom floor, Gracie curled comfortably between her older sisters.

As I bent to kiss them, Maggie murmured, "No tears. She was happy all night. We even bathed her."

I could have done without knowing that, but all was well.

Wearily Mike and I climbed the stairs to our loft hideaway, leaving Gracie behind where she was. The thought flitted through my tired brain that not only had Mike and I not had any time together in the last forty-eight hours, but this was the first time we'd been alone in our bedroom since Gracie's birth. But I was too exhausted for romance.

We brushed our teeth and got ready for bed without any conversation, almost like mechanical robots. After we both were settled in bed, Mike reached for me, and I prepared to sleep cuddled next to him. But he had something else in mind.

"Kelly? The mayor has asked me to be in her office at nine o'clock sharp Monday morning."

Mike saw the mayor from time to time as part of his official duties, so I was neither surprised nor worried, not even, I admit, curious. Sleepily, I murmured, "What do you suppose she wants?"

He took a deep breath. "I think she'll ask me to be interim chief." He held his breath as though in suspended animation.

A bell went off in my befogged brain and brought me awake and to attention. I sat bolt upright. "Mike! Al Johnson told me he was seeing the mayor Monday morning."

He looked a little crestfallen. "Did he say what time? Did she call for him?" Then, sheepishly, he added, "I wasn't sure I wanted the job, even on an interim basis, until you said that. Al Johnson would be awful for the force."

I was back to sleepy again and muttered, "He patted my bottom."

"What?" It was a yelp, not a real question, and I settled down to sleep.

* * * *

Next morning the girls again took care of Gracie, and Mike and I slept until almost nine thirty. I couldn't remember when I'd done that the last time. A cup of coffee and some granola readied me for the day, and I put returning Anthony's call first on my list.

"Miss Kelly, I got to tell you. I got a bad feeling about that White-whatever-his-name-is."

"Whitehead," I supplied. "Why? Dishwasher not fixable?"

"No, no, it's not that."

I could see him running his hand through his white hair, a gesture he did whenever puzzled, angry, concerned.

"House is neat as a pin, real clean. My Teresa couldn't do better. And the dishwasher, I got it fixed securely to the wall this time. He shouldn't have no more trouble with it. But it's what he's got on the walls."

I waited impatiently. Anthony always told his stories his own way and at his own speed.

"What you call them, like my boys have on their walls? Posters, that's it. My boys, they have posters about football and soccer players. This Whitehead, he have posters that say, 'You will not replace us,' whatever that means."

"I know what it means," I said grimly.

"Whatever. There were two signs I know about. One said, 'White Lives Matter,' and the other was a swastika. Believe me, I recognize that. We got Nazis living on our property." His voice rose in agitation.

Anthony's family, or most of them, had survived WWII in Greece. He was a very young child but undoubtedly had heard family tales. And he'd lost two uncles in the resistance. Of course, he recognized and feared that symbol. I tried to calm him. "Not Nazis in the sense you think of, Anthony, but they're better called white supremacists. They think whites are better than any other races and should rule. But they like Hitler's belief in the Aryan race, so they use the swastika."

"I know about them, Miss Kelly. I watch the news, see the protests and trouble they cause. I don't want them in that house."

I sighed. Not the way I intended to start my day. "I don't want them there either, but I signed a lease. I can't evict them because I don't like their ideas. If they do anything to break the lease, I'll get them out of there, believe me." After a second, I asked, "Did you meet a roommate named Morty Berman?"

"Yeah, he came in, tried to be helpful. Whitehead was rude to him, wouldn't let him talk."

"I think he may turn out to be a help to us," I said, already contemplating a call to Berman Jewelry.

At last, somewhat reassured, Anthony ended the conversation with a mutter about protecting his boys. I thought it a non sequitur, but I was glad to get him off the phone.

Joanie was next on my list, and I punched in her number reluctantly, dreading to hear what she'd come up with overnight. It wasn't all bad.

"McKenzie and Nicolas are home," she said, "and I'm going to spend the day with them, reassuring them. And I've got to sort through all this food. Someone from church called and is bringing dinner tonight. I wanted to say, 'Wait, no! Don't do that,' but of course I couldn't. Please come take anything your family will eat."

I promised and added a quick trip to Joanie's to my daily agenda. And then my mother called. She wanted to talk about how awful that shooting was and wasn't the chief a friend of ours.

"Mike and Buck Conroy worked together for many years now, Mom, and his wife was a friend of mine." Her hair would curl if I went into details, so I spared myself.

"You know, Kelly, I do wish Mike would find another line of work. Being a policeman puts him in danger, and it has even gotten you in trouble. Have you ever talked to him about a change in careers?"

Me? Talk to Mike about a change in careers, especially when he was probably going to be appointed interim chief? I don't think so, Mom. Aloud, I said, "No, Mom. Mike loves his work, and I wouldn't dream of suggesting he quit the force."

And then, "Yes, Mom, of course I worry about him too. Gotta go, I think I hear Gracie waking up from her nap." *How big a sin is it to tell your mom a white lie?* I ended the conversation with a vague suggestion that we have lunch soon, just the two of us, but I set no specific date.

And I was done with the phone for the day. I switched it to vibrate and went to visit with Gracie, who in reality was happily playing on the living room floor, with Clyde watching her.

* * * *

In the afternoon, Maggie came out of her bedroom, obviously dressed to go someplace special. Charcoal leggings were topped with an oversized tunic of light gray that she'd brightened with a colorful red-and-blue scarf. Her hair was freshly shampooed, and she wore a bit more makeup than I usually sanctioned.

Before I could say anything, Em asked pertly, "And where do you think you're going?"

Maggie's answer was equally pert, "I'm taking Dave for pizza. Mom said I could."

"Can I go?" Em is my ever-hopeful and optimistic child.

Maggie was scornful. "Of course not. It's a date."

Good thing she didn't see my facial expression. It was hard for me to think of Maggie as dating. But I did remember that promise, a thank-you for her care of Gracie yesterday. Still, we had just had lunch. What time she did plan to go? Seemed too early now, but I didn't want her to be out driving around very late at night—and I certainly did not want her to drive Dave home after dark. I didn't mind if they went to a pizza place nearby on Magnolia and came home after dark, but across town was out. Gracie's near-escape had truly made a helicopter mom out of me.

"When are you going to pick Dave up?"

She shrugged. "I thought I'd go now, and we could hang out here for a little while. Then we can go eat about four. Dave is always hungry." She laughed a little at that.

Sounded like a plan to me, and I gave my okay.

"Mom, while I'm gone, could you…uh …kind of change clothes, maybe work on your hair a little?"

"What? Stretched-out sweats and a T-shirt aren't acceptable?" I grinned and promised to do as she wished. I knew another battle loomed. Em always wanted to "hang out" with them, and I could hardly lock her in her room to prevent that. On the other hand, Maggie was forbidden to take Dave into her bedroom. "Em, you want to go upstairs and do a puzzle with Mike this afternoon?"

I totally forgot that Mike wasn't home and probably wouldn't be all afternoon, until I called him to take Dave home.

Maggie came to my rescue, much to my surprise. "Good idea, Mom. Maybe we can all do a puzzle on the dining room table. Can you see if Mike can come home?"

And that's what happened. The three youngsters—did I dare use that word?—settled at the dining table with a thousand-word puzzle that was a montage of brand names and logos. They had almost completed the outer edge when Mike came in.

Dave jumped to his feet and held out his hand. "Afternoon, sir."

Mike shook his hand and said how glad he was to see him.

Dave seemed to want to engage Mike in conversation. "I never did a puzzle this way, figuring out the edge first. We always just put pieces together that look like they fit."

Em gave him a withering look as if to ask, "How dumb is that?"

They worked on the puzzle with small talk buzzing, touching on everything from the weather to school, but they pretty much avoided politics. Mike, a proud liberal, had told me before he was afraid Dave followed his dad's beliefs and was "pretty conservative." You could read a lot of things into that, but this afternoon Dave confirmed it with an out-of-the-blue question.

"I guess that black cop is going to lose his job for shooting that unarmed kid, huh, sir?"

I could see Mike stiffen. "Not necessarily," he said. "Internal affairs is investigating, as is the district attorney. It depends on whether or not Jason Pickard was justified in shooting and followed the departmental guidelines he learned in training. He's got a good record as a police officer."

"But the kid was unarmed," Dave protested. "And he was white." As soon as he added that, he regretted it, if for no other reason than the astounded look Maggie gave him.

"What color either of them is or was has no bearing on the case," Mike said mildly. "The way I understand it, the young man had a bad drug habit and was breaking into a store with intent to rob it. He ignored Pickard's order to stop."

Dave didn't give up easily. "But did he have to kill him? I mean, we all know they like to kill white people."

The word "they" hung in the air like a giant cloud, and I half expected Maggie to repeat her earlier words about not being able to go to the dance, now less than a week away, with Dave. She didn't. Very slowly, she asked, "Who is they? Police or black people?"

Dave knew his mistake and shrugged. "You know."

Mike sat back and let Maggie handle it. Em, to my great relief, was silent at least for the moment.

"No, I don't know, Dave. You need to get rid of some old-fashioned ideas about people, like that skin color matters."

Dave looked down at his hands, which were clasped in his lap. "My dad always told me it does matter."

She looked straight at him. "Your dad is wrong. Dead wrong."

Saved by the bell. The doorbell broke the tension, and I almost ran to see who was there. Claire Guthrie, my close friend, family friend, and at this moment a welcome angel. Even Mike threw his arms around her in gratitude. Claire and Mike had once had a long standoff before they finally decided to embrace each other. But that's another story.

"Hi, Aunt Claire," Em piped up. "We're doing a puzzle. Want to help?"

"Sure, sweetie, if I can have some iced tea while I do."

That was my cue, and I went to the kitchen for snacks for everyone—iced tea and the cookies Em had baked this morning, with my supervision. As I got things together, I heard Maggie introducing Dave to Claire. Her manners were perfect, and so were his.

Maggie and Dave declined tea and cookies, and Maggie looked pointedly at her watch. "Let's go get that pizza, Dave."

I was unsure what kind of experience awaited Dave when the two were alone, but I had a feeling it might be a tad unpleasant.

Dave said how nice it was to meet Claire, thanked Mike and me, and said his dad would come pick him up. And with that, they left, and the rest of us let out a huge sigh of relief.

"What's wrong with everybody?" Claire asked innocently.

Chapter Nine

Claire's first reaction was instant. "Just tell Maggie she can't see the young man. When you explain why, she'll see it. She's a sensible girl."

I decided I'd let Mike handle this one, and he did. "I don't believe that's the way to do it, Claire. Maggie knows what the problem is with Dave, but she likes him. Maybe you could say she has a crush on him. In that case, if we don't welcome him, she'll resent us—last thing I want. She's trying to show him how wrong his thinking is. He's a good kid, and his ideas are not his own. It's how he was brought up."

"Well and good," she replied, "but did you read about the incident in New York where a young neo-Nazi boy shot and killed his girlfriend's parents when they told her she couldn't see him anymore?"

"Point proven." Mike shifted uncomfortably in his chair and rubbed his hand across the top of his burr haircut, a sure sign that he was agitated. "That's what happens when you issue categorical rules instead of getting the teen to work with you. Besides, Dave isn't a neo-Nazi. He just happens to hold the faulty belief that white people are better than others."

"Keisha?" she asked, and I piped up. "I'm trying to keep Keisha out of this. She had an unpleasant encounter at the office with some guys who rent a property we manage, and her discrimination radar is pretty sensitive right now."

Em was listening to all this wide-eyed, and a part of me thought it was a good lesson, but another, motherly part wished she wasn't hearing what she was.

Claire never gave up easily. "Why is our Maggie, who's been raised right, interested in a boy who comes from that kind of background?"

"Why did you fall in love with Jim Guthrie?" Mike asked.

Except for my involuntary gasp, silence fell on the room. Claire's ex-husband had been a wife-beating alcoholic, and from what I'd heard secondhand they had some rip-roaring physical battles. She'd once shot him in the butt, and he'd nearly succeeded in throttling her. Jim Guthrie died in a single-car crash, his driving ability impaired by too much alcohol on top of an opioid drug he'd taken thinking it was aspirin. For a long time, Mike thought Claire had deliberately planted that pill, and he would have nothing to do with her. But it came out that one of her daughters had slipped it into her pill case, thinking it was a tranquilizer, and Claire had innocently given it to Jim. The case went to court, and Claire was completely exonerated. It had taken a long time, but she and Mike now had a cautious friendship.

Just as she said, "That was a low blow, Mike," he realized he'd overstepped and apologized. "Sorry, Claire, that was out of line. I just meant that there's no accounting for how or why people are attracted to others. You'll admit now that your attraction, long ago, to your ex is out of character and beyond explanation?"

Head down, she said, "Yeah, it was. But I'm still nervous about this boyfriend of Maggie's. He seemed like a nice kid, but …"

Her sentence drifted off, and we turned our attention to the puzzle. Two hours later, we had made some progress, but there was a lot left to go. Em sighed in frustration when Claire said she had to go home, and we all scattered in different directions.

Maggie and Dave came back about six, reporting that the pizza was the bomb and they'd had a good talk. Neither of them gave away what they'd talked about, but we all thought we knew. Dave's father came for him pretty quickly, and Maggie walked Dave to the door, punching him lightly in the arm and saying, "See you Monday."

Nope, it wasn't a romance yet, and I was glad.

The rest of the weekend was lazy and laid-back. I checked on Joanie from time to time, but she was fully occupied with her children, said they'd been deluged with food and visitors until she'd put a "Do not disturb" sign on the door. I wasn't sure that was the way to handle the well-intended visits and I was half-temped to go run interference for her. Mike suggested I stay home—he liked the idea of all of us together without any outside activities or obligations. It didn't happen often enough.

Togetherness was fine, but in truth he spent much of Sunday at his desk, sometimes on his computer, though I often caught him staring into space, and I knew he was thinking about his interview with the mayor in the morning. In the afternoon, he put a roast in the oven, with potatoes nestled around it, and suggested I stir-fry the Brussel sprouts he'd bought.

"Stir-fry? Brussel sprouts? The girls have never eaten them."

"Cut off the stems, peel the outer leaves, and quarter them. Then stir-fry in a bit of olive oil and dress with salt and pepper and butter. You can do it when I take the roast out of the oven to rest."

I bit off the question on my tongue. Why wasn't he doing this?

When Keisha called to say she and José were going to Joe T.'s to eat on the patio since it was a pleasant evening and did we want to go, I declined with, "No thanks, we're having Brussel sprouts."

"What?" I could hear the disbelief in her voice.

"It's a long story," I said. "Mike put a roast in the oven."

"Okay. I'll see you at the office. I'll be there eight thirty sharp. I'm ready to get back into the routine and forget shootings and who's black and who's white."

"Me, too," I said fervently.

Of course, it wasn't possible, and it didn't work out that way.

* * * *

Monday morning Gracie and I arrived at the office a little after eight thirty. Keisha was there and already had lights on, coffee made, the day started. Gracie seemed happy to be in her little corner play area, and I settled down to answering messages, skimming the real estate section in the paper, and pretending I was working.

In truth, my mind wouldn't stay out of the mayor's office where Mike was at his appointment. Mayor Shirley Goodwin was a tall, stylish woman of, oh, I'd say sixty. She had a commanding presence and, from the little I could tell, was doing a good job of running the city. She was also a woman of color.

If she asked Mike to serve as interim chief, there would be a lot of changes in his life, new and complicated responsibilities, of course, but also a change in the physical location of his office—from the Central District to City Hall. He'd have to leave

José and others he'd worked with for years. He'd have less time for his family and less free time. But Mike, first and foremost these days a family man, was also a dedicated law enforcement officer. He saw it as both a major calling and a major challenge, and if he felt his contribution would be important, he'd take on the job.

These thoughts distracted me most of the morning. I started to write a contract and discovered so many holes in it, I gave up. I picked up the phone to call someone and couldn't remember who I was calling. I gave up more than once and played "hide the toy" with Gracie. Keisha watched me carefully but said nothing.

Mike finally called about eleven, but he was neither solemn nor ebullient. In fact, he was kind of terse. "Meet me at home for lunch? We need to talk."

My heart did a little flip. How serious was this? "Of course." I began to review mentally the refrigerator contents, sensing that peanut butter would not do. "See you at noon?"

"Good," and he disconnected, not so much as "Bye" or "I love you." Just that empty sound in my ear.

No word on the interim position, no hint about what was on his mind, except that it sounded big. I marched over to the coffeepot and managed to splash half a cup everywhere in my frustration. Mike could be calm and collected, but I sure was not.

Keisha said nothing, just watched, even when I bundled up Gracie and left without a word about when I'd be back. We got home about eleven forty-five. The refrigerator turned out to be a non-starter, so I whipped up a batch of tuna salad, defrosted four slices of rye bread, and got out some pickles. Gracie would get the peanut butter. It was almost ready when Mike walked quietly into the kitchen, surprising me because I'd been so absorbed in hurrying to get lunch ready.

He wrapped his arms around me and rested his chin on my shoulder. "Thanks for meeting me. I needed to see you."

He acted as though it were a big favor and maybe a sacrifice on my part, but that man knew I would meet him anywhere any time he asked. As lightly as I could I asked, "What's up?" I really wanted to demand, "What did the mayor want? Did you say yes or no?" Instead, I squirmed a little in his arms.

Mike can read me like a book. "I told the mayor that I had to talk to you, Kelly, before I gave her an answer. If I take the interim position, it will probably lead to a permanent position, and that means a big change in our lives."

I'd just thought of it as a promotion, so I guess I hadn't thought it through. Mike knew that and went on, "I'd be a public figure, have to go to a lot of receptions and formal events. You'd be expected to go with me."

Was it serendipity or a warning that Gracie chose that moment to dump her bowl of sliced strawberries on her head. Solemn as he was being, Mike laughed, but my only thought was "Who would care for Gracie while I went to all those functions?" I wasn't ready for babysitters, probably wouldn't be until she was twenty-one. And I couldn't, wouldn't leave the older girls home alone with her for more long evenings. The evening at Joanie's had been a necessary exception.

"She'll be fine," Mike whispered. "We'll work it out. In fact, we'll start this week. You'll need to be at Buck's funeral, sitting with the officials—and no, you can't take Gracie." He pulled away and looked me square in the eye, "That is, if you want me to accept the job."

"Of course, I do." Perhaps I said it too quickly, but there was no way I could hold Mike back because of my fears. Still, those fears were very real. "Will you be a target like Buck?"

He nodded. "Are you ever going to feed me?"

He cleaned up Gracie and gave her recovered strawberries, while I finished the sandwiches and got them on the table, with glasses of ice water. We both ate in silence for a few minutes, but I was waiting for him to say more.

"I'll be the symbol of the police in the eyes of a lot of people who don't like us. It's always a risk."

"Why do it then? We're safe, or relatively so, and we're comfortable. We don't need you to earn more or have more prestige. Why don't we just stay as we are?"

He shook his head. "Kelly, you know I can't do that. I think I can do some good for the city. And there are problems that need cleaning up in this city. Unless you're a part of the force, you don't see them. But you yourself do—you've run into those problems more than I like. Given the opportunity to make a difference, I can't just say, no, my wife and I are happy as we are."

A part of me, big part, recognized that, but I also wanted to scream, "High and mighty words, but what happens when you get shot and leave us." I wouldn't put that into words, for fear it would jinx him, and I'd never say it anyway.

"One problem we haven't really run into before, but it seems that racism is being felt more these days in odd corners of the city. I don't know how the Hardin boy's death or Buck's fit into that, but first thing I'll put a team on it."

I started to tell him about Tom Whitehead and Anthony's description of the things he'd seen in the house, but Mike suddenly looked at his watch.

"Gotta go. Meeting with the mayor and Joanie at one about Buck's funeral."

I smiled, the first smile of our lunch. "Call me if you need help with Joanie. She's liable to have some wild ideas."

He smiled too. "Forewarned is forearmed. Listen, let's celebrate tonight, as a family. Why don't you make dinner reservations at that new Chinese place? I'll meet you all there at six." With a quick kiss for me and one for the top of Gracie's head, he was gone.

After I cleaned the kitchen, Gracie and I went back to the office. She could nap there, and I, frankly, didn't want to be alone with my thoughts.

Keisha didn't ask—she would never pry—but I poured out the whole story to her, including the need to find care for Gracie. That, of course, was what she fixed on. With a glance at the now-sleeping baby, she said, "Kelly, you got to loosen up about that child. It's not good for her to have you hovering over her."

I started to protest that she didn't realize how scared I was, but then I saw the flaw in that. She *did* realize. She'd lived through every minute of the kidnapping scare with us.

"I'll keep Gracie here at the office during Buck's funeral. I can't always keep her at night for you, but we'll start with this week and go from there."

I hugged her tight and then went back to my desk. As I picked up the phone to make dinner reservations, I asked, "Want to go for Chinese tonight?"

"Everybody going?"

"Sure. I'm not sure the girls ever have had Chinese food. Should be fun. I'll make reservations, and we can check the menu online."

We never did check the menu and when I thought of it later, I decided to be surprised, because I was actually getting some real estate work done and didn't want to quit while I was on a roll.

Contract for Chaos

Chapter Ten

"I don't believe I've ever had Chinese food." Em's very precise statement carried clear as a bell from the back seat, where Gracie sat ensconced in her car seat between her two older sisters. "I don't expect I'll like it."

Before Keisha and I could respond from the front, we heard Maggie ask, "Why not? Chink food is good."

I stiffened when I heard that racial epithet come out of my darling daughter's mouth, but while I thought about reacting, Keisha was faster. "How about n-food?" she asked.

Maggie gasped. "Keisha, you know we never say that word."

Keisha shrugged. "Same thing. Calling a Chinese person a chink is just like calling me by an epithet. Or some Jewish fellow a kike. You get my drift?"

Maggie's voice was subdued. "Yes, ma'am."

"Don't let me never hear any of those words from either of you. And I expect you to have your best manners on tonight, and not be squealin' and gigglin' over foods that seem strange to you."

"Yes, ma'am," they chorused, but Em added, "Don't they eat weird, squishy things like snails and grasshoppers?"

My turn, and I jumped in. "The French consider snails a great delicacy. They call them escargot."

"Well I'm not eating them," Em said with determination, and Keisha almost ruined the golden teaching moment by muttering, "Me neither, Em."

Mike was not, as I hoped, waiting at the restaurant for us. As we got settled, before we even looked at the menu, he texted he'd be late and to go ahead and order. The girls were a delight, after the scare they'd given me in the car. They asked our server, a young woman, about various dishes, seemed interested, and made good choices. Em had the vegetarian stir-fry and did not even ask them to leave out the eggplant if there was any in it. Maggie and Keisha both ordered beef with broccoli, and I had the sweet and sour pork ribs. I ordered spring rolls and wonton soup for appetizers and explained that the way to eat the meal was for everybody to taste a bit of everything. Except for Gracie, who was content with rice and the hard-boiled egg and banana I'd brought.

I hoped Mike would appear while we waited for our order, but no. He texted he'd be a little longer and to please order him the seared bean sprouts and duck stir-fry.

"Spring rolls are good, Mom. Can you make them at home?" Em was now an enthusiastic fan of Chinese food.

"I'll make lettuce wraps. Easier to do and doesn't require the soy wraps and all that."

She looked puzzled but agreed.

Maggie and Keisha loved their beef and broccoli, but Em found it a bit spicy for her taste.

"I can't get the food to stay on my chopstick," Maggie laughed, holding up empty chopsticks. The server demonstrated again, but the broccoli still fell off. "I'll have to practice at home," Maggie said, and the server reminded her she could take her chopsticks with her.

"I'll stick to my knife and fork," Em said, and again Keisha sided with her.

For dessert we had chrysanthemum panna cotta, which everybody loved. Even Gracie liked the taste she got. We all used spoons, and I tried to envision eating panna cotta with chopsticks.

"Are we really eating flowers?" Em demanded of the waitress and was assured that she was. "Well, I like them!"

Mike texted, which by now I expected, and I asked to have his food boxed so we could take it home. He'd see us later, maybe after the girls were asleep. There were a few other leftovers, and we asked to have them packaged too.

"Some celebration for his new job," I muttered, and Keisha, without sympathy, replied, "Get used to it."

And that's how I ended up reheating leftovers in my kitchen at midnight.

Looking exhausted, Mike sat uncharacteristically slumped in his chair. "I feel like I've been rode hard and put up wet," he said. "I sure hope every day isn't like this. I may resign before I'm officially approved."

He had changed into sweatpants and a T-shirt and now looked oddly vulnerable to me. We didn't speak as I heated his dinner, plated it, and set it before him. For a long moment, he just looked at it. I poured wine for both of us and sat opposite him, while he toyed with his food. If it had been Em, I'd have scolded her.

Finally, he said, "It was a long day. I didn't expect half what happened."

I wanted to scream, "What did happen?" but some better instinct told me to tread softly, and I simply asked, "What?"

"There's more trouble in this city than I dreamed. Lord knows I thought I saw I all in the Central District, and I did—gang shootings, violence, hatred. But I didn't know for instance how racist we are, what undercurrents are always bubbling in this city. Today the mayor appointed a task force to study racism, since it's been rearing its ugly head across the country."

I reached for the hand he wasn't using to eat and held it. "Did something happen to spark her interest now?"

"Yeah. Someone applied for a permit for a public gathering the day of Buck's funeral. In that open space across from the church. A guy they've been watching for racist tendencies. A hatemonger. Name of Tom Whitehead. Ironic name, no?"

In my absolute alarm, I jumped up from my chair and said, much more loudly than I meant, "Mike! That's our tenant, over on Alston. The one Anthony was so worried about. The one Keisha had a run-in with and won't speak about to this day."

Mike was dumbfounded. His fork clattered to his plate, and he got up from his chair to stride to where I stood and grab my shoulders. "You knew about this guy, and you didn't tell me?" He wasn't exactly angry, but neither was he pleased.

"I didn't know what to tell. I can't report someone because they have tiki torches and a swastika in their living room. That would make us a police state. But now that I know he's planning a protest—oh, I don't know what to do. But he hasn't broken the terms of his lease. I can't evict him."

As Mike let go of my shoulders, I slid back into my chair and buried my face in my hands.

He took his seat, but pushed his half-eaten dinner away. "Another group has also applied. Not exactly Antifa but one that opposes white supremacy. That's the combination that led to the violence in Charlottesville. And I don't want it to happen in Fort Worth. That's what we spent the day on—preventing violence at Buck's funeral."

"And I suppose Joanie wouldn't go for a small private ceremony."

"No. And neither would the city. There are times you just have to give in to protocol or whatever, and this is one of them. Let's go to bed."

His dirty dishes, stuck with food and yucky, would be waiting for me in the morning, but I took the offered hand, and we headed toward our bedroom.

* * * *

The next week was one of the longest of my life. The office was slow, not something I could tie to the very public funeral looming at the end of the week, though I tended to link everything to that spectacle in my mind.

Mike worked long hours, came home late, and used me for a sounding board for all he'd discovered. He'd always been close personal friends with Buck and, as a district captain, he been part of the so-called leadership team. But now he was looking at the way things were done, and he pretty much decided Buck had a one-man show going, with little delegation of authority in the ranks.

"I gave more authority to the heads of the various districts," Mike said, "and I made enemies right away. It made sense to me to put a Hispanic in

120

charge in a district with a heavy Hispanic population, and a black in a heavily black district. Buck has white guys in every district, so some guys got sort of demoted—just two or three districts. And I guess some who've been with the force a long time expected longevity rewards by being transferred to head a district, if I was making appointments."

His logic made my head spin. We were sitting at the kitchen table, late at night again, with a quiet household. I had spent the evening reading one of Susan Albert's China Bayles mysteries, and I had a hard time drawing myself out of her small town in the Hill Country and back into our city. I had momentarily forgotten about Buck's funeral, now just two days away. Mike made it all come back. "Are you saying there's racism in your police force?"

"Yeah, that's what I'm saying, I guess." He reached into the fridge for a beer and poured me a glass of wine. "How can I combat racism in the city, if it exists in my department? 'Course, that's what they're saying all along about the Pickard shooting—calling it reverse racism."

"Because a black cop shot a white kid?"

"Yeah, doesn't help that he was a kid. Some of the worst trouble we have comes from kids, but people always think they're innocent. This one clearly wasn't."

I decided this new job was not a good thing for Mike or for us as a couple or a family, but I couldn't say that, so I just sat silent.

"I offered José a transfer and a promotion, but he turned me down. Says he liked Fairmount, and Keisha would kill us both if I moved him out of the neighborhood."

"Probably right," I said. "She would, and I'd probably help her."

As usual, these talks went nowhere, led to no solutions for Mike, and only served to open my eyes to problems I'd ignored or didn't even know existed. Blind ignorance is really comfortable sometimes.

* * * *

Keisha stormed into the office the next morning, late enough that I was there before her. No bright colors this morning, but black jeans and a black-and-white top. "What does Mike Shandy think he's doing, moving José out of the neighborhood?" She picked up the coffeepot with such a flourish of anger that she splashed coffee everywhere. Setting her cup down, she attacked the mess with paper napkins.

I stayed quiet and watched. When at last she had her coffee and had slammed herself into her office chair so hard it rolled backward and almost unseated her, I said mildly, "José said no, so why are you so upset?"

Angry and noisy shuffling of papers was followed by a loud sigh. And, then, suddenly, she laughed aloud. "You're right, Kelly. Why am I upset? That boy knows what I want, and he did the right thing. Guess I'm just mad at Mike for even offering."

Keisha and logic were not always on the same page, so I changed the subject.

"Buck's funeral is tomorrow. Guess I better call Joanie."

Keisha gave me a long look. "Is this your way of saying you're nervous about it and asking me what my sixth sense is telling me?"

"I wouldn't dream of asking," I said with as much pride as I could muster. My fingers were crossed behind my back. My mama told me a little white lie never hurt.

Suddenly, she whirled her chair around to face me. "I'm getting mixed messages, Kelly. I have no idea what will happen tomorrow. It's been bothering me. Maybe why I flew off the handle just now."

Hadn't her mother told her about the value of a little white lie? Why couldn't she have just told me it would be all right, so I could relax. Instead, my fears came crashing down on me. A vision of Mike, shot, came out of nowhere, and my ears manufactured the sound of sirens. A full-blown hallucination.

It took me a full minute or longer to gain control and stop the shaking in my hands. "You still keeping Gracie tomorrow?"

"'Course I am. José's goin' to the funeral, with the officers of the Central District. Sure hope criminals keep quiet, at least while that's goin' on. I don't think there'll be a loose officer in the whole city." Then, abruptly, she changed directions and grew solemn once again. "You talked to Joanie? Everything okay with her?"

I had talked to Joanie every day in the week since Buck was shot, but I hadn't seen her. I told myself she had other officers' wives around her. I knew they'd set up a meal delivery chain—I'd even made and sent a batch of spaghetti one night. By phone, I listened to her grief, her anger, her determination to raise her children well, her burning desire for revenge on the as-yet unknown shooter. I'd counseled her on talks with the children and her outfit for the memorial service. But I hadn't been to her house, I hadn't given her the hugs I knew she needed. Joanie was still hard for me, because of her betrayal with my ex-husband, but now she was even harder. I didn't want her grief to come too close to me. If she could lose Buck, I could lose Mike—and I couldn't face that.

"Yeah, she's okay. I'll call her again. Maybe we should take her to lunch." Reluctance echoed in my voice and bounced off the walls as I slowly picked up my phone and punched in her number. Joanie was not on speed dial.

"Yeah. We should do that." Keisha cocked an eyebrow at me.

Joanie's neighbor was keeping her children this morning while she ran some last-minute errands. I caught her in her car, and she replied breathlessly that she'd love to meet us for lunch. Even as I told her Keisha would be with me, I knew I was taking Keisha for my own comfort, not Joanie's.

* * * *

We met at Lili's Bistro, a little early so that we beat the crowd. Joanie may have had a babysitter, but I was lugging Gracie. I could hardly ask the interim chief of police to take a long lunch and babysit his daughter. Keisha and I beat Joanie to the restaurant by ten or fifteen minutes, so I was tasked with keeping Gracie occupied, which meant crackers and trying to prevent her from crowing with delight every time someone smiled at her, which they did often.

Joanie breezed in, hair tousled by the wind, breathless with apologies. "I just had no idea it would take so long to pick up the shoes I was having polished. There was the slowest, pickiest woman ahead of me. I swear she found fault with everything. And then I had to go to the cleaners for my dress. It needed slight alteration, but I had to have it perfect for the service."

She looked wonderful in a what was probably a pricey beige pantsuit with a silk blouse and a contrasting scarf draped attractively around her neck. I never could drape scarves, always ended looking like I'd been in a fight with the thing and lost. I envied Joanie just a bit.

She paused for breath, and Keisha asked, "How are you? What's your week been like?"

Joanie looked startled, as though this were a question she hadn't expected. Her rapid rush of words slowed. Brushing her hair out of her eyes, she said slowly, "It's been busy and crowded. I'm never alone, except in the middle of the night. That's the only time I've had to miss Buck."

"That's kind of what people intend," Keisha said. "I'm glad they've been good to you."

"Oh, they have. And the mayor has been ever so kind. Consults me on everything about the service. There's going to be a bagpiper. Buck loved them. I think it's so much screeching, but he'll be happy."

That present tense sent a shiver down my spine. "What did you decide to wear?"

"Basic black. A dress I've had for years, one that's always in style. And I got one of those widow's hats, you know—the veil that hides your face. Scared McKenzie when I tried it on." She giggled at the memory, though I didn't find it funny.

We ordered. I had the vegetarian slider sandwiches, Keisha chose the King Ranch casserole, and Joanie, the tilapia. I didn't tell her all the bad I'd heard about tilapia.

Joanie's exuberance faded while we waited for our food. "I do miss Buck. Even miss his cigars. He was a good man, as good a father to McKenzie as to Nicolas, even though she's not his biological child. He provided a good home."

"Did he make you happy?" Keisha asked.

Thoughtfully she replied, "Yes, he did. He really did. Most of the time."

I guess that's all any of us could hope for—most of the time. I didn't feel it was time to say that Buck made me unhappy most of the time. We clashed over everything from my accidental involvement in crimes and murder to his cigars and sometimes boorish manners. I was glad he made Joanie happy.

"I've got a mission," she said. "I'm going to find out who killed him and why. I think the police should have nailed the shooter by now. Truth is, I'm pretty unhappy that there's someone out there walking around who killed Buck."

Truth was I was pretty unhappy about it too, because I was afraid they'd try again with Mike. "Did you ever think there might be trouble at Buck's service?" I should have bit my tongue.

"No, of course not. No one would dare do anything tomorrow. I won't stand for it."

"Joanie, a group of white supremacists have gotten a permit to demonstrate. I know they'll be kept far from all of us, but you should know they'll be there."

She threw down the napkin she'd been holding. "They can't do that. I'll call the mayor right after lunch." Then she shrugged. "Whoever shot Buck must have meant the bullet for someone else. They won't be back tomorrow."

I wondered who else could have been the target. Mike was probably right next to Buck. He usually was at department affairs.

With a bright smile, Keisha asked, "Have you thought beyond tomorrow? What will you do? Stay in Fort Worth?"

"Oh, of course. This is my home. Kids and I are comfortable here. We have friends. I may move us to a small house—hey, maybe I should find something in Fairmount with you all. Keep me in mind."

Our food arrived, and we all took that first bite. But then Joanie continued as though there had been no interruption. "I think I'll try to get my old job back."

Scattered as she sometimes seemed, Joanie had held a responsible job with one of the major ad agencies in town before Buck, before McKenzie. I had no doubt she'd do a good job if she focused on the job and not the kids during the day.

Conversation sort of petered out as we ate our lunch. Food at Lili's was always good, and I enjoyed my sandwiches. Gracie, full of milk and crackers and a banana, was heavy-lidded and quiet, ready for her nap. We paid the bill and left.

Outside, I gave Joanie the tight hug I should have given her all week and told her I'd see her tomorrow. Arrangements had been made to chauffeur her and the children and to take care of them all day. I was free and at loose ends to be part of the official party.

Holding on to me, she said, "You've always been there for me, Kelly, even when I didn't deserve it. I'm grateful, and I'm glad you'll be there tomorrow."

That noise I heard was my conscience beating me up.

Keisha put an arm around Joanie's shoulders, explained she was babysitting, but said she'd be there in spirit. "It's all gonna be okay. I see it in the future."

Joanie looked reassured and went to her car, while we started the short walk back to the office, this time with Keisha carrying my baby. I had to learn to bring that stroller!

Chapter Eleven

A cold front moved in during the night, and we woke to temperatures in the low forties with a stiff wind blowing. Outside the church, flags, both national and state, whipped on their poles, and trees bent and danced in the wind. The church itself, Gothic in style with arches and tall thin windows, looked like a small Notre Dame. Men and women ducked their heads into the north as they hurried across the street from the parking lot to the cloistered courtyard where they gathered in small groups and whispered softly. A phalanx of police stood at attention, their badges taped with black, and watched the crowd dispassionately.

Later than I meant to be, I pulled into the parking lot at First Methodist and found most places taken, so the attendants shunted me to the far side of the lot. And there they were—protestors, much closer to me than I liked. For a minute, late or not, I sat in my car gaping. They were almost all young men in their twenties. Despite the stereotypes, they weren't all skinheads. Shoot! Mike wore his hair shorter than most of them. If it weren't for the placards they waved and the anger on their faces, they could have been at a college fraternity picnic.

But oh, those placards! "No Black Cops!" "Take Back America!" "White Lives Matter Most" and similar sentiments that appalled me. Three grim-faced police officers made sure these young men stayed behind their barricade, occasionally waving Billy clubs menacingly. But there was no violence, and there were, to my amusement, no tiki torches.

Tom Whitehead was in the front line of protestors, going from one to another, apparently exhorting them to heightened anger. He stopped and happened to glance my way long enough that I know he recognized me. Then he hastily turned his back. If my other tenants were there, I didn't see them. Or maybe I'd only met them so briefly that I did not know them when I saw them. I was dumbfounded at the ideas on the protest signs and the anger in the faces.

Apparently, others felt the same way. As they left their cars around me, mourners glanced at the young men and then turned determinedly away. White supremacy found no friends in this crowd. But there didn't appear to be any counter-protestors either, certainly not the dreaded Antifa that Mike had hinted would be there. Mike could relax, I thought.

Slamming the door of my car harder than necessary, I too turned away and followed the others across the street, fighting the wind. I hurried across the cloistered courtyard, glad to be out of the wind. A quick look up at the fanciful tracery made me wonder at the stone carver's ability to make the hard medium come alive. Then I noticed that the surface had a slight glaze on it. Terra cotta, a way to mold clay so that it looked like stone. Stone or terra cotta, the elaborate building stood as a symbol of the strength and solidity of the church and, to my mind, countered the ugliness of the protestors. I vowed to get Mike and the girls to Sunday services sometime soon. It would make my mom happy, though she never could drag Otto to church.

Entering the narthex, I asked the nearest usher where the mayor's party was assembling. He kindly directed me to a small antechamber where several people gathered, coffee in hand. Mike was not among them, not that I really expected him to be. He would process in as one of the honorary pall bearers. Neither was Joanie there, and I suspected she and her family were sheltered somewhere else private in the church.

I'd met the mayor before, but it seemed good form, being new at all this protocol as I was, to reintroduce myself as Mike's wife.

"Oh, my dear, I'm so grateful to you for joining us. Do I understand correctly that you are close to Mrs. Conroy?" Before I could answer, she went right on, "You'll be a help in comforting her, I know. There will be a long line of mourners wanting to pay their respects. I'd like to ask you to stand by Joanie, as sort of support. And, of course, you should introduce yourself to them as they come through. Awkward time to have to meet your husband's public, but it is what it is." And she flitted away to greet someone else.

I was making my way to the coffee urn when a small, slightly overweight man blocked my path. From behind thick, wire-framed glasses he squinted at me. In his hand, he held a small ring notebook and a pen. "Mrs. Shandy? You're the wife of the new chief, aren't you? I'm working on a little story about the transition of power. Wonder if I might talk to you a minute, ask you some questions."

Transition of power? My warning radar shot up immediately, but I knew it was important, in this new role I was playing, to be polite to the press. I nodded, wishing for that coffee.

"How long did you know Buck Conroy?"

Had it really been eleven years since Tim Spencer was murdered, since all that mess with the skeleton in the house? "A little over ten years."

"You friends outside his job?"

Now there was a question. "Yes and no. He married one of my best friends and, of course, he and my husband worked closely together."

"You like him?"

What was this man's agenda? I could hardly say that most of the time I found Buck boorish and crass, but there were times we saw eye to eye.

While I hesitated, the reporter, whose name I never got, said, "I know you've had some unpleasant tangles with the law—or folks on the wrong side of it—and I wondered if you and Conroy saw eye to eye."

"Sometimes," I said, edging closer to the coffee table.

"Your husband okay with that?"

He made it sound like I was having an affair with Buck. Okay with what? Occasionally but not often being on the same page as Buck? "I really can't speak for my husband. You'll have to ask him."

"Just one more question: do you have any theories about who shot Buck Conroy?"

"Of course not. That's none of my business. I just hope the shooter is found and brought to justice. Now, excuse me, but I need some coffee, and I have to check with my babysitter."

He thumbed his notes backward for a minute and then said, "Oh, that's right. You have a baby. Almost kidnapped a while back, wasn't she?"

I turned on my heel and left him without a word.

Keisha didn't make me feel any better. "Girl, why are you callin' to check on me? Little one and I are doin' just fine. Quit your worryin' about us and go be the proper chief's wife." She was laughing as she hung up, but I was not amused.

Too quickly, we were organized into a parade of sorts and led into the sanctuary and shown to pews just behind those reserved for the family. I was grateful not to be seated next to the mayor, where I would have had to make small talk. As it was, I knew neither of the people on either side of me. I introduced myself quickly—one was a city council member, a woman I should have recognized, and the other was the superintendent of schools. I probably could have blabbed about my girls' school experiences, but I chose an attitude of worshipful silence.

The family was led in next, Joanie in the lead with a child tethered by each hand. She did indeed wear a widow's veil, and peer as I might, I could tell nothing about her state of mind, but I saw that she held her head high and walked with enough determination that Nicolas struggled to keep up. Buck's parents, looking hollow-eyed, came next, followed by relatives that I assumed were brothers, sisters, cousins, and the like. Joanie's parents had come from wherever—Ohio?—but they weren't close enough to offer her any support.

When the family was seated, the music changed from the soft prelude to the stronger tones of "A Mighty Fortress is our God," and the clergy processed in, followed by the honorary pall bearers. Mike had the audacity to wink at me, a move that greatly relieved my anxiety. It told me he was on top of things and not to worry.

The service was predictably long. Readings from the old and new testaments, three hymns— "How Great Thou Art," "Here I Am, Lord," and "Just As I Am." Was Joanie sending God a plea to take Buck with all his warts and bumps? The pastoral prayer was long and eloquent, as was the minister's eulogy. I didn't figure Buck graced the church doors often, so the minister must have visited with Joanie to find out about him. Then the mayor gave a shorter eulogy, as did one of Buck's brothers. I was squirming in my seat by the time we got to the benediction and recessional, "For All the Saints."

And then came the reception. The mayor and Joanie had decided to hold it in the church fellowship hall rather than asking people to move from one location to another. Burial would be later and private, family only, which meant neither Mike nor I had to attend.

The mayor's party was led out following the honorary pallbearers, and the rest of the congregation held for a bit to give us time to organize into a receiving line. I found myself by Joanie, as the mayor had requested. The children had somehow been spirited away to a nursery. Joanie's only question to me was about the protestors.

"Are they causing a scene?" she asked, and I assured her all was peaceful outside. And then we were greeting people, shaking hands, plastering smiles on our faces, telling people how glad we were to meet them. It seemed to go on for hours. Occasionally I glanced up to see someone with a plate of food or a cup of coffee, and I hoped my tongue didn't hang out. Was that really my stomach grumbling in hunger?

"My feet hurt," Joanie whispered.

"You may *not* take your shoes off," I retorted.

Next was, "I am so hungry."

"So am I," I whispered back. "Look, I think I see the end of the line."

"Thank the Lord."

"I already did."

The line did end, Mike brought me a plate of food, and I sank down in the nearest chair to wolf it down. A check of my phone showed that Keisha had not called. Mike had disappeared as soon as he handed me my plate, and someone had spirited Joanie off, so I sat in blessed solitude and tried to collect myself. I breathed a sigh of relief and briefly closed my eyes, wishing I could kick off my heels, unaccustomed as I was to them. After telling Joanie she had to keep her shoes on, I figured the same rules applied to me.

"I bet you're tired."

My eyes flew open, only to see the same pesky reporter. "I am exhausted," I said tersely.

"You got any reaction to the trouble outside?"

Trouble outside? No wonder Mike had disappeared so quickly. I rose to the reporter's bait. "What trouble?"

"Protestors. White supremacists have been attacked."

The worst-case scenario galloped through my mind. "Anybody hurt?"

He shrugged. "Not that I know of. Haven't heard gunshots. Was this what your husband was afraid of?"

"I can't speak for my husband." Suddenly I was desperate to get out of there, to leave that crowded hall, to lay my eyes on Mike and see that he was okay. I stood up, managing to mutter, "Excuse me" and dumping my plate on a serving stand. Halfway to the door, I realized I still had to tend my manners, and I whirled to find Joanie and the mayor.

The mayor was easier. She was talking to someone but turned to me as I approached. "Kelly, thank you so much for standing by Joanie."

"Glad to, but I have to run. Babysitter needs relief"—okay, my fingers were mentally crossed as I grabbed her hand in both of mine and said my thanks. Then I hurried to find Joanie, who was surrounded by family. Growing more desperate by the minute, I almost barged through a couple of layers of people to hug her and whisper, "Keisha called. Got to go. I'll call tomorrow."

She returned my hug. "Everything okay?"

Then of course I felt guilty for my little white lie. "Yes, yes, of course."

I headed for the exit, only to be waylaid this time by Al Johnson, who put a menacing hand on my arm. "Don't think this is over," he growled. "I know I should be chief, and I'm not forgetting."

Stunned, I jerked my arm away and turned away from him. But my heart was pounding. *How dare he? And how dangerous was he?* As I hurried away, I heard a derisive chuckle behind me.

And then at last I was back in the courtyard and headed for the street. Even there, I could hear voices raised in anger. When I reached the street, the parking lot seemed filled with men in blue, far outnumbering protestors. In fact, I had to look to identify the protestors. But they were there, now held in two opposing lines by the police. They shouted taunts and insults at each other, but no one came close to violence.

"Where's your car?" Mike's voice came from behind me, and I tried to be cool, not let him know how unreasonably afraid I'd been.

When I pointed out my car in the far end of the parking, close to the protestors, he said, "Let me get it for you. You don't need to go near that unpleasantness."

"Is it safe?"

He scoffed. "Those folks don't worry me. They're all talk and no show. Now a hidden sniper, that worries me." He brought the car to me, and I made a beeline for the office and my baby, glad to leave the funeral and protestors and Al Johnson behind me.

Chapter Twelve

There was no violence, and no new problems came out of Buck's funeral. Mike came home that night almost at the usual time, and we sat down as a family to roast chicken, French green beans, little potatoes roasted around the chicken, and a fruit plate for dessert. It felt wonderful. I was ready to put racism and protests and funerals behind me, to sit and play with my baby, to find out what was going on with my big girls, to spend some time with my husband. In short, to sit on the couch and read a book.

I did have one worry, but it was of a different kind. The fall dance, which it seemed we'd been anticipating forever, was the next night. Maggie and Dave were in a happy place in their friendship, and she was excited about the dance.

"Mom, I didn't mention this all week, because of Joanie and all, but I don't have a thing to wear to the fall dance," she said that night at dinner.

"Maggie, you've got a closet full of clothes," practical Em said. Her sister favored her with a dirty look.

"Maybe we could look together through your closet and see what we could find," I suggested. "Maybe a new combination of some of your outfits...."

Now Mike was frowning at me. "Kelly, I think you're missing the point. A girl deserves something new, to make her feel special."

Maggie looked at him with shining eyes and then turned to me. "Jenny and I were thinking we could go shopping tomorrow morning. Not the mall"—she said those last words with disdain—"but University Village. They have J. Crew, Banana Republic, and lots of others. I'm sure we'd find something."

I was a little behind here. "Is Jenny going to the dance?"

"Yeah. She's going with Brian Porter, a friend of Dave's. We're going to double date, sort of. We thought we'd meet at HG Sply for dinner before the dance. Brian has his own car, so he can drop Dave off here, and I'll drive us. Then after the dance, I'll drive us home, and Brian will pick Dave up here so his father doesn't have to get him. Dave is getting a little embarrassed about his dad having to take him to and from dates." She paused a minute, and then the truth came out. "It's awkward, too, that I'm the one who can drive, and he can't."

My nonfeminist daughter, with a firm grasp of traditional roles, at least about who drove the car. I bit my tongue when I saw Mike's stern look. Instead, I included him in my glance when I said, "I think University Village would be fine."

Mike added, "I'm really glad you aren't going to the malls. We get too many reports of trouble from them."

"None of the good stores are there anymore," Maggie said a bit snobbishly.

So it was settled. Maggie would spend the night at Jenny's, and they'd go shopping in the morning, with lunch at one of the sandwich shops in the shopping center. As a sop to Em, I asked if she wanted to call someone to spend the night.

"Can I go spend the night with Keisha?"

I was startled, but I said I'd call. I explained Maggie's agenda and said that Em, offered a sleepover, had instead asked to stay with Keisha. And the answer of was, "Of course that sweet baby can come stay with me. José's on patrol—he got a little sleep after the funeral—but he'll be glad to see her. I'll fix her up in the guest room, and she and I can do girl stuff, like paint our nails. In the morning, we'll take her to the pancake house. Who knows? We might just go shopping in University Village." She laughed heartily.

Mike and I would have an evening alone, with Gracie that is. I almost wished I felt comfortable enough to ask my mom to take Gracie, but truth was, I didn't. She'd go to sleep early, and Mike and I could have some private time. I had no idea he would fall dead sleep before Gracie, but I woke him when I went to bed, and he made me glad I did.

All my girls were home by noon the next day. To my surprise, Maggie bought a dress, well under the limit I'd given her. It was short, of course, but not so short as to make Mike and me raise our eyebrows. Below a V-neck, it was fitted at the waist and then flared. Short sleeves flared to match the hem. It fit Maggie perfectly, and the soft shade of green became her. Still within her price range, she'd found a pair of light brown sandals. She modeled all this proudly, but when we asked about jewelry, she was astounded.

"No jewelry. It's not a dressy dance."

Keisha, who had brought Em back and was watching the style show, said, "Well, shut my mouth and call me old-fashioned. I think you need a necklace with that neckline."

Em, meanwhile, was sporting nails painted a shade called Alice Blue, presumably the favorite of Alice Roosevelt. I doubt Em knew that, but it was a nice thought. What bothered me more was that she had a matching streak in her lovely light brown hair. Keisha saw me frown, and whispered, "Now, Mama, don't say nothing." I didn't.

That evening, Dave arrived about six, thanks to Brian. Dave was wearing new, creased, starched jeans, a starched white shirt, and a tweedy sport coat. But something was different, beyond the spiffy outfit, and I couldn't put my finger on. Suddenly I knew.

"Dave! Your glasses are gone."

He looked down in embarrassment. "Yes, ma'am. I got contacts."

"Doesn't he look great?" Maggie asked enthusiastically.

He pooh-poohed our praise, but I could tell he was secretly pleased. They set off for supper and the dance in high spirits.

Later that night I sat alone in a darkened living room. Mike and Gracie were asleep in our bedroom, and Em had fallen asleep over a book in her room. I'd peeked at her just minutes before Maggie got home. Then I was sitting on the couch, my book open in my lap but my eyes not on it. Holding a glass of wine, I stared into space and felt happy with life.

Just minutes before Maggie's midnight curfew, I heard the front door but didn't turn, because it opened but didn't close. Maggie and Dave were waiting for Brian. I could hear soft voices but couldn't hear what they said. It seemed forever that I sat, controlling both my curiosity and my impatience, but at long last, Dave came in to say goodnight.

"I knew you'd be up," Maggie said, her tone just a bit critical.

Dave jumped in with, "I hope you had a pleasant evening, Mrs. Shandy. We had a great time at the dance, and then we went to Ol' South for pancakes, a whole bunch of us."

"Sounds like fun. I'm glad you enjoyed yourselves."

With polite words, he said goodnight to me and then to Maggie, and I heard her close and bolt the door. Wordlessly, she came and hugged me and headed for her bedroom. Then, over her shoulder, she said, "Thanks for trusting me."

For the second night in a row, I woke Mike up. I had to share the evening with him, and I was glad I did.

* * * *

Sunday morning lazies. We all slept late—well, Gracie slept until a little after eight, which was really late for her. Mike got up with her, since he'd gone to sleep much earlier than I had, and headed for the kitchen to make sausage and waffles. We were still at the breakfast table at eleven, none of us in a hurry to do anything. I had conveniently put aside my resolve to get my family to church. Next week, I told myself.

It was a banner day for our family. Gracie was pulling herself up on everything—footstools, chairs, the couch. She edged around a hammock, never letting go because she'd learned if she did, she'd plop down on her bottom.

When we finally cleared the kitchen so I could start supper (this is a lazy Sunday?), Mike was reading the newspaper on the couch, and Gracie was crowing at him from her stance by the footstool. Idly Mike held out a hand, just a bit away from her, and she took that all-important, first-ever step to get to him. They both laughed in delight, and Mike demanded the girls and I come see.

After that the girls tired that baby out, encouraging her to walk. By the end of the afternoon, she had taken four consecutive steps before landing on her bottom and gleefully clapping for herself while her sisters cheered.

The weather had again turned cold, with November right around the corner, and I'd made a pot of chili for supper. Mine is a basic and simple chili, and contrary to Texas folk wisdom, I put pinto beans in it. My family likes to eat it with grated cheddar, chopped red onion, and a good glob of sour cream.

As I chopped onions and garlic for the chili, my cell phone rang. Caller ID showed a number I didn't recognize, so I automatically started to ignore the call. But instinct is a funny thing, and without a second thought I punched the talk button and said, "Kelly O'Connell."

A man's voice, vaguely familiar but I couldn't put my finger on who. "Ms. O'Connell. Tell your husband there's going to be trouble tonight. I wanted to warn you."

A noise in the background and then a hurried, "I have to go now."

I rushed to find Mike, who was still on the couch with his book. "Trouble tonight," I blurted out. "I just got a call."

So calm I could have strangled him, he put his book down and looked at me. "Trouble where? What kind of trouble? Who called?"

I had to confess that I didn't know the answers to any of those questions. Not even who called.

"Describe the voice." Mike still seemed unperturbed.

I did the best I could and added the thought that had just come to me. "It was an educated voice. He spoke precisely, slowly, even though he was in a hurry at the end."

Mike sat up, took my hand, and pulled me down on the couch next to him. "Kelly, I think someone's messing with you. Sounds like a prank call. Put it out of your mind." He gave me a kiss and muttered, "Onions."

Chastened, I went back to my chili.

As the five of us sat at the table, I remembered Em's longing for one of our big potluck suppers, with all of our nearest and dearest—my mom and Otto, Claire Guthrie and her daughters, Anthony, his boys, and his daughter Teresa and her husband, Joe, and their new baby. And, of course, Keisha and José. And sometimes Maggie's friend, Jenny, and her mom, Mona, who owned the flourishing small hot dog stand on Magnolia. Em frequently clamored for these suppers. Perhaps even at her age she realized that reconnecting as a family was essential to our recovery from the trauma of the kidnapping threat that hung over us for so long.

Now, I thought, it's about time. Maybe next week. I dished up the second helping that Mike asked for and was about to solicit family opinion on a potluck, when his cell phone beeped. From the instant look on his face, I knew there was trouble.

Almost knocking the chili on the floor, he said, "Gotta go" and headed for the closet and his warm jacket. Watching, I saw him take his service revolver from its locked box on the high shelf, but he didn't stop for his uniform. Just his shoulder holster. Wearing khakis and a sweatshirt under the jacket, revolver shoved in the holster, he was almost out the door before I could ask, "Where?"

"Jason Pickard's house. Better watch the ten o'clock news."

He didn't expect to be back before ten. This was not a quickly solved situation, whatever it was. While the girls cleared the table and Gracie gnawed on a hard biscuit, I sat and thought about what I knew about Jason Pickard. I'd never met the man, but ever since he shot Douglas Hardin, I'd heard a lot about him.

A family man, married to his high school sweetheart, two young children—my mind jumped to when my older girls had been young, and I felt a wash of nostalgia. But back to Jason. He lived in an upper middle-class neighborhood, homes mostly owned by black businessmen. His wife worked in public relations, and the children were in a church preschool. They attended church on Sundays, didn't go out much, and were generally an all-American family. Except, some would object that they were black and therefore not typical.

Since the shooting, protestors with obnoxious signs had shown up outside the Pickard home. The same signs, perhaps literally, that I'd seen at Buck's funeral. The house had been egged, and a black swastika painted on the brick. The air had been let out of the tires of their cars, stranding them.

Instead of fading, the protestors seemed to get bolder recently and some signs demanded action in the investigation into Hardin's death. After the death, Jason had been immediately taken off patrol and assigned to a desk job, but lately he'd talked of either quitting the force or taking a leave of absence. He wanted to be home with his family, protecting his house if necessary.

Jason had strong support from his fellow officers and the Pickard family had the same from their neighbors, who rallied around with food and fellowship, chasing off protestors at some risk to themselves, until the police asked them to stay inside and notify authorities. I tried to tell myself that a few protestors had probably shown up and someone had called police.

But deep down I knew Mike was more concerned than that when he left. I got up and went to the kitchen to turn on the TV, thinking if it was bad, they break in with news. But all I got was

Sunday night football. The girls were doing the dishes, so I fetched Gracie into the kitchen to play and began putting away food and laying out things for breakfast and school lunches the next day.

When the phone rang again, I jumped, hoping it was Mike. A quick glance told me it was that unidentified caller. Only then did I remember his earlier warning. My "Hello" was cautious.

"Ms. O'Connell, this is Morty Berman. I tried to warn you before, but Tom caught me on the phone. He doesn't like me, and frankly I don't like him. I'm only here because Jim Johnson is a special friend of mine."

I wondered for a nanosecond how to interpret that.

"Tom tolerates me because I cook. But I can't overlook what's going on here, and you seemed the best person to whom I should turn."

Tentatively I asked, "What *is* going on?"

"The encouragement of racism, blatant racism."

The gay Jewish cook had a moral streak a mile wide. Good for him.

"Tom organized tonight's protest, called people to get them to turn out. They're all gone now."

My next question was desperate. "Did they have guns?"

"No, ma'am. Only signs and their voices. That's bad enough."

I let out a huge sigh of relief.

It turned out that my sigh was premature. Nor did we have to wait for the ten o'clock news. Mike called a little before nine. My always unflappable husband was almost incoherent.

"Keisha's been shot. Get to JPS right away. José will send someone to meet you at the entrance and take your car. Go!"

Chapter Thirteen

Keisha, shot. At JPS. My mind was spinning. "Mike, the girls …" Keisha was who I always called if I had to leave the girls alone.

"They'll be fine," he said tersely. "Keisha needs you."

"Mom, what is it? You look scared to death." Maggie's voice brought me back to reality.

"It's Keisha," I stammered.

Em was suddenly clinging to me, her face fearful, her eyes brimming. "What's the matter with Keisha?"

I hesitated and then reached out to them both with my arms. This would rock their world worse than anything they'd known, worse even than the kidnapping threat. Keisha had been the rock that they relied on.

"What happened?" Maggie demanded, her tone strident and adult.

"She's been shot." It came out as a whisper, and I realized I didn't have anything else to tell them. I didn't know how, why, when. I had no idea how threatening her condition. "I have to go to her. To the hospital." We were all crying now, our arms wrapped around each other. From her crib in the dining room, Gracie sensed the atmosphere and began to wail.

"I'm going with you," Maggie announced in a tone that said she'd not stand for anything else.

Em echoed, "Me, too."

I took a deep breath. "Girls, we can't take Gracie to JPS. I need you to stay and look after her."

The word "Keisha" began to form on Maggie's lips and was cut off just as suddenly as she realized that Keisha couldn't help us this time. We had to help Keisha.

"Will you call as soon as you find out anything?" The demanding tone was still there.

"Of course. Em, can you find my purse?" I stumbled to the closet to grab a jacket. Some impulse made me reach to the locked box on the high shelf and get my handgun. I slid it into my pocket, hoping the girls wouldn't notice.

Em was too quick for me. She came up behind me, carrying my purse. "Why are you taking your gun?" Alarm was written all over her face.

"Just a precaution, Em. I won't need it. But you know, the parking garage at JPS is a scary place." I turned to give my lecture to both of them. "Please get Gracie in pajamas and give her a bedtime milk in a sippy cup. When you both get ready for bed, finish your homework. I'll call. If you need anything in a hurry . . ." What could I tell them? "Call Claire. Only call Nana in a desperate emergency." I did *not* want to deal with my mother and answer her questions. She'd find a way to put blame on Keisha, and I couldn't bear it.

One more instruction about locking doors, calling police, and I was in my car headed for the hospital just blocks from our house. My hands gripped the steering wheel so tightly they ached, and my vision was blurred with tears. I sped and slipped through stop signs and prayed for an officer to stop me, but none did. I roared up to the entrance to the hospital and skidded to a stop.

Before I could open my car door, a young police officer beat me to it. "Ms. O'Connell? Chief asked me to take you to José, We'll take care of your car."

My first thought was that I was surely an embarrassment to Mike. I took mental inventory of my appearance—this morning's makeup, if it survived, was streaked and faded, my hair had not met with a comb in hours, and I was wearing stretched-out sweats, a T-shirt, and a jacket that clashed with everything. All while carrying a gorgeous soft leather handbag from Talbot's that

Mike had splurged on. To top it all off, I was sure my eyes were wild and frantic.

My second thought was that Mike had told me never to go with anyone who claimed his authority unless they knew our secret code. As I opened my mouth to ask if Mike had sent a message, the young man said, "Keisha asked for you." Ironically, that was it. We just never knew it would be truth.

The ER waiting room at JPS, the area's trauma hospital, would be a zoo, and I said a silent prayer that was not our destination. Keisha and I had once spent a day there, and it ranked high on my list of experiences not to repeat. As I followed the young man through labyrinthine corridors, I knew we had passed the waiting room, but where was he taking me?

We finally stopped in a hallway full of doors. My escort knocked softly and then, without waiting for an answer, opened the door and stood aside for me. The small room, the size of an examining room, was crowded with a couch and two overstuffed chairs. José sat in one of the chairs, elbows on his knees, head buried in his hands. He did not look up. The other man, in policeman's uniform but with a clerical collar, looked up and nodded gently to me.

"José?" I spoke softly, but he jumped to his feet and threw his arms around me, holding tight and long. My face was scrunched into his shirt front so hard I could hardly breathe.

"Kelly, she's gonna die. I know she is." He was sobbing, forcing the words out between gulps of grief. He finally relaxed his grip enough that I could pull back and look at him. He was a mess, looked worse than I did.

"She's not going to die, José. Has anyone told you that? A doctor?"

He shook his head. "I just know. Because I don't know what I'll do without her. But, Kelly, she was shot in the head. People die when that happens." He said it with a kind of strange authority.

Shot in the head! Yeah, people usually do die from that. I looked to the clergyman for affirmation, but he simply nodded. "Sit," I said, practically pushing José back into the chair and then sinking into the couch myself, so that our knees were touching, and I could hold both of his hands. "Tell me what happened. Where was she?"

Again, words punctuated by sobs. "Coming up Jason Pickard's driveway. One shot. That's all it was. One lousy shot, and it got her in the head. Oh, God, Kelly. There was blood everywhere. I never seen so much blood."

"Where is she now?"

He shook his head in misery. "I don't know. Some doctor—too young to trust—told me they had to clean away all the blood and whatever that they could and then they'd do something and take her to surgery if there was any chance to save her."

It was the "whatever" that I didn't like, could barely think about. Bone fragments? Oh, please, Lord, no!

I shifted uncomfortably on the couch, which was so well used that a spring was poking at me where I sat. "Why was she there? I know Mike went because there was trouble. But why would Keisha go?"

José straightened up a bit, and pride crept into his voice. "She's been takin' food to Jason and his family. Part of something called a meal train. I didn't know about it, till someone told me at the scene. Just like her."

It was just like Keisha to walk into danger because she wanted to help someone. Lord knows, she'd done it often enough to save me.

José went on. "Whatever she had fixed, she put it in her grandma's good dish. She's gonna be royally pissed that the dish got shattered."

For the first time I grinned. Yes, she would be royally pissed. In my mind, I could hear her fussing about it.

With a start, I remembered to call the girls. I was talking to Maggie, leaving her as uncertain as we were, when Mike burst in the small room without knocking, his large presence filling the room. Mike was still in civilian clothes, now rumpled. His face wore a mask over fatigue.

José jumped to his feet again, and the two men stood locked in a long bear hug. The clergyman rose and sidled his way by them, not an easy task, indicating to me he'd be outside if needed.

Mike suddenly drew back from the hug and demanded, "Why the hell did you let her go over there?" His tone was angry, accusing, and completely out of character.

I drew in a sharp breath, and looked at José, who had drawn a fist, ready to strike. Holding my breath, I did the only thing I could think of. I stepped between them, praying that each would look and think before striking out.

José deflated first. "Man, I had no idea what she was doing. Far as I can guess now, she's been goin' over there when I was on duty."

"Mike." I said it slowly and softly but in a firm voice that finally drew his attention to me.

He caught himself, stared for a minute at both of us as though he didn't know us, and then slowly sat on the couch, shaking his head. "Sorry. I'm just so damn upset. I couldn't believe she was there, and I tried to shout out, but I was too late. She . . . she just crumpled, like a sack of meal, and I couldn't do anything. Nothing!" He buried his face in his hands.

"Yeah, I know," José muttered.

We sat in silence for what seemed forever, until I finally asked, "Everything quiet at the Pickards' house now?"

Mike roused himself. "Yeah. We got the crowd to disperse. Had to arrest your tenant, Kelly. That Whitehead fellow. Wouldn't put his sign down, wouldn't stop yelling about white rights and stuff, wouldn't try to lead his people away. Actually got into a scuffle with him." He looked down at his clothes. "Guess you can tell. He's in a cell now, and I hope he's thinking about the consequences of disturbing the peace, resisting arrest. Maybe trespassing. What kind of a fool tries to fight with the officer who's just trying to get him to move on?"

He stared off into space for a minute and then looked at me. "Officer who collared him brought me his ID. He had membership cards in things like the National Socialist Movement and the Covenant Nation Church of the Lord Jesus Christ. That so-called church believes Christianity is for white folks. And the other group is a national neo-Nazi one. Our guy is flirting with some big stuff."

"Are their branches of those groups here?" I asked.

"Not that I know of. That's sort of a saving grace. If there were, I'd have to dig a lot deeper about your tenant."

I chewed on that for a while, but I had no legitimate reason to evict Whitehead and his roommates. Made me nervous, though.

José asked, "Pickard okay? His family?" José probably was truly concerned, but he was also trying to distract himself.

"Pickard says he's putting the house on the market. May leave Fort Worth but says at least he'll move to an all-black neighborhood. Seems to think neighbors would come out to support him then. He's pretty bitter. I'll talk to him but sure not tonight."

Slowly, more of the story came out in bits and pieces. José had been on duty but responded to an "all officers" call for help at the Pickards' home. He was helping with crowd control when he happened to turn and see Keisha, with that covered dish in her hands. He started to run toward her when he heard that shot. "I don't know what I was going to do," he said. "Probably something dumb and dramatic, like throw myself on top of her. But I couldn't even shout. It was like my voice was frozen."

Aside from those snippets of conversation, we sat in agonized silence. My insistence that no news was good news fell on deaf ears.

When we finally heard a soft knock, I thought it must be midnight. It was only nine o'clock. I had been with José barely an hour.

Chapter Fourteen

José was right. The doctor who edged into the room was far too young to be out of college, let alone tell us anything about Keisha. His white coat was immaculate—so much for all that blood José worried about—and he wore a stethoscope around his neck, something I'd always heard doctors-in-training did but "real" doctors never did. His close-shaven beard hid much of his face, but tired blue eyes looked out from above it.

Looking in puzzlement from José to Mike and back, he held out his hand and said, "Mr. Thornberry? I'm Dr. Carmichael."

José stood, looking much like a person on trial and about to hear the judge impose the death penalty. "I'm Thornberry," he said in a tight voice.

"Please, sit again. Your wife is going to be fine. She's asking for you."

We all stared at him for a minute as though he were speaking in tongues. How could she be fine? She'd been shot in the head. Was this some kind of macabre joke?

José finally asked, "Say that again?"

Dr. Carmichael obliged and elaborated. "The bullet grazed her head, but it didn't penetrate the skull. We've cleaned the wound, sutured it, started her on antibiotics. I'm pretty sure she has a concussion, mild we hope, and I know for sure she's got a whopper of a headache."

José put his head in his hands and sobbed. "Thank you, Lord, thank you." Then he seemed to remember his manners, because he jumped up and began pumping the doctor's hand. "Thank you, oh, Lord, thank you so much, doctor."

"I'll take you to her." He looked regretfully at us. "I'm afraid she can only have one visitor."

Mike rose. "We understand. I'm Chief Mike Shandy. José is one of my men and also a part of my family. His wife and my wife"—he nodded at me—"are partners in real estate. Would you come back and give us a fuller report?"

The doctor promised, and they left. As José passed to the door, Mike laid a hand on his shoulder and squeezed. "Give her our love."

True to his word, the doctor was back in less than five minutes. When Mike asked, he explained that if you thought of the flesh covering the skull as earth, you might say the bullet plowed a furrow in it. "'Bout the size of a pencil. Bullets are dirty things, though, carrying lots of crap with them, including dirt and grease. We've started her on antibiotics, and we've given her some pretty strong narcotics to ease the pain, both of the scalp wound and the headache."

"Where's the bullet?" Mike asked, his police antenna ever on duty.

The doctor shrugged. "Who knows. It just didn't stop with her. You can do a search of the area where she was shot, but it may be like looking for that needle in a haystack."

I asked about scarring and he said, yes, there would be scarring where the graze mark is. "Depends on how she wears her hair."

I thought about that spike hairdo she'd been wearing lately.

The doctor went on, "There's some bruising around the site, and it will get worse before it gets better. But most of her symptoms should disappear within a few days. If not, then she needs to be seen by a professional. So far, she doesn't seem to have many symptoms. If she starts complaining about blurred vision or interrupted sleep, we'd need to know about that."

We asked the usual questions about hospital stay, recovery, and the like and were surprised, even alarmed by the answers. The doctor allowed as to how she might stay the night for observation, but she'd go home tomorrow and back to work whenever she felt like it. Which meant whenever her head stopped aching. He wouldn't begin to predict when that might be.

It all seemed too informal to me. I wanted lists and times and symptoms to watch for. When I asked, the doctor clarified a bit. "While we have

Mrs. Thornberry, we'll be watching for several things—fuzzy thinking, tendency to stumble and fall, slurring speech, uneven disposition.

"We'll send home a list of things to watch for and a do and don't do list. We won't just send her out cold." He smiled at his own small joke.

"I imagine her husband will spend the night. Why don't you folks go on and get some rest at home."

We left, but of course home is not where Mike went. Saying he had a few details to work out, he kissed me and sent me on my way in my car, which had magically appeared at the hospital front door just when I needed it.

"Don't be too late," I whispered.

"Soon as I can."

On the way home I called the girls, struck by sudden guilt that I hadn't checked on them. All three should be asleep by now, but of course the two older ones were wide awake. They cheered when I told them Keisha would be fine.

"I'll be home in five minutes," I said.

When I got there, they met me with a glass of wine and a snack tray of cheese and crackers, and I knew I was in for a blow-by-blow repeat of the evening. It was almost midnight when we went to bed, and after one when Mike came in. I knew he'd gone back to the Pickard house.

* * * *

We dragged ourselves and the girls out of bed the next morning, but we were running late. While I tended to Gracie and tried to gently hurry the older girls along, Mike made breakfast—or tried to. He burned the bacon and brewed a pot of hot water because he forgot to add the coffee. He was even a bit short with Em when she couldn't find her homework that she absolutely knew she'd done the night before, and she burst into tears. Finally, tears dried, stomachs fed, the girls left for school.

"Okay," I turned to Mike, who sat at the kitchen table, obviously absorbed in his own thoughts to the extent that he was ignoring Gracie, who clamored for more eggs. "What's on your mind?"

"That bullet. I tried looking last night, but it was no good in the dark. I'll get a team out there today. If we can find the bullet, we stand a chance of finding out who shot Keisha. If, and it's a big if, we find the rifle. But last night I was so sure we could nail your tenant for it. Now I don't think so."

I shuddered, remembering the initial unpleasant first contact between Keisha and Tom Whitehead. There would have been a certain symmetry if he'd been the one who shot her, besides which it would have solved it quickly and given us all some relief. "Why don't you think it was him?"

"Angle is all wrong, if I've got this figured right. Bullet came from almost straight behind

169

Keisha as she walked up the driveway. We were containing the protestors way over on the street on the far side of Jason's property. No way Whitehead could have gotten over there. And we didn't see any protestors with rifles."

"What's across the street from the house?"

"A park." He said it grimly, and I knew he was thinking bushes and trees could easily have sheltered a shooter. But if it wasn't a protestor, then who? And why?

I remembered that Morty Berman had said his roommates were not armed, and I relayed hat message to Mike, who said it only confirmed what they had decided.

"Got to get going. I got a lot to do today." He kissed me quickly and went to finish dressing in his uniform.

I had a lot to do too, but I had trouble collecting myself and my thoughts. First order of business was to call José and hope I didn't wake him.

* * * *

José was at the hospital. In fact, he'd never left and had slept, uncomfortably, in a chair in Keisha's room. She'd woken him at five thirty with a demanding, "José? I got to get out of here now!"

His efforts to placate her fell on deaf ears. She was not going to be a sweet model patient. She was Keisha, and she was determined—and not pleasant about it.

"Started pulling out IVs and all. I had to call the nurse, and I was truly afraid they were going to strap her down. Either that or I'd have to slap some sense into her. One nurse told me it isn't too unusual for people with concussions to be unreasonable. Can you come try to quiet her?"

There I sat, holding Gracie while she drank juice from her sippy cup. I could hardly take Gracie into the ICU unit. "I don't have anyone to take care of Gracie."

"Shoot! I'll hold Gracie in the lobby. I can reason with her easier than I can with Keisha."

And that's how I found myself at Keisha's bedside, while elsewhere in the vast hospital José held my infant daughter who, when I handed her to him, was sleeping soundly. Trouble was belligerent Keisha had been replaced by sleeping Keisha. Under the white sheets, she looked smaller and darker than usual—and a lot more frail than the woman I was used to. She snored gently and ignored my light hand on her arm. I couldn't stay all day waiting for her to wake up.

Softly, I whispered, "Come on, Keisha. It's me, Kelly. Open those eyes and look at me." I stroked her arm, fluffed her pillows, tried to create a quiet commotion that wouldn't disturb her, though I was half afraid of what would happen when she woke up.

"Kelly? My head hurts somethin' awful. Where's José?"

"Downstairs watching Gracie, so I could come up and watch you sleep."

She grinned. "Sorry. I'm just so tired, and so mixed up about what happened to me. I think I got shot, but I'm not dead so that can't be." She moved uncomfortably, twisting the sheets until she had them in a knot.

I explained the best I could about the bullet grazing her head, and she put a tentative hand up to the left side of her head, where bandages covered the wound.

"I'm not gonna die?"

"Not unless José or I kill you for being difficult. You fought with him this morning, told him you had to get out of here at five thirty in the morning."

She sat up a little and then winced at the pain. "Well, I do got to get out of here. Got work to do at the office." Then she seemed to remember something. "The Pickards. There were all kinds of people there, and I was taking them King Ranch Chicken. In my granny's best dish. Where's the dish?" She looked clearly at me.

I tried to divert her with a question. "What were you doing at their house? Why would you go there when you knew there was a protest?"

"Protest? I didn't know about it." She stared off into space and then seemed to have another of her moments of recall. "Oh, all these people off to one side. And a lot of police officers. But I didn't know about it. I was taking food to the Pickards. Been doing that every two or three days." Another pause, and then, "Something hit me in the head, hard, and I remember knowing I was falling, couldn't help myself."

"It was the bullet."

"Yeah, must've been, but as I fell, I could hear José calling my name. From far off."

I remembered José saying his voice froze but Mike saying he tried to call to her. She thought it was José, and I wasn't going to correct her. I asked a different question "Keisha, did anyone know you were going to the Pickards?"

She started to shake her head and then regretted it. "No. José was on duty. You're the only other one that keeps track of me, and I don't call and tell you everything I'm doing. Oh, and Momma. But I don't bother her much. She worries, just like Miss Cynthia. Don't tell either of them I been shot."

She was beginning to ramble, which I thought was a prelude to sleep so I started to sneak away, only to be stopped by a demanding voice, "Kelly. You tell that no-good José to come here and get me. I got to get out of this place."

Yep, concussion sufferers could be irrational.

* * * *

I collected Gracie from José. She'd woken up hungry, which he solved by getting her soft-serve ice cream that she was happily licking from the cone he held. When he handed her to me, she was a drippy, sticky mess.

"Keisha?" he asked.

"You're right. She's not herself. I promise not to tell her you fed the baby ice cream."

"Yeah, right. Guess I better go back upstairs. I hope they keep her another night."

"Me, too," I said.

Gracie and I went by the house for me to clean her up and give each of us a bit of lunch. After the ice cream, she wasn't hungry and played with the cheese I gave her. I finally packed a snack for her, and we left for the office.

As I expected, phone messages were stacked up, and when I turned on my computer, the email almost exploded at me. I was about to find out what life without Keisha was like, at least for a while. Gracie played nicely by herself and finally took another nap, leaving me free to deal with the chaos.

Slowly I returned calls, including one from the owner of the house Tom Whitehead had rented. She was concerned about the nature of her tenant and understood he'd been in trouble the night before. I couldn't figure how she knew that for the life of me, but I knew only too well how bad news travels. I told her the tenant had given us no justification for breaking the lease and that I was aware of the situation and watching it.

Two, not one, but two people called with potential listings. One house sounded wonderful on the outside but unprepossessing on the inside. The other was just the opposite, beautiful Craftsman woodwork throughout but on an unusually small lot. Both owners asked when I could do a walk-through, and I had to put them off. Normally I'd have turned Gracie over to Keisha and been out the door right away, but I had a sleeping baby to care for. And even if she were awake, it was hardly professional to take a one-year-old on a real estate call.

The girls didn't get home until almost four thirty, and since the days were growing shorter as winter approached, it would be dark by the time I inspected a house if I waited for them to babysit. My only option seemed to be do walk-throughs on Saturday when Mike could play home parent. This was Monday, and that meant putting people off an entire business week, during which time they could easily call another realtor. I promised to drive by and report to each owner.

I made a good dent in the mess that had greeted me and was just thinking about packing up Gracie and driving by those two potential listings on the way home, when the door opened, and Tom Whitehead came in. I wasn't particularly pleased at the thought of being alone in the office with him and the baby, so I gathered all my psychological strength. And I refrained from saying, "Did you post bail?"

"I want to know if my lease is in jeopardy," he demanded. "I know you're married to the cop who arrested me last night."

Another instance of news getting around. "No, I'm married to his boss, the one you fought with," I said. "So far, you've done nothing that gives me cause to break the lease."

He wore jeans and his work shirt and had apparently come directly from his job. Now, he paced in front of me, his hands caught in the pockets just below his belt—a pose I associated with cowboys and thought looked out of character on him. "That repairman you sent...I suppose he reported on the posters on my wall."

He was sounding me out. "Yes. I've gathered you believe in white supremacy. But I could have told you that from your first encounter with Keisha." I looked toward her desk. Behind me, Gracie stirred. The loud voice had woken her.

He seemed to notice for the first time that Keisha wasn't at her desk. "I'm sorry she got hurt," he said and sounded like he truly meant it. "I thought there were to be no guns at the meeting."

"You call that a meeting? I call it a protest."

He whirled on me. "The term doesn't matter. We gathered to express our opinion that the two races should live separately. I hear that officer is thinking of moving to a black neighborhood. He should. That's where he belongs."

The innuendo in this whole thing made my head ache. "I don't happen to believe that way at all," I said boldly. "We are all created equal."

"That's bull. We should not be sharing neighborhoods, schools, churches."

"Churches?" I know my voice squeaked.

"Christianity is a white man's religion." His tone now was haughty.

I did the worst thing I could. I laughed. "What makes you think Jesus was a white man?"

He turned toward the door. "As long as there is no problem with my lease, I have no reason to talk to you."

"There's no problem," I said equitably, "but Anthony will make frequent inspections to be sure you haven't damaged the property. We have a key."

"I'll change the locks," he threatened, every fiber of his posture shouting controlled anger.

I didn't want to break that control, but I said, "That would break the lease."

He stormed out.

Shaking, I stuffed papers into my briefcase, gathered up Gracie and her things, and headed for the car. I'd lost enthusiasm for the curb inspections and only wanted to be home.

* * * *

Not surprisingly, Mike was exhausted when he came home. He sank into a chair in the living room, and without asking, Em brought him a glass of red wine, which he sipped gratefully. Finally, he surprised me with, "I've a bit of good news. We found the bullet that hit Keisha. We're pretty sure there was only one shot, so we have it."

"Who found it?" Em asked.

He looked a bit chagrined. "One of Pickard's kids. My men combed those bushes forever, but his son, maybe eight, crawled in there and was behind the bushes so long I thought we might have to pull him out. But when he crawled out the other end by their garage, he was holding this bullet."

"I want to see," Em said.

"Can't. It's in the evidence room at headquarters. If we ever get a suspect, we can test the bullet against the gun or guns that may have shot it. I'm keeping that bullet under lock and key. It's the only clue we have to who shot Keisha." He turned to me, "How is she?"

I described my morning visit with Keisha, and he frowned. "Not like her," he said, and I agreed.

"Will she be back to herself?" Em asked hopefully.

Contract for Chaos

Chapter Fifteen

José called the next morning just after the girls and Mike left. I was spooning Cream of Wheat into Gracie's mouth. Since I'd sweetened it with it a bit of brown sugar and butter, she opened her mouth like a young bird, but some still dripped down her face and onto her clothes. It was pretty much a two-handed job, so I talked with the phone wedged between my raised shoulder and my ear. Not good for concentration.

"Doctor says she's going home today," José said. "Says he's not alarmed by her…ah…behavior, but I am."

I could see long, lanky José slouched against the wall, holding his phone in one hand and scratching his head in perplexity with the other. "Here's the thing, Kelly. I'm on duty the next four nights, and I don't like the idea of leaving her alone at night. Shoot! I don't like the idea of leaving her alone, but I can handle it during the day and get some catnaps."

He knew what I'd say. "She'll stay here."

"I thought maybe we could both stay in the guesthouse. Don't want to trouble you."

"José, it's no trouble." The phone slipped out from its wedge, and I had to shout, "Hold on." I picked it up and said, more calmly, "Can you hold on for a minute?"

He said "Yeah, I'm out in the hall. Don't want her to hear me. She's gonna say she's fine."

I got rid of the Cream of Wheat, gave Gracie a chunked-up banana, and went back to José. "Of course she's not fine. She'll stay here, you sleep in your own bed during the day, and come see her before you go on duty. It's only four nights and then we'll reassess."

"Sounds like heaven. We'll be there whenever they cut her loose."

Keisha's pending arrival made for a busy morning. I cleaned Gracie up, shoved her, soiled clothes and all, into a jacket and ran to the office to fill my briefcase with things I'd left behind the previous day, transferred phone calls to my cell phone, checked that I hadn't overlooked anything, and headed home. By three o'clock, when José and Keisha finally arrived, I had a clean, well-rested baby girl, and had done the two curb inspections and a lot of annoying paperwork.

Keisha didn't start things off on a good note. "I can't stay here. We got that feral cat to look after."

"I can take care of the cat," José said.

"Well, we can't impose on Mike and Kelly."

"You can and you will," I said firmly. "The girls will sleep on pallets and you'll get Maggie's new bed. Much better than the cot-like thing she used to sleep on." We'd recently bought Maggie a double bed. It didn't leave much room around it for pallets, but I thought I could make it work, and they'd be there if Keisha started wandering in the night or something. Upstairs, Mike and I might not hear her.

Keisha sighed and headed for the kitchen table. "My whole life has changed, because of one person's hate. And rifle. It's not fair."

Not the time to remind her that life was rarely fair and so on. "We'll find out who shot you. Mike's working on it, and I have some ideas."

"I don't even care who it was. I just want that two seconds of my life back."

I didn't think that was a good sign at all. I wanted her to burn to know who it was, to see that the shooter was properly punished. Instead, she was apathetic.

Then she added, "And maybe I want my granny's casserole dish back." But then she asked, "It wasn't that Whitehead fellow, was it? I remember he was there, kind of leading that pack of fools."

"No. Mike suspected him at first too, but the angle of the bullet was wrong. They've found the bullet. One of Jason Pickard's children found it in the bushes. Mike says it's important evidence, and he's got it in a safe place in the evidence room."

"It'll just disappear," she said prophetically, and I hoped she was wrong.

I almost threw my hands in the air. Instead, I turned on the teakettle and got cups out for tea. That's where the girls found us—sitting around the kitchen table with our hot tea.

"Keisha!" Em dropped her books unceremoniously and rushed to hug her.

"Hi, baby. How you been? I missed you."

"Oh, I missed you and worried about you. I'm so glad you're all right."

Maggie was more restrained in her welcome but nonetheless sincere. Keisha rewarded her by holding her at arm's length, examining her critically, and saying, "You put on weight, Miss Maggie. You got to watch that."

Maggie was crestfallen, and I said, "I don't think she's gained much in three days, Keisha."

And that's how the evening went. José left to get into uniform and start his patrol, promising to swing by during the evening. Mike came home, bringing with him cheeseburgers from the Grill.

"Sorry, Keisha. Doctor said no wine for you yet."

She uttered what I could only describe as a profanity I'd never heard from her before, and both girls looked stunned. "I'll settle for one small glass," she said. I poured it and felt guilty about it.

The rest of the evening, she'd seem fine, but then something weird would come out unexpectedly. Once, when Mike had gone upstairs briefly, and the girls were changing for bed, she took my hand and said softly, "I'm afraid, Kelly. Very afraid."

"Of what, Keisha? Seems to me about the worst that can happen has, and you've been lucky. Not many people survive being shot in the head."

"I'm afraid I lost my sixth sense." She hung her head in despair. "I can't see the future. I don't know if you're safe, if José is, even little Gracie."

I thought about her prediction that the bullet would disappear and hoped that the sixth sense was gone, just temporarily, but that the prediction was off-base.

Mike came back downstairs and asked why we looked so glum.

"Just girl talk," Keisha told him, and I didn't correct her.

* * ** *

Keisha stayed with us four days, and every day I saw improvement. She slept a lot but told me she slept restlessly, waking frequently. I mostly worked from home those days, but when I had to go to the office I took Gracie with me. Mike agreed that he could watch Gracie Saturday, so I put off walking through the new listings until then.

Most afternoons, Keisha was up, dressed, and in the kitchen with me by four o'clock. Or she was in the dining room with the girls while they did their homework—I had to caution her not to do it for them. And some days, she played with Gracie, encouraging her efforts to walk around the coffee table while holding on for dear life and occasionally letting go for one or two free steps.

One afternoon the doorbell rang, and I answered it to find a tall man and a young boy.

"I'm Jason Pickard," the man said, quickly flashing a police identification badge at me, "and this is Henry, my son. We came to see Keisha, if that would be okay."

I realized that for all he'd been in my thoughts and, unconsciously, had a major impact on my life, I'd never met Jason Pickard. He looked younger than I thought he was, younger than me for sure. His skin was a warm cocoa color, and he looked like he knew his way around a track or a baseball field. Something kept him in good shape.

Henry was probably in fourth grade, missing a tooth in front, and smiling happily. He held out a proper hand to shake in greeting.

I welcomed them both and called out, "Keisha, you ready for company?"

"Sure." She sounded hearty and welcoming, so we all turned into the living room, where she had ensconced herself on the couch. Looking up, she quickly greeted Jason by name.

"Jason, thanks for coming to see me. How are you?"

"Question is, how are you?"

She reported that she was doing fine, and I chimed in to support her claim.

"Henry here is the one who found the bullet. He really wanted to come tell you about it."

With Keisha beaming at him, Henry described in great detail how he crawled to the back of the bushes along the garage wall. "I could fit where big people couldn't," he said proudly, "and I seen…"

"Saw," his father corrected.

"Saw this tiny glint. I had to dig with my hands to get it out, but I knowed I found it."

Keisha clapped her hands in admiration and exclaimed, "You are my hero, Henry. That bullet's gonna be important one day, so they tell me." Her purse was next to her on the couch, and she reached in and fished out a five-dollar bill that she handed to him. "I want to reward you."

"Oh, no," Jason said. "He doesn't need a reward. He was excited enough by the find."

They bickered back and forth and, finally, Henry got to keep the money. His eyes danced with happiness as he stuffed it in his pocket.

"Em," I called out, "would you take Henry out in the kitchen and get him a snack? Maybe lemonade, if he wants it."

Em came in, greeted our guests, and departed with Henry. I asked Jason how long he'd known Keisha, because I was really puzzled by her appearance in his driveway.

"I didn't know her till all this happened," he said. "When it got to the point that Carol, my wife, couldn't go the store for fear of people harassing her, Keisha brought us food. I think Sunday night was the fourth trip she'd made. I didn't know her, and José says he never told her what was going on with us."

Keisha broke in mournfully, "My sixth sense was working. I knew they were in difficulty. And taking food is what you do. I wish my sixth sense had told me about the protest Sunday night. I didn't know until I got there, and then I wasn't going to turn around and go home with my casserole. It looked safe enough. I'd like to relive those two seconds."

Jason sighed. "I'd like to relive that collar I made on that kid. I was horrified the instant I shot him, but it's what I was trained to do. He advanced on me, and I had no choice. But it sure has messed up my life, his family. I don't guess when a teen does something like that, he thinks about how many people he's gonna hurt."

I asked about his status with the department, and he said, "I been cleared by internal affairs but the DA hasn't checked in yet. Anyway, the chief, your husband, won't put me back on the street. Says it's not safe, until he decides who he trusts with my back. I hope it's José."

Out of the corner of my eye I saw Keisha shudder, and I knew she sensed danger in such a reassignment of her husband.

"Seems there some trouble in the department," Jason went on. "You probably know about that." His hands twisted in a nervous knot in front of his knees as he sat on the edge of one of our big Craftsman chairs.

I had a choice. If I bluffed and said I knew, would he elaborate and tell me more? If I was honest and said I didn't know a thing about it, would he clam up out of deference to his chief? "Mike has indicated something about it," I said cautiously, fingers crossed behind my back. It wasn't exactly a lie, maybe just an exaggeration.

"Some people on the force are apparently trying to start trouble...or keep it going. It's just a handful at most, but they're devious. They're quietly supporting the position of those protestors, saying we blacks shouldn't be police officers, shouldn't be allowed to have a gun."

Keisha gasped. "José ain't told me nothing about that," she said. "Who are they?"

Fleetingly I wondered if this was what we needed to get Keisha more interested in who shot her, to get her anger up, and maybe her sixth sense back.

Jason shook his head. "If the powers that be know, they aren't telling yet. Means for me and some of the other guys and a few women we watch our back all the time, 'cause we don't know who we can trust."

I know my face gave away the fact that I didn't know this before, because Jason quickly said, "I've said too much. I shouldn't have spoken."

Mike changed the discussion totally when he walked in the front door. "Jason! Glad to see you, man. Welcome." They shook hands, and Mike said "Get you anything? A beer?"

I had forgotten my manners—offered the child refreshment but not his dad. I blamed it on my total absorption in the conversation.

"Naw, thanks. Me and Henry got to get home. Carol wanted hot dogs, and Henry and me came to see Keisha on the way to that Bun Appetit place."

Our friend Mona owned Bun Appetit, a family favorite for us. "Good idea," Mike said "What's for dinner here, Kelly? Do we need hot dogs?"

190

I admitted that I hadn't started dinner yet, and Maggie, who'd apparently been eavesdropping from where she did her homework, called out, "Hot dogs! I want hot dogs."

Mike said, "Settled. Jason, call your wife and tell her to meet you here. You and I can go get the order."

Jason looked down and finally said, "We don't want to intrude. And I don't want her drivin' out alone. Not while things are still chancy."

Mike understood immediately. "How about if you and I go pick her up? Leave Henry here. He can watch TV."

And that's how we had a hot dog party. Carol proved to be tall and athletic like her husband, soft-spoken and gracious. She was angry about her husband's situation, but she wasn't cowed. I liked her immensely.

José was the only one missing from our party, and we got two extra dogs for when he dropped by later in the evening.

Late that night, after José had taken his dinner break to eat hot dogs at our house, Keisha said, "Tomorrow it's time for me to go home."

"Tomorrow's Saturday," I said.

"Right. And Monday's time for me to go to work." She sounded more determined and more like herself than she had all week.

Chapter Sixteen

If I thought Mike Shandy was going to talk to me about racial tension in his police force, I was sadly mistaken. I waited for him to elaborate on what Jason Pickard had hinted at, that there were a few bad-apple racial supremacists in the force. I watched Mike and knew he was upset about something. When I finally asked, he diverted my attention—or tried to.

"We're seeing a pattern of increased gang activity on the far West Side. Some home break-ins that are all too much alike. I'm afraid it's the same guys. Got to figure out how they're targeting victims, so maybe we can anticipate their next strike."

I asked who, what, why, when, and where, and got vague answers.

Meantime, Mike was gone a lot, which robbed me of my ambition for cooking. The girls and I subsisted on peanut butter sandwiches or scrambled eggs, and they grew cranky, partly I thought from the diet and partly because their world was out of whack. Well, mine was too. I wanted a husband whose attention was at home when his body was.

I was fairly certain that while some West Side break-ins concerned him, the problem he was carrying around had to do with race, Keisha, and prejudice among those who reported to him. I waited.

Meantime, Keisha went home on Saturday and was at work before me on Monday, as she promised. She wore her signature pink, flowing top of some kind of pleated material, pink spike sandals, and tight blue jeans. The front of her hair was tinted pink. She had earlier confessed to me that the now-healing scar, that long trough on the left side of her head, was a continuing concern to her. She announced she was going to let her spiky haircut grow out, and I had visions of dramatic upsweeps that left hair on one side tight to her head and fanned out in fanciful curls on the other side. With appropriate tints of pink and blue and lime green, of course.

Monday morning, she asked briskly, "So what have I missed?"

I told her briefly. "A wonderful house on College—light and sunny inside but needs a lot of work. Total redo. And a house on Henderson that is interesting inside, lots of Craftsman woodwork, but it's a mess on the outside. Deferred maintenance. They're both gonna need that special person who falls in love with the house, regardless of its problems."

"Let me see the spec sheets," she demanded.

"Uh, I haven't got them done yet. Had a few other things on my mind."

"Place is goin' you-know-where without me. Good thing I'm back."

I pulled my notes out of the briefcase and immediately went to work on the spec sheets. No wonder I sometimes asked who was in charge in this office.

That first day we went to lunch at the Grill. Peter, the owner, exclaimed over Keisha's scar and fussed over her until I could tell it made Keisha uncomfortable.

Over salads, I asked, as casually as I could, "Keisha, don't you care about who shot you?"

She shrugged. "I'd like them caught, so they don't shoot anybody else. But if you're asking about revenge or seeing them punished, no. I'm not particularly interested. A part of me doesn't even want to know who it was. Why would I want to know someone that full of hate, to shoot me just because of the color of my skin? José won't talk about it, and he's convinced me that's best."

Every fiber of me longed to find the culprit, and I found it difficult to understand her calm attitude.

After a long minute of silence, she said, "Kelly, I think it's coming back."

"What's coming back?"

"My sixth sense. Something's gonna happen, though I can't tell what. I don't think it's very bad."

"That's cold comfort," I said, trying to laugh it off.

In truth, I didn't laugh off Keisha's slight premonition as easily as I tried to pretend. It echoed the dread I felt, and I carried it with me when I went home that night.

Maggie had volunteered to make spaghetti for supper. She was a fledgling cook but seemed to be enjoying it. If she wanted to cook, I was going to stand by and encourage, hoping she learned far earlier and better than I had. So I was in the kitchen cooking with her, when for some reason Dave popped into my mind. I've no doubt it was linked to Keisha's premonition, but I couldn't make the connection. Maybe Maggie could make it for me.

"Maggie, we haven't seen much of Dave lately. Everything okay?"

She smiled, half coy, half a knowing smile. "Yeah. We've both been busy. Lots of homework. But we talk."

"So how is he?" I persisted. I was rubbing toast slices with cut garlic while she stirred her spaghetti sauce. It smelled wonderful.

"He's okay. He's been over to see your tenant on Alston a couple of times, and we sort of argued about that."

A moment of enlightenment. Maybe that was what my instinct had been trying to tell me. Cautiously, I asked, "Why do you argue?"

She turned away from the pot momentarily, and I sensed exasperation, just from the way she stood. "You know, Mom. He's a racist. Dave still thinks he's kind of cool. After all, he was a big kid when Dave was younger, and he was apparently good to him. So now Dave pooh-poohs my warnings not to get involved."

"Involved how?"

She turned back to her sauce, and her voice was almost strident. "Why do you think that Whitehead character keeps inviting Dave over? It's called recruitment, Mom."

I was floored, both by my daughter's sophisticated understanding of things I wished she knew nothing about and by the forces that operated on our children. I almost stammered, "Well, bring him around here more. Maybe we can be a good influence."

She softened a bit and said, "I will. He's a good guy. I haven't given up on him yet."

The spaghetti was excellent, and Maggie was pleased that we all complimented her and asked for seconds. I even gave Gracie some cut-up bits of spaghetti with a smidgen of sauce. She ate it with her hands and smeared it all over her face.

I didn't tell Mike where Dave was hanging out these days.

* * * *

Em, my little social planner, still wanted a big potluck supper. Circumstances had gotten in the way of my earlier resolve to plan the party, and it never happened. Now she pointed out that Halloween was Saturday, and we could have a big Halloween party on Sunday. Invite everyone, and she reeled them off: Anthony, his daughter Teresa and her husband Joe, and Anthony's sons, Emil and Stefan; Claire and her daughters Megan and Liz, and Brandon Waggoner if Megan was still dating him.

"Don't forget Mona and Jenny," Maggie chimed in from the dining table, where she was supposed to be studying but was listening to Em instead.

"And Nana and Otto," Em added, with an air of being self-righteous.

"What about Keisha and José?" I asked.

"Of course." Both girls almost chorused that, and Em added, "I just assumed you knew I meant them. We couldn't have a party without them."

"Can I bring Dave?" Maggie asked, and Em frowned at her, but I thought that would be okay.

I agreed tentatively to all of it, depending on what Mike said, but I was pretty sure he'd agree. Might bring him out of his funk. We planned a Halloween menu. Em wanted to duck for apples, and I thought Mike could probably arrange that in the back yard. I didn't think Em had any idea how difficult it was.

I held firm against recipes for witches' finger cookies or spider candies or all those weird-looking dishes concocted to sell prepared foods. We considered huge pots of chili, but the girls finally thought hot dogs would be suitable—we'd ask Mona to help provide a variety of toppings. Em got quite excited about a chocolate cake she'd ice and then draw a spider web on. I volunteered to make a pumpkin dip for apple slices (those apples no one could get by bobbing) and a spinach dip. I promised to send out email invitations as soon as I talked to Mike.

Poor guy. The minute he hit the door, the girls said, "Mom wants to talk to you." Or "Mike, Mom's in the kitchen. Go talk to her." It was all settled soon, and I got the invitations out before supper. By early evening, I was hearing back. Keisha would bring candy-corn clusters, whatever they were, and Claire promised a nonalcoholic brew called Witches' Punch. Mike said he'd stick with beer. For some reason, Nana thought coleslaw sounded like Halloween. It was her second choice. She first volunteered a chocolate cake, and I got the chore of telling her Em had already spoken up to make that.

Halloween used to be a nightmare for me, with the girls wanting costumes at the last minute. I'd run everywhere from the Dollar Store to Hobby Lobby putting together homemade costumes, because of course we couldn't get a ready-made and look like everyone else. Now, thank goodness, the older girls were beyond costumes and trick-or-treating. They preferred to stay home and answer the door. But they collaborated on making Gracie into a puppy dog, starting with some fuzzy brown pajamas she already had.

That night, when all the girls were asleep, Mike and I retreated to our hideaway. As he sat on the bed, wearily taking off his shoes, he said, "I had to pull Al Johnson and his partner off patrol today. Brutality. I think the charge will stand up to investigation, unfortunately. Don't know what he was thinking."

Caught in the midst of changing for bed, I sat in sweat pants and a silk blouse to ask what happened.

He shook his head. "They caught an eleven-year-old boy, unarmed, stealing groceries. When they got through with him, kid's in the hospital with a mild concussion, broken arm, cuts, and bruises. They worked him over good."

I clasped my hand to my mouth in disbelief. Police brutality had long been like white supremacy—it happened, sure. I read about it in the papers, saw it on TV. But it didn't happen in Fort

Worth. Not my city. Finally, I managed to ask, "What color is the boy's skin?"

Mike gave me a withering look and let his other shoe drop on the floor. "What do you think? He's black, of course."

"And the officer with Al Johnson?"

"Young white rookie. Probably thought if a seasoned cop thought it was okay, that was his permission to beat on the kid. I have to look into it more. And of course, internal affairs will investigate."

Eleven years old! I couldn't imagine two grown men beating a child that age. I thought about my girls at eleven and wanted to wrap them in the proverbial bubble. "Child's parents?"

"Mom's single, has four other children. Says they were hungry, that's why the kid—his name is Ezekiel—was stealing groceries. We're doing so much wrong when a kid has to feel that kind of responsibility for a hungry family. It's not just the beating. It's the whole situation."

"Did Al say anything in his defense?"

Mike shrugged. "He said it was a black kid, and he was stealing, as though that settled it. The rookie didn't say much but did tell me Al said the kid had a knife. There was no knife."

"So what happens next?"

"We got some praying to do for the boy, some hospital bills to pay, a family to reach out to. And Al and the rookie are suspended until the internal investigation is done. He could lose his badge. Bad for him, because it would affect his retirement, but worse for the rookie. End of a career before it really starts. And now he probably hates the department."

My mind was going lickety-split, and I knew I'd never be able to go to sleep. "I'll get Keisha to put together a basket for the family and deliver it."

"That's how she got shot," Mike said bitterly. "She may not want to do it."

"She will, when she hears the story. And, Mike, I'm not sure why this brought Joanie to mind. I've neglected her, what with Keisha being here and all. I'd like to invite her to bring the kids and join us Sunday night."

"Sure. The more the merrier."

I didn't think he meant that. Talk about a self-fulfilling prophecy. At three o'clock, I was still awake, tossing and turning, while Mike slept soundly. I wished for his ability to turn the world off. In my occasional rational moments while sleepless, I decided I should tell Mike about Al Johnson calling Keisha "Joanie's girl." When I finally slept, restlessly, I dreamed that Al Johnson was chasing me. He looked suspiciously like Herman Munster.

Chapter Seventeen

I called Joanie but instead of inviting her over the phone, I asked if Gracie and I could stop for coffee. Joanie's kids would be in school or day care, but Gracie could play with their toys while we moms talked. Joanie welcomed the idea so heartily that I almost had second thoughts.

Domesticity had somehow hit along with widowhood. When I got to Joanie's, the coffee smelled fresh and there was a warm coffeecake, just out of the oven. Okay, it was one of those you buy in the store and bake yourself, but it was the effort that counts, so I told myself. We settled around the kitchen table, with Gracie contentedly banging on pots with a wooden spoon Joanie provided. No toys needed!

"So how are you?" I asked.

"I'm fine," she said with just a little too much perkiness. "I'm working my way through the mess. Closing bank accounts, opening new ones, closing Buck's accounts at the cleaners and the local pub and a lot of other places, some of which I didn't know about until he was killed."

I noticed that she never said "died." She always made the point that he was killed. "Must be hard," I muttered, shooting up a quick prayer that I'd never have to do it.

"I've cleaned out his closet and dresser drawers and put aside some keepsakes for the kids. But what I can't work through in my head—or in reality—is why anyone would shoot Buck."

I didn't think this was the time to point out that Buck Conroy could be pretty aggressive and there were times I wanted to throttle him myself. The logical side of my mind could see Buck being shot with a handgun in the midst of one of his scenes or arguments but shot with a rifle from a distance—that was a different story. A sniper planned what he did—or she, but I doubted that.

Joanie had reached almost the same conclusion. "I've decided it wasn't random. Someone was aiming at Buck, someone who's a good shot with a rifle. So who had it in for Buck?"

All I could offer was a sort of lame dance around the question. "Mike hasn't said much about the investigation. The department apparently is in a mess...." I hastened to add, "Not that Buck left it that way, but some problems have come up."

She looked at me knowingly. "Yeah. Race problems. I hear things. Some of the guys talk to me, and a couple of the wives have taken me to lunch."

A pang of guilt swept over me. We can't live by should, but I should have taken her to lunch, invited her to supper. She seemed not to notice my discomfort.

Stirring her coffee kind of absently, she asked, "Do you think the same person shot Buck and Keisha?"

I'd thought about it, of course. Who wouldn't? I'd run it by Mike but got one of his police platitudes: "You can't convict on coincidence, Kelly. We have to have evidence, and we don't have it now."

I'd asked about bullets, since Keisha's bullet had been recovered, only to find out that the bullet that killed Buck had never been found. It hadn't stayed with its victim, but Mike refused to go into gory autopsy details.

None of that helped with Joanie. "I think it's possible, but you can imagine what Mike said to me about evidence and proof."

She sighed. "Yeah, I know almost word for word. I keep thinking if they find out who shot Keisha, they'll know who killed Buck. Or at least they'll be able to focus their investigation, lean hard on the suspect, all that stuff."

Gracie began to pull up on my leg and whine. Before I could lift her up, Joanie said, "I bet she needs a snack." She produced a sippy cup of milk and some dry cereal in a bowl. Finger food that would keep Gracie occupied for a while. And that was enough to change the topic.

"Your kids going trick-or-treating?"

Joanie shook her head. "They're too little, and I frankly don't have the heart for it. Buck took McKenzie last year, but I don't think she realizes it's an annual thing. Of course they hear about it at day care, and they want costumes. So I'll dress them—gosh only knows as what?—and maybe invite some neighborhood kids in for a party."

There was that thread of domesticity again. I could barely recognize the Joanie I used to know, the one who agonized over her broken hearts (several), drank too much wine, and was terrified when she found herself pregnant out of wedlock. And all that was before Buck charged onto the scene, her knight in shining armor who rescued her.

"Em wants a Halloween party this Sunday," I said. "We'd love to have you bring the kids. They'd probably be the only ones in costume and would be a huge hit."

"We'd love to come," she said with enthusiasm.

So we settled time and all that, and I told her the menu and said she should not worry about bringing anything.

"Oh, I've saved some recipes and pictures for scary snacks. You know, like those witches' fingers that are all over the internet."

I shuddered. If I were Nicolas and two years old, I'd run screaming from those fingers. I might still, even at my age.

When I said I had to get back to the office, Joanie asked, "Do you have five more minutes? There's something else on my mind."

Of course, I agreed. Something else proved to be finances. She'd been to see Buck's accountant, and it was clear that Joanie not only could not afford to keep the house, she would have to return to work. Buck was generous but not good at saving for the future.

"Will you go back to the ad agency?" She had hinted at this before. I had no idea if the agency would want her back or not. She was personable and pleasant, great attributes, though I sometimes wondered how much hands-on knowledge of advertising she had.

"No," she said slowly. "That's not what I want to do."

With an unexplained feeing that I was walking into a trap, I asked, "What do you want to do?"

"Work for you." She said it straight out, and I, standing with my purse in hand, sat down hard, the wind almost knocked out of me.

"Work for me? I don't have anything for you to do. Keisha does everything I need."

"I could sell real estate. If I could sell advertising, I could sell real estate."

She had a point there, but I plunged ahead. "You need a real estate license. That takes time, money. You don't just walk in the door and make money."

"I know that," she said impatiently, rising and beginning to pace about the spacious kitchen. Finally, staring out the window, she said, "We can live on what we have for a while, if I'm frugal. And I will be. I can learn real estate from you."

Keisha, who really wanted her license, was not going to take this well. I tried another tack. "Why do you want so badly to sell real estate?"

"I don't give a flip about real estate. I want to be around you, because I desperately want, no I need, to find out who killed Buck. You solve murders. I know eventually you'll get to the bottom of this, whether you set out to find Buck's killer or the shooter who got Keisha. I'm real serious about this, Kelly."

I was speechless, but my first thought was, "She really loved that loud-mouthed, crude piece of work." I didn't say that aloud. In fact, I didn't say anything for a long time. Finally, my voice weak, I reminded her that Mike wanted me to keep out of police matters. "I have no leads, no ideas. I'm just waiting for the police to uncover something."

"You'll find the truth," she said with confidence. "I can start next Monday. My neighbor will keep the kids. I'll pull them out of day care to save money."

Joanie had thought this through carefully, and she'd left me no escape, except to walk away from our friendship. "What about pay?"

"If I bring you a sale or make one, pay me a commission. Maybe a smaller one if I bring you a listing. I can open a new neighborhood for you. You don't do business out here in the so-called suburbs."

She was right. Reluctantly, I said I'd see her Sunday at the party. As I gathered up Gracie, I was thinking that I'd have to give this news to the two people who meant most to me—Mike and Keisha. Neither would be pleased.

As Joanie opened the door for me, she put an arm around my shoulders and said, "Thank you, Kelly. More than I can say." There were tears in her eyes.

I left wondering what I'd gotten myself into.

That evening, Mike let me know clearly what I'd gotten myself into—trouble. Joanie was a holdover friend from my days with Tim, the girls' father and my first husband, and Mike had none of my old-time loyalty to her. Plus, he thought she was an airhead.

"Kelly, how could you? It's one thing to invite her Sunday night, and I'm all for that. But having her in your office? Among other things, you can't afford to pay her."

"I'm only paying commission, small ones at that," I muttered, feeling somewhat like a schoolgirl getting a strong scolding.

"You know, since she's not licensed, you're opening yourself—and our finances—to a whole lot of liability."

I bristled. Did he think I didn't know my own industry? "I thought of that. I won't exactly use her as a real estate agent. She'll be more like a PR person. You know, she can design an ad campaign for me, stuff like that I never have time to do." I couldn't tell him the real reason she wanted to be in my office. He'd really blow a gasket if he knew she was doing this to find out who killed Buck. A thought went through my mind—Joanie said she still heard things from the department. She might hear things Mike wouldn't tell me. I didn't say that to him either.

"Very well," he said, jamming his hands into his pockets. "Don't come to me when she's driving you crazy or when you bottom line sinks."

Maybe telling Keisha would be easier.

It wasn't.

"You did what?" was followed by "We're gonna have that featherbrain in the office, chattering at us all day every day."

"I'm sure she'll work a shortened day because of her children." I tried the PR angle on her, but she scoffed that she could do that better herself.

My final plea. "She's changed, Keisha. Motherhood and then losing Buck. It's all kind of sobered her up. And if we can help her get back on her feet, good for us."

"She better not mess with my filing system," she muttered. "I finally got it like I want it." She paused. "My sixth sense really has failed. I sure didn't see this one coming at all."

I took her to Ellerbe's, the toniest restaurant on Magnolia, for lunch and told myself it would all be all right.

* * * *

With all that was going on, I was afraid Sunday's Halloween potluck would be a dismal event, but it was just fine. Well, it almost was.

Bobbing for apples turned out to be a hit with the adults, but not so much the younger generation who gave up in exasperation. I cut up fresh apples and added grapes for a kid-friendly snack tray. Of course, guess who actually walked away with an apple in her teeth? Keisha, of course.

José was heard to mutter, "I told you she has sharp fangs."

Apple still in her mouth, she walked over and literally shoved the other side of the apple in his mouth, I think each one got one small bite before it fell to the ground, amid laughter and clapping.

211

I made a chip dip of canned chili and melted Velveeta, and the kids mostly filled up on that. Poor Gracie had to be content with diced apple and diced Velveeta (no, I don't ordinarily feed her processed food). Later, she got her own grilled hot dog, cut in small chunks. My mother frowned at me but said nothing. She didn't have to. I knew she disapproved of my child's diet.

Mike and Joe grilled the hot dogs until they had nice burnt patches on them. Most of the youngsters ate them with my chili-cheese concoction, but Otto and I stuck to sauerkraut, and the others tried a lot of toppings that Mona brought, from Thai to pineapple relish.

Dave looked a little bewildered by the crowd and overwhelmed by the laughter and noise. Maggie told me later he pulled her aside to ask anxiously, "Are you related to all these people?"

She explained about extended families, and he shook his head in confusion. "My mother would never have half this many people in the house, and certainly not some of the people who are here." He glanced at Keisha and José. "Sometimes my dad has guys in to play poker. They drink a lot of beer and get so loud Mom hides in her bedroom. Other times they may have our neighbors in for pizza and beer, and they sit and stare at the TV. Nobody talks." He stared at Joe and Teresa, who were a captive audience as Otto waved his hands while talking about something important, like his own narrow view of politics

Keisha and Claire were in a corner, heads together in talk that, every once in a while, exploded into laughter, and Brandon was trying earnestly to teach Nicolas a game on his phone. Joanie seemed to have settled on the couch and let it all flow past her while she nursed a glass of wine. Mom went over to talk to her, and I quickly went to head off the hand-wringing sympathy and accusations I knew Mom would give. All in all, it was my family, and I was blessed to have them in the house. I did think Dave looked a little shell-shocked, but Maggie was happy to have him there.

Em's cake was the pièce de résistance of the evening—a chocolate cake, it was decorated with white icing in the pattern of a spider web. She even created a spider of icing in one corner, and she was so proud of what she'd done. Just as she walked majestically into the dining room to place it on the table, Clyde the watchdog let out one of his deep growls, the kind that came from far down in his chest and built to a frightening crescendo. He ran to the front door and began barking furiously. The dog had simply been hanging out around Gracie all evening, which is what he generally did. The sudden alert seemed to come out of nowhere.

José, who'd been responsible for Clyde's training, followed him. I froze for a moment and then, in remembered terror, screamed, "Don't open the front door."

José turned. "Just gonna show him there's nothing there."

"You don't know that," I yelled, completely out of control.

Mike came from behind me and put his hands on my shoulders. "It's okay, Kelly."

By then I was sobbing. "Gracie. I've got to get to Gracie." I didn't care that a room full of people stood staring at me. They were all silent, eyes going from me to José.

Mike knew what few others did. I was having a flashback to the awful time when we lived in fear that Gracie would be kidnapped, when every sound was a threat, when Clyde had become our watchdog, one of several barriers between us and the unthinkable.

José, one hand firmly on Clyde's collar, opened the door just a bit, peered out, and said loudly, "See, Clyde? Nothing there." He closed the door firmly, but the dog was still agitated, whining, jumping at the door, pacing in front of the windows. By then it was dark outside, and though several people peered out the windows, they could see nothing.

"Streetlights must be out," Anthony remarked. "It's black as pitch out there."

By then, I was on the couch, clutching Gracie, who wriggled to be free of my tight grasp. I paid no attention to anyone else.

Em was on the edge of tears that Clyde had ruined her moment in the spotlight, but Mike comforted her. After wiping her eyes, she cut the cake, and Keisha helped her pass plates. Mike went around filling wineglasses, offering new soft drinks, assuring everyone that things were okay. I wished I were that sure.

Joanie was the first to leave. Her little ones were rubbing their eyes, and Nicolas had a meltdown over the game he could not master. "Bedtime," she said philosophically, beginning to gather up their scattered clothes.

When Joanie had everything together, McKenzie by the hand and Nicolas in her arm, I walked her to the door. The streetlight was apparently still out, because it was black as pitch out there. "Mike, would you bring a flashlight and help Joanie to the car, please?"

He responded quickly, and after a quick hug for Joanie, I watched them go down the walk to the curb where she'd parked. But I was puzzled when they stopped on the sidewalk and appeared to be studying something on the ground. Mike shone his flashlight all over the sidewalk and the low retaining wall, while I watched with growing apprehension. Finally, he helped Joanie load the children, saw her into her car like the gentleman he was, and watched her drive off. Then he came back up the walk, but the bounce was gone from his step.

216

Chapter Eighteen

He wasn't the same man who had happily been reassuring people not five minutes ago. "Streetlight's been shattered. And there's graffiti on our sidewalk and retaining wall." He sounded tired, as though the graffiti had taken all the joy out of his evening.

"Graffiti?" I echoed stupidly.

He nodded. "That's what upset Clyde. We should learn to listen to that dog and not try to think we're smarter than he is. It looks to be spray paint. It will come out, but not easily. Anthony will have to look at it in the daylight. Meanwhile, José and I need to call the neighborhood officer on duty. I'm sure it's too late, though."

I was finally getting the picture. "What does it say?"

He looked at me, hesitated, and then said, "'Whites only' and some other racial slurs in big, bold, black letters that sparkle with some kind of glitter, just to be sure the neighbors don't miss it."

I was so stunned it's a wonder I didn't drop Gracie.

Everyone crowded around, wanting the details, muttering and murmuring in anger. The one clear voice I remembered later was Maggie's when she said, "At least we know it wasn't Dave. He was inside with us."

Dave muttered, "Gee, thanks, Maggie. Would you have thought it was me?" He was crushed, and Maggie had some fence-mending to do.

Keisha looked grim but said nothing, and her silence was almost more than I could bear.

* * * *

Next morning, Keisha appeared early, dragging a reluctant José behind her.

"I told her we should just go on and go to breakfast at the Grill, like we do every morning of the world. But, no, she had to come over here and see it in the daylight." He slumped over a cup of coffee.

The older girls and I went out with Keisha to look at the lettering. It was done with spray paint. You could tell by the fuzzy edges and sometimes irregular lettering, but it wasn't crude. No backward letters or misspelling. Then again, who would misspell those words? The letters were in bold black with an iridescence to it, the better to show up at night, as Mike had said.

"Lordy, lordy," Keisha moaned. "Who hates me this much?"

"I don't think it's you, Keisha. I think it's Mike they're trying to get to. They won't succeed. You know Mike. Unflappable."

"No, it's me. It's someone after you because you've made me family. You haven't done that with Jason Pickard or that poor child who was beaten. It's me, and it's my responsibility to get this obscenity off your sidewalk."

I really protested at that. "No! Anthony will rent a power scrubber this morning and get it off. Do not think you have to do a thing." I was in her face, hands on my hips, mocking her determination.

She backed off but only a few physical steps. Her determination never wavered. "I don't want you to do that. Can you live with this a few days? Object lesson to the community?"

Believe me, I hadn't thought of it that way, selfishly hadn't thought of its effect on anyone except us. It was a blot on the house that was my haven. "Why?" I asked cautiously.

"My momma's real active in her church, and they got a good youth group. Black kids, white kids, brown kids. They come in all colors and stripes. They clean this off as community service, they'll learn a lesson they won't forget. Make them activists at a young age. Let me call the minister."

"Can we help?" Em asked.

"Let's talk to Mike," I said, and we all trooped inside to where the two men still sat with their coffee cups. Mike needed to go to work; José needed to go to sleep. But they listened to us.

Mike rarely makes snap judgments, but this was as close as he ever came. After a long moment of silence, he said, "I like it. It's a community role model. We'll get some newspaper and TV coverage. Might be a good antidote to what's goin' on in this city."

I stared dumbfounded at Mike, who usually avoided publicity like the plague.

"I'll talk to the mayor this morning," he said. "Keisha, go ahead and call your mom's minister."

And that's how we ended up with a crew of teenagers at our house at nine on a cool, fall Saturday morning. But it was a long week between Monday and Saturday. Word spread, and we noticed a lot of drive-by traffic in front of our house. My phone rang off the hook at the office, with calls ranging from expressions of support to crude accusations that echoed the sentiments on the sidewalk. Granted, those calls were in the minority, but they were there. I heard loud, ugly voices in my ear. Fortunately, only a few friends knew my private cell number or Mike's, so we were not bothered at home in the evening.

Both Maggie and Em reported buzz about the whole thing at school. A few kids were like Em and wanted to help. Most seemed glad it wasn't their house, but the girls encountered little of the ugliness I occasionally heard on the phone. Maybe,

I thought, the younger generation has learned some lessons their parents haven't.

Of course, Mom and Otto drove by to look at the letters, and she called me. "Why haven't you gotten that cleaned up yet?" she demanded. "What an awful thing for the girls to see."

I explained, but she was not mollified. "I don't see how you can live with that on your sidewalk, like a badge of shame."

I didn't tell her it was sort of a badge of pride. She wouldn't understand.

"It would never happen in Chicago," she said. In some ways, Mom still rued the day she left her longtime home in Chicago to move to Texas. After several years, she still considered Texas barbarian country. It was no good pointing out the murder rate in Chicago or anything like that.

I simply assured her that Mike and I were doing what we thought best and were in control of the situation. With a muttered, "I worry about my granddaughters," she hung up. Otto, I decided, had a negative effect on Mom. When she first moved down here, she was brighter and more cheerful, more outgoing. She went to church and made friends, but now Otto preferred to stay home and let her wait on him. A problem for another day.

* * * *

Saturday morning, we were all up early. I had buckets of iced soft drinks and an urn of hot coffee for adults. Mike made a quick run to the donut shop and came home with four dozen. We had no idea how many kids there would be.

Our work crew arrived in a van just before nine. Ten young people, and Keisha was surely right. They came in all colors, sizes, and shapes, but I figured they ranged from fourteen to about seventeen. They were armed with pails, scrub brushes, and detergent, and they were chaperoned by three church members. To our surprise, Jason Pickard was one of the adults.

"You all been good to me and mine. I want to do what I can to repay the debt," he said.

Eight-year-old Henry was with his father, but Jason explained hastily that Henry knew he was too young to help and had promised to stay out of the way.

"I bet he can eat a donut or two," I said, and the child grinned happily.

The young people set to what proved to be hard work, requiring a lot of elbow grease. If the paint had been any color other than black, their job might have been easier. But they scrubbed diligently, and when one's arm tired out, someone else stepped in. I was proud that Maggie and Em, both wearing old jeans and hand-me-down shirts from Mike, joined the work crew and worked as hard as anyone else. They soon developed a camaraderie with these kids, none of whom they knew, and fit right in.

My only hesitation was that it would have been so much easier if Anthony had at least loosened the paint with a power washer, but I kept quiet.

About ten in the morning, newspaper reporters and photographers began showing up, followed shortly by TV vans with camera crews. "Mayor must be on her way," Mike whispered. "She said she wants to make an announcement from here."

Unfortunately, protestors, seeking their moment of fame, showed up before the mayor. It was only a handful of young men, and I recognized each one—Tom Whitehead and his roommates, except Morty Berman, carrying signs that said, "White Lives Matter" and "Take Back America." They ignored the kids and walked back and forth in the street, their faces impassive. The kids stared curiously for a couple of minutes and then returned to their work.

I noticed that Berman wasn't with them and resolved to get in touch with him. His cell number should be on his application on file in the office.

While we waited, reporters talked to the kids, took pictures, tried to take shots of both Mike and Jason, who ducked. They panned a few views of the protestors but seemed disinterested in talking to them.

One woman who called herself Beth was determined to get me on camera. She did the usual intro for the camera, identifying herself, telling where she was and why. "Mrs. Shandy, how do you feel about this invasion of your privacy?"

I squelched the urge to tell her my name was O'Connell and tried to be reasonable and polite without being flip, but I really wanted to say, "I hate it, and I'd like to get the morons who did this." I didn't. I stressed my gratitude to the young people and my confidence, which I wished I really felt, that the police would find the vandals. She asked how my kids felt about it, and I pointed out that both older girls were helping scrub. When she veered into discussing race relations in the city, I told her to wait for the mayor.

Mayor Shirley Goodwin arrived with little fanfare and no entourage. She chatted with us for a few minutes, greeted the kids, and sent a disapproving frown in the direction of the protestors. Mike and Jason had subtly moved into position to keep the young men out of camera range and away from the mayor. She stood in front of our house, mic in hand. Her few words were brief—I guess she knew they'd be cut at the TV station. She simply said she was deeply disturbed by some tensions in our city.

"If you live in this city," she said, a slight smile on her face, "you are my neighbor, and I am yours. We must all act as neighbors, good neighbors, not enemies in small groups pitted against each other. I am declaring December 1 Neighbors Day so that we can celebrate our neighborliness, our support for each other. There will be activities at various designated spots through the city. Please watch newspapers and television for further announcements."

The look on Mike's face told me this announcement was a surprise to him and not necessarily a pleasant one.

Mayor Goodwin posed for a group picture with the kids and was gone as quickly and quietly as she had arrived. Her visit lasted less than fifteen minutes, but I supposed she had a busy schedule even on Saturday morning. The protestors disappeared as soon as the reporters and cameras did.

By noon, only faint traces of paint remained here and there, and those would disappear with time and rain. The kids were exhausted, and so was the supply of drinks. Mike's declaration of hamburgers for everyone met with a great cheer. A conversation with Jason convinced us that it would be easier to bring the hamburgers to the kids than to take them somewhere in a group, so they all trooped into the house, while Mike and Jason went to Whataburger armed with a variety of orders—pickles for this one, no tomato for that one, mustard on one and mayo on another.

When it became obvious that the tired kids needed rest, Jason and the other leaders loaded them up in the van. We waved them off with profuse thanks and invitations to come see us again. Then Mike, the girls, and I went in the house to collapse.

It occurred to me I hadn't seen José and Keisha. They'd deliberately stayed away.

* * * *

My entire household shut down for a nap that afternoon, while Gracie took her usual afternoon sleep. The older girls were exhausted by their labors, and Mike and I were emotionally exhausted by all that had been going on. I was vaguely aware that he got up about four, but I snuggled down in the covers and dozed.

When I finally wandered downstairs, he had been to the grocery for steaks and salad makings, and he had a plate of good Irish cheddar and thin, wafer-like crackers waiting for me. With a glass of cold white wine, of course. A fire, comforting on an afternoon that had turned chilly, burned in the fireplace, sending off warmth and, even better, cheer.

I sank down onto the couch. Mike, red wine in hand, settled in next to me, and I cuddled close.

"I wish the mayor had warned me," he said. "Told me about that Neighbors Day plan of hers."

"Why?"

"I'd have tried to talk her out of it, that's why," he said, almost smiling but shaking his head. "It will be a security nightmare, especially now, with those tensions she talked about in the air."

I turned to look him square in the face, and for a minute I just studied him. He looked tired to me, maybe older, and I thought his responsibilities were wearing on him. He waited for me to speak, a

226

quizzical look on his face. "Mike, do you want this job on a permanent basis?"

He tried to laugh it off. "Oh, Kelly. A lot has to happen before we can even think about that. The mayor has to call for a national search, and she's told me she's not about to do that until things settle down in the city. But, to your question, I don't know. I was pretty happy as district chief, but if I can do more good in this job . . . I don't know." His voice trailed off.

"I don't either," I said. "I think I worry less about you than I did when you were more often on the streets—"

He made a wry sound. "Buck was in this position when he was shot."

I moved close to him again, began tracing the bones on the back of his hand with my finger. "I know. And that means you have to find out who shot him. You won't live with yourself unless you do."

Restlessly, Mike pulled his hand away and stood up. "There are a lot of things I have to solve if I'm going to live with myself—and with you—in peace. I can't leave Jason Pickard behind a desk forever—he'll resent it, maybe leave. And I've got to do something about Larry Peterson, the rookie cop with Al."

I was instantly alert. "The one who beat up the young boy?"

"I think there's more to the story," Mike said, beginning to pace. "Larry came to me, and we talked a long time. He says he wasn't complicit, tried to pull Al off the kid, but Al just sort of went crazy. I believe the rookie. He's young and sort of naïve, but I think he's honest, has his head on straight."

"And his heart in the right place?" I asked gently.

"Yeah." He kept pacing, and I sat silently, sipping my wine now and then. Suddenly, he turned. "I actually have a plan. Going to run it by the mayor first thing Monday morning. I want to appoint José sort of a special deputy, an assistant to me. Oh"—he threw his hands in the air—"I've got deputies, guys in charge of patrol, and finance, and support but I want a kind of jack-of-all trades guy to back me up. José's young, but he's the perfect candidate, because we know how each other works, we've worked together, and I have confidence in him."

I couldn't resist adding, "And he's Hispanic, married to a black woman. I think you're rehearsing your speech to the mayor on me." What I didn't say was that it both amused and saddened me to hear him call José young and realize that he no longer thought of himself as young. From our perspective in our late thirties, José was young, but it was a strange thought. Times and life had toughened us.

"Sounds like a plan," I said. "José will hate giving up Fairmount. He'll worry about the neighborhood."

Mike was warming to his subject. "I got a plan for that too. I want to make Pickard the neighborhood officer and attach Larry Peterson to him. It will be a real test of Peterson—well, of both of them. But my gut tells me it will work out."

I pondered. "Young white cop accused of beating black kid assigned to Hispanic cop in a racially diverse but heavily white neighborhood. Did you shoot off fireworks when you were a kid?"

"Aw, come on, Kelly. Stand by me on this one."

I put my drink down, got up, and hugged him. "Always, Mike. I always will."

Maggie walked in just then, carrying the book she'd been reading. "Oh come on, you two! When's supper? I'm hungry."

We celebrated that night. I never was sure what we were celebrating—maybe just steaks on the grill, but I thought it was more.

* * * *

As it turned out, Joanie never did come to the office. She called to say the advertising agency had offered to let her begin with some freelance consulting work. She would be paid by the job—more than I could ever pay her—and sharpening up those skills that had gotten rusty. Plus, she saw it as a way back into the agency, and I agreed.

"But, Kelly, I'll still keep my eyes open for properties and clients for you. It's what friends do for each other, and you've been a good friend."

With fingers crossed, I muttered my thanks.

When I told Keisha this she said, "Praise the Lord! He does work in mysterious ways his wonders to accomplish."

I threw a crumpled piece of paper at her.

* * * *

I carried through on my resolve to talk to Morty Berman. His phone number was indeed on his rental application, and I caught him in the family jewelry store one morning the week after the great graffiti scrubbing. He willingly agreed to meet me for coffee and suggested a Starbucks near his office.

"Neutral territory," he said with a chuckle. "Not likely to see anyone either of us know."

Without explanation, I handed Gracie to Keisha and took off. "Coffee, back in an hour," was all I said, but she looked at me knowingly. The sixth sense was back.

Tall, cheerful, not overly attractive, with wire-rimmed glasses, he was utterly without pretense. One of the few totally unselfconscious people I ever met.

When I asked about his unlikely living situation, he laughed and said he had to get out of his parents' house before his mom drove him wild. At his age, she was still overprotective, hovering over him at meals, wanting to know where he was every minute. "And then there's Jim." He sighed. "That part of my story didn't go over well with either of my parents."

His frankness encouraged my own. "How ever did you and Jim end up with Tom Whitehead? I would think the mutual dislike would be intense."

"It is, believe me, but he's Tom's cousin, and Jim has this quixotic idea that he can protect Tom from himself. I'd say let the fool hang, but Jim won't and of course I couldn't let him do this by himself. His dad is on the police force, so I figure he won't get too deep in trouble."

I knew Jim's last name was Johnson. *Surely not, but then maybe.* "Is his father Al Johnson?"

Morty regarded me skeptically. "Right on. You know him? I'm sure your husband does."

"Yes, I know him," I said slowly.

"Then you can understand Jim had to get out of the house too, and Al thought it was fine he went to live with his cousin."

Cautiously, I asked, "How do you and Tom Whitehead get along?"

"Not at all, but as I told you, I'm a damn good cook. My mom taught me. Look, Ms.

O'Connell, I like to think I'm also a damn good citizen, so I justify this to myself by watching and anticipating what Tom and Robert are doing. If I see something truly alarming, I'll tattle. I was always encouraged to tattle as a kid. Imagine that!" He laughed wryly and sipped his coffee.

"But Jim goes with Tom to protests. I saw him at my own house."

"Yeah." He stirred his coffee, thinking. "Sorry about that. I know that Tom and Robert painted those awful slogans—honestly, I expect something about kikes next. But I don't know how they knew to protest when the kids cleaned." He stared off into space. "You might tell your husband that I think there's a snitch in the police department."

I almost said, "My husband thinks so too," before I remembered I was trying to be cagey and bit my tongue. "Why?"

"Tom knows things that aren't public, and in turn, I think he feeds information to someone. It's probably Al, but we don't talk about it. I know, though, that's how the guys ended up at that black cop's house that night and how they ended up at your house."

"Makes sense. And you're telling me all this why?"

"Ever read Martin Niemöller's poem about the people who remained silent during Nazi occupation? That's my inspiration. Next, I could be

232

the target. Tom already refers to me as 'the kike,' and pretends it's an affectionate nickname. I know better. And Fort Worth is my hometown. I don't like to see this stuff go on. I'm not about to be an out-of-the-closet activist. I'm not that brave. But I'll do what I can behind the scenes. More coffee?"

I declined, thanked him for meeting me, and complimented him on his position.

"Call me anytime," he said, "I'll be in touch if I need to be."

Morty Berman wasn't quite the lighthearted jokester I first took him to be. I bet he played the fool for Whitehead's benefit. When I got back to the office, I looked up Martin Niemöller.

First they came for the Socialists, and I did not speak out—
Because I was not a Socialist. . . .

Then they came for me—and there was no one left to speak for me.

Chapter Nineteen

Mike was both preoccupied and busy that next week. Busy I could understand. He had official functions to attend, meetings that lasted well past the hour when I thought the girls should have supper, one dinner, one reception, and a happy hour that far as I could tell did not add much happiness. None of it bothered me the way preoccupied did. When Mike was at home, his mind wasn't with us. He was always staring off into space, lost in some problem he couldn't or wouldn't discuss with me.

One night when I knew he would be late, the girls and I decided to have fried catfish for supper. Crisp and mild, with lots of lemon, it sounded good. I left them in charge of Gracie and took off for the Grill to get takeout.

As I stood in line to place my order and wished I'd thought to call ahead, I heard a familiar voice. "Where's the man, Kelly?"

I turned to see José grinning at me. Behind him stood Jason Pickard, who smiled and ducked his head a bit shyly. "What are you two doing here?" I asked.

"Far as I knew, anyone can eat here," José said. "Jason's on patrol with me, second night. He's learning the ropes, so he can become the neighborhood police officer."

We placed our orders—catfish to go for me, chicken-fried steak for them—and retreated to a booth. José even brought me a glass of wine, setting it down with a flourish and the comment, "You look tired. Thought you might need this."

I thanked him and asked Jason how he liked Fairmount so far. My underlying but unspoken question was what kind of a welcome he'd received in the neighborhood. Had his history preceded him? I thought Fairmount folks were inclined to be fair and, yeah, a bit liberal, but there could always be unpleasantness. I'd learned that lesson too well over the years.

Jason looked straight at me, fingered his flatware, and said slowly, "It's been better than I thought. I was ready for trouble—ugly comments, if nothin' else. But José's been taking me around, introducing me to business owners, like Peter"—he nodded his head toward the cash register where Peter was taking orders, and I remembered that Peter had greeted him by name.

"Shoot," Jason said, his tone lightening a bit. "I'm ready to move to Fairmount."

I laughed. "Bet I could show you a few houses." Out of the corner of my eye I glanced at José to see his reaction, but his eyes were on his cell phone.

Jason replied easily, "I bet you could, but I already saw one that intrigues me. Over on Allen . . . no, that's not right. Alston, that's where it is. Too close to Hemphill, but it's a great house."

My heart lurched, but I managed to hold my voice steady as I asked, "What's the house number? You remember it?"

"Yes, ma'am. It's 1860, big old two-story. Needs work, but Carol and me, we've been talking. We're ready to move—that fancy house we got when Henry was born doesn't feel good to us anymore, what with all that happened, 'specially Keisha being shot in the driveway. And we sort of like the idea of fixing up a house, making it our own."

How could I tell him the one big problem? The house was next door to the one Tom Whitehead and his pals leased. They would not make good neighbors for a black family, and I didn't give a hoot about Whitehead, but I wanted to spare the Pickard family. They didn't need any more trouble. I coughed and took a sip of wine while I thought about my options.

Was I obligated to tell Jason about potential neighbors? Especially this early in the game? He might well find another house he liked better, he might not want to pay the asking price on this one, all kinds of things could happen. A real estate deal is never final until it closes, and he was months from that. But, yeah, I had an obligation as a person.

I began tentatively. "You'd have neighbors."

José laughed aloud. "So what's unusual about that, Kelly? Everybody in this neighborhood has neighbors, mostly pretty close. We got those really religious folks next door to us, but they're nice, and we get along good." José wouldn't have recognized an enemy if he had one.

Jason was more serious. "What are you talking about, Kelly?"

"We lease out the house next door to the one you're interested in. Bunch of guys, four to be exact. They're racists, extreme." I didn't add except one, but I sent a silent apology to Morty Berman.

José was scornful again. "Come on, Kelly. How do you know that?"

"They picketed at Jason's the night Keisha was shot, and they were at our house last Saturday morning."

José sobered, and Jason looked thoughtful. "I got to think about that," he said. "We can't spend our lives running, but I don't want to put Carol and the kids in the line of hate, or something worse."

José spoke up. "Those are the guys I got on my list for us to go see. Ever since they showed up last Saturday, Mike's been after me to talk to them, see how deep they are into this stuff. Maybe put the fear of the Lord into them."

"I don't think they're subject to the fear of the Lord," I said.

With a cheerful, "Here you go, Kelly. You and those girls enjoy." Peter handed me our food.

As I stood to leave, I said, "Jason, if you decide you want to pursue this, I can show you the house. We'll take Anthony, my redo man, to tell us how solid it is, what the potential is for renovation."

Jason stood politely, which caused José to scramble to his feet. "Thanks, Kelly," Jason said. "I'll talk to Carol and get back to you."

I was already burning with curiosity to know how their talk with those "boys" went, and they hadn't even rung their doorbell yet.

* * * *

We all like to think that our lives go on as normal, no matter what's going on in the larger world, and that's how I felt that week about my family, only it wasn't true. Oh, the girls and I went about life, Maggie and Em went to school, Gracie and I went to the office, we ate supper together and really enjoyed that catfish. But for Mike, the world seemed frozen in place.

Friday night, to my great relief, he came home early and demanded, "What's for dinner?" I had made chicken tetrazzini, a favorite of everyone's, and right then I was grateful. At the table, Mike quizzed the girls about their week, school happenings, twitted Maggie about Dave, fed Gracie small bits of pasta and chicken while she opened her mouth hungrily, and generally seemed to have fallen back into the fatherhood role he usually relished.

After dinner, when the table was cleared, Em dragged out a thousand-piece jigsaw puzzle. The picture was of an ice-bound castle in Europe, the forest around it covered in white. In short, it was a study in shades of white and a challenge as a puzzle. We all fell to it with dedication, fishing out edge pieces, trading with one another, and having a really good time.

A little after eight I excused myself to get Gracie to bed. When I returned some twenty minutes later, the atmosphere had changed and not for the better. The girls worked at the puzzle, but I could tell their hearts weren't in it. Mike had wandered away, poured himself two fingers of Scotch neat, and sat in morose silence on the couch. The Scotch alone was a warning flag because he was pretty much a beer-and-wine person.

I plopped down next to him and asked, inanely, "What are you thinking about?" I really wanted to ask what had happened since I left the room barely five minutes ago.

"The world," he said, "and how I sometimes really don't like it." He reached over to give me an affectionate hug, but given his attitude, it was cold comfort. I had the good sense to sit and wait. Maggie and Em looked at us and silently got up and went to their rooms to watch TV, read, probably talk on their cell phones. I waited.

Finally, shifting so he faced me more, he said, "José called. He and Jason stopped for supper on patrol and got to talking. Jason finally said he'd been feeling ostracized in the division since he's back on street duty. Says all kind of rumors are going around about him, and some guys openly question why he's still on the force. José thought I should know."

"He thought you should know badly enough to interrupt you on a Friday night at home?"

"Yeah. It's relevant. José knows I had the usual weekly meeting with the division chiefs this week, and I'm worried about it. Six patrol divisions, and two of the guys had officers who requested partner changes. One had two. A total of three." He turned toward me, and I saw despair in his eyes.

"Kelly, do you realize what a big deal that is? If a cop doesn't trust his partner, doesn't think he's got his back, neither one of them can be effective. Oh, and don't ask—they're all men, white guys with black partners. In the years I've been on the force, I've never heard of this."

"Where's it coming from?"

"This is going to sound paranoid, but I think it's Al Johnson."

"I thought he was on paid leave."

Mike shook his head. "He is, but he hangs around with the guys, meets them for coffee and such. Some newer ones especially think he's the old, seasoned guy telling them how it is. He's not. He's spreading hate and fear. Larry Brown learned that the hard way, but he can't go around badmouthing Al, even though it's deserved."

He paused for a minute, took a sip of wine, stared at the fire. "Oh, and he tells everybody how I stole the job that was supposed to be his. Tells 'em Buck anointed him. Mostly they don't listen to that. But I think some listen to that racist stuff. It's like a disease, a cancer spreading from one small spot out through the department."

I didn't have much to go on to keep my end of the conversation up, but I tried. "When's the internal affairs report due?"

He shrugged. "Don't know. I can't bug them about it. DA has taken an interest in the case, though, and we've sent copies of the paperwork up to his office. I think that's because some legal counsel for the poor got hold of Ezekiel's mom and is walking her through a civil suit. She should get compensation—or the child should, even a college scholarship. But she needs money to pay the medical bills."

None of that answered the most important question or me. "How's the boy?"

Mike's face brightened. "He's doing well. Been home from the hospital for several days. Concussion healed, no problem. Cuts and bruises clearing up, maybe a couple light scars. Right arm is still in a cast, but he can grab a pencil. School system's sent teachers to the home, and last report I got he's doing really well in school. Mom's getting help with the groceries."

I couldn't help interjecting, "She doesn't have Ezekiel to steal them for her." I meant it lightheartedly, but Mike didn't take it that way.

Very quietly, he said, "She's not that way. She was as horrified that he was stealing as she was that he was beaten. That lady works ten at night till five in the morning cleaning an office building. Leaves those kids alone in the motel where they're living. Probably drug dealers and all in the same building. She feels safe 'cause they got good locks, but no lock is good enough. Habitat for Humanity is working to get her a home, a quick deal, not one where she waits while the house is built."

"Can we feed them, do something?"

He shook his head. "Best not for us to get involved. That would threaten my neutrality in the whole deal. Al would really blow that out of proportion. Keisha's been helping, even babysat the younger kids." He grinned. "I think we'll be hearing about a baby from the Thornberry household soon. She's getting the urge."

"Keisha beats all. I'll talk to her. See how we can quietly help, especially with Thanksgiving coming up and then Christmas. What about the rookie?"

I had of course instantly condemned him in my mind, without knowing him.

"He's still on leave, waiting for internal affairs. They've interviewed him a lot, more than Al, I think, though I'm not really on top of it. He's been to talk to me. Says he tried to pull Al off the kid. Seems genuinely upset."

"What does Ezekiel say?"

"Doctors say not to push it too hard and bring back the trauma. And he's only a kid. All he really remembers is someone beating on him and yelling at him." He put his head in his hands. "I can't imagine it, simply can't imagine a grown man doing that. But it happens all the time. This is just one instance that got brought up close and personal."

"What will you do with the rookie?" I asked.

"I think I'll put him on desk duty in my office, so I can watch him, judge for myself."

"He's white, isn't he?"

"Very," was all Mike said.

The girls had long since come to tell us goodnight, and I had hugged each one fiercely, so grateful for how safe they were in their sheltered little world.

Mike and I sat, each lost in our own thoughts for a long time, until we finally got up and made our way upstairs. The weekend lay ahead of us, and I hoped it would be restorative, but the world looked pretty gray that night.

Ours was a blessedly quiet weekend. The girls had busy things to do with friends—Maggie went bowling with Dave and then later spent Saturday night with her BFF Jenny. Em and a friend were treated to a shopping trip by the friend's mother and then the friend spent the night with us, a quiet, shy girl who I didn't get to know well in spite of my best efforts. Sweet Em mother-henned that girl the whole time she was with us—"Susie, do you want milk?" "Susie, let's make cookies," and "Susie, what do you want to do now?" By Sunday noon when Susie's mom came for her, I think Em was worn out with being an event planner.

Mike and I pretty much hung out, that young people's phrase, around the house, playing with Gracie, taking Gracie and Clyde for a long walk down on the trails by the river because Saturday was a beautiful fall day, the kind that would soon give way to the gray and damp chill of winter.

Sunday morning Mike fixed shaped pancakes for Em and Susie—he was pretty good at doing pancakes that looked like the child, and Susie was so thrilled with her pancake she refused to eat it, wanting to save it to show her mom.

Sunday night, we fixed a big supper. I experimented with beef stroganoff, using hamburger, and cooked a big pot of egg noodles to go with it. Crusty French bread, salad, and fresh asparagus. We feasted. When Maggie came home from Jenny's, she brought Jenny and her mom, Mona, with her, and we called Claire, who was home alone that night. It was a party, and Mike joked all night about his harem. He rather enjoyed it, despite complaints, including, "Where's Dave when I need him?" At the dinner table that night, talk was of school. The girls rattled off the spring sports they were going to try out for, though Jenny said she'd rather work in her mom's hot dog shop than try out for swim team again. She'd done it in the fall and hadn't liked it all that much.

Jenny was less outgoing than Maggie, and either she hadn't discovered boys yet or they hadn't discovered her, but she was a bit shy around Dave, one reason we'd left him out of Sunday night dinner. Besides, Maggie explained that he was having dinner with his mother's parents, who were visiting.

"I don't like his grandfather," she said honestly. "He's always putting his arm around my shoulder. He talks to me about stuff, but I never know what to say back. Now I know where Dave got some of his bad ideas."

Mike and I exchanged looks, and he nodded slightly, which I took as assurance he'd talk to Dave's father and check out the situation.

It was a school night, and everyone left before eight. The girls helped with the dishes, without a single squabble. Of course, my conscience dinged me when my mother called later in the evening just to say how much she missed the girls. She invited us to supper Wednesday night, and I accepted without consulting Mike or the girls, though I warned Mom not to count on Mike.

Keisha called too. She'd been appointed to the Neighbors Celebration master committee and would be out of the office Monday afternoon. "I knew you'd approve of me being civic-minded, boss lady, so I volunteered, and they accepted me. I'll report tomorrow night."

Mike wanted me to be active on that committee and I had good intentions, but if Keisha would be going to meetings I'd have no one to leave Gracie with. If I said that to Mike, I knew I'd get a lecture about having to learn to trust more people with my sweet baby. But fear still lingered in my heart.

"I'll try to manage the office without you, but it will be hard," I said with a laugh to cover the discomforting thought her announcement brought. And then, changing the subject, "Keisha, why didn't you tell me about Ezekiel and that you'd been visiting and helping that family?" Between Ezekiel's family and the Neighbors committee, I suddenly felt left out of everything. And I wasn't above pouting about it.

Her reply was serious. "Kelly, there's just some things I can do better than you. You think Mike or I would let you go to that motel on Lancaster? No way. You just rest easy and let me take care of this one."

I felt like a child who'd been scolded, but I managed to say, "I'd like to gather some groceries or toys, whatever you tell me is needed."

"Oh, I got long lists. We'll talk about it tomorrow."

I told her I'd work from home in the morning, and we could confer over lunch at the Grill.

* * * *

I did work at home Monday morning, though not the kind of work I'd led Keisha to believe. I straightened the house after our lazy weekend, picking up laundry left on the bathroom floor—a forbidden act in my house, searching for puzzle pieces on the floor before Gracie found them to chew, sweeping the kitchen floor, and putting away clean dishes. I'd used every dish in the house to make our Sunday night supper.

By a little after eleven thirty, Gracie and I were in the Grill waiting for Keisha, who breezed in ten minutes later with complaint after complaint.

"That Whitehead fellow called again. Wouldn't talk to me. Just asked when you'd be in. I told him this afternoon. I'm not messing with that kind of trash any more. And then Jason Pickard called, wants you to show him a couple of houses. Jason tells me one of them is right next door to that Whitehead piece of work. Just asking for trouble, that's all it is. There's plenty of houses in Fairmount."

"What happened when José and Jason went to see Whitehead?" I couldn't believe I'd forgotten about it all weekend, but then I guessed Mike hadn't heard a report or he'd have told me. Or would he?

Keisha never answered my question but dodged it by saying, "I'm mighty hungry today. Guess I'll have chicken-fried steak."

Knowing not to push her for the answer, I ordered cheese grits, without jalapeño, for Gracie and a cheeseburger for myself. Keisha righteously ordered a salad and then kept staring at my burger. "What else happened?"

She sighed. "I think I was on that darn phone all morning. Got two new listings on your desk to talk to people about, and two other people called asking if we do property management. I almost told them no. Finally, I said you did, but I didn't. And that's the God's honest truth."

I could hardly wait to get to the office. But I never heard about the official visit to Tom Whitehead, and I was still curious.

Chapter Twenty

With Gracie settled in her play corner and rubbing her eyes in anticipation of a nap, I turned to the messages on my desk. Among the notes and calls to return was a list of toys—things Keisha said Ezekiel and his brother and two sisters would like. I put it aside—Em would probably love a toy shopping trip to the Dollar Store later that day. A part of me wanted to show Keisha and take the toys directly to the motel, but I heard Mike's voice in my ear and knew that wasn't smart. Especially if I had Em and Gracie with me.

I called Jason first, hoping I wasn't waking him since he was on night duty these days.

"Kelly? Thanks for calling."

I could hear rustling in the background and feared he was indeed sleeping.

He quickly sounded alert. "Carol and I had a long talk last night, and we're serious about Fairmount. And about that house on Alston. Can you show it to me tonight? Then, I'll ask to go back with Carol, the kids, and your contractor. But first I want to check some things out."

Like how much distance you can get from your neighbor? I wanted to ask that, but I didn't.

251

Keep it professional, Kelly. I did ask, "What happened when you and José called on Whitehead?"

"The guy's a jerk," he scoffed, "but he's small time, nothing to be real concerned about." I heard a chuckle. "He really didn't know who to talk to—a brown guy and a black guy at his door. He kind of chose the brown guy, I guess as the lesser of two evils. But, you know, my skin's barely any darker than José's. It's kind of all in how you think about it. If you think blacks are worse than Mexicans, then you'll talk to José. I suppose some others would take it another way."

"Did he admit to picketing at our house last Saturday?"

"Couldn't deny it if he wanted to. I was right there. He says it's a public street, and it's his right to be anywhere he wants. You know the argument. And of course, he denies having anything to do with the spray-painting or shooting Keisha. I didn't expect anything else. But now he knows he's on our radar, and we're watching. I think he tried hard to look like we didn't make an impression on him, but we really did."

"I hope. What time tonight do you want to see this house?"

I could hear him draw in his breath. "Tonight? On my supper hour? I want to go when Whitehead's at home and while our visit is still fresh on his mind."

"Is that a good idea?" I asked, wondering what Mike would say.

"It's the best idea I got," Jason said simply.

I did some quick calculations in my mind. Toy shopping might have to wait a day, and the girls would have to keep Gracie. I'd also have to tell Mike. He couldn't exactly forbid either Jason or me to go there, either as a boss or a husband, but he could sure offer strong discouragement if he saw fit.

Mike didn't see fit to discourage at all. In fact, he supported Jason—unofficially. Over the phone, he said, "It might do that Whitehead nut some good to have an example next door to him. And I agree with Jason. He needs to know we're watching." He hesitated. "But none of that can be the basis for Jason's decision. He should only consider that house if he thinks it would be a good fit for his family in all ways." Mike said he'd try to get home by six to help the girls with supper and Gracie.

Mike's words, echoing Jason's about keeping an eye on Whitehead, made me wonder if Jason was really interested in the house or if our excursion had more of a surveillance, even harassment, motive.

Maggie and Em not only agreed to watch Gracie, they suggested grilled cheese sandwiches and tomato soup for dinner. It sounded heavenly to me, but I warned them not to grill until they saw us. Soggy grilled cheese sandwiches are no fun.

Jason came to the house, and I drove us to Alston in my car. When we pulled up, I saw Tom Whitehead's truck in his driveway with its "White Lives Matter" bumper sticker. Made my stomach turn.

The house was red brick, a fairly standard Craftsman design. Red brick with five or six steps leading up to the roofed front porch, which was supported on either hand by white wood pillars set above square brick foundations. The porch was rimmed with a low brick wall, and the wood trim all painted white. Evenly space windows with decorative vertical grilles in the upper half marched two on either side of a wide front door with a stained glass insert.

I drew in my breath sharply and realized why I had so far overlooked this beauty. It was sadly in need of renovation, steps showing large cracks, rot beginning at base of pillars, paint peeling to expose bare wood. Over many years, the house had shifted so that the door no longer hung straight, and I could envision cold winter air and hot summer blasts coming in through the crack at the bottom. The sign said, "For Sale by Owner," so it had not come to my attention on an MLS listing.

Involuntarily, I murmured, "Oh, Jason!"

He beamed. "You like it?"

I sobered immediately. "That's not the point," I said. "This house almost needs more work than I can think about."

"I can do a lot of it," he said. "My dad was a carpenter, and he taught me. But I'll want your guy to look at it."

Jason called the owner, who assured him the house was empty and would be open—the occupant had died, and the owner didn't live in town. Leaving a house unlocked was a big warning sign for me, but we entered a spacious and very empty living room that once again took my breath away, not in a good way. Someone had gone crazy with white paint, covering all the lovely built-ins—bookcases, sideboards, French doors—that should have been natural wood. Even the tile fireplace was white. The result was dazzling but oh so wrong. All I could think was what elbow grease would be needed to get rid of all that paint.

The kitchen was the disaster I expected, with an ancient gas stove, a sink that stood on four metal legs, and scarred and stained wooden countertops. The two bedrooms downstairs had peeling wallpaper, and the bath was outmoded but did have the tiny octagonal floor tiles original to the house and a wonderful, if short, clawfoot bathtub. Upstairs was what I guess was the master, with windows on four sides and a much larger bathroom, with the same tiles and footed tub.

I thought about my house. The two were of the same vintage, but mine had been lovingly maintained by three generations of the family that built it; this one had also remained in its original state, except for the explosion of paint, but little to nothing had been done to maintain it. It would take thousands of dollars and hours of work to make it the terrific home it could be.

"Jason, Anthony is likely to discourage you. And you'd have to have a thorough inspection done to check heating and electricity—they could be dangerous." I could see all kinds of code violations just looking around. "And the plumbing. Who knows what lies hidden in these walls."

Jason was so obviously in love I doubted he heard me. So much for surveillance or harassment.

"Can't you see what it can be?" he asked.

"Yeah, I can. But I can see all the hard work it will take."

"Let's look at the backyard."

The house was so old the yard sported a storm cellar and a clothesline anchored to two iron pipes. The fence to the north was a fairly new, six-foot wooden fence—our lease property. The other two sides of the yard were fenced with six-foot hurricane fencing and opened to an alley and the neighbor's yard. No privacy.

I had made up my mind quickly that this was a fool's errand, and Jason would be a fool to buy the house. But you know about those places where angels fear to tread. He wanted to wander through the house again at leisure. We were there probably an hour before I finally said Mike would be waiting at home.

As we left, Tom Whitehead was standing on his porch. One look at Jason, and he demanded, "What are you doing here? Spying on me?"

Jason broke into a smile. "Hey, man, I might be your new neighbor."

Coldly, Whitehead said, "That would be a cold day in hell. I don't live next door to no blacks."

I gasped, but Jason seemed unperturbed. "Hey, man, talk nice now. There's a lady with me."

"I know that lady," was the steely response. "And her husband."

We drove back to our house in silence, but a kind of nervous energy radiated off Jason. I could feel it in the air. At the house, he came in to speak to Mike, but I think he only did it as a courtesy. He was clearly itching to be gone.

"Stay and have a beer, Jason," Mike urged. "Tell me about the house."

Almost bouncing from one foot to the other, he said, "Thanks, but I got to get home. Got to tell Carol about this house. It's got our name written all over it."

After he left, I told Mike about my doubts about the trip, how I thought it was a surveillance and harassment mission on Jason's part, but I'd changed my mind. "He's truly infatuated with that house. And, oh, Mike, it needs so much work."

"What's the asking price?"

I stopped dead in my tracks. I had no idea, and I bet Jason didn't either. "I'll do some research tomorrow. Find that out and the history of the house. Whatever they're asking, they better be prepared to come down."

The girls wanted to hear about the house at supper, and they were aghast that someone had painted it all white, stem to stern. So was I. I still couldn't get over it.

Next morning, Keisha was so full of plans for the Neighbors Celebration—that was the official title now that the mayor had decided on—that she blasted all thoughts of Jason and the house on Alston right out of my mind.

Her opening statement blew me away. "It's going to be in the coliseum, instead of all over town like the mayor originally decided. She changed her mind."

The coliseum? The place where they held rodeos and filled the arena with bucking horses and bulls, calf-roping and clowns, and western music? Surely not.

"Think about it, Kelly. They don't always have dirt on the floor—sometimes it's even ice for skating. But they can make a nice, flat floor for booths. There's space outside, where the Midway usually is, for a few kiddie things like a bounce house, a kid's Ferris wheel, bumper cars. None of that stuff for adults, because that's not what this is about."

"Is the coliseum big enough?"

She shrugged. "Mayor says that's where it's gonna be, so that's it. Booths are mostly going to be food vendors—you know, that stuff they call ethnic. So we get to all be neighbors. Greek church will have a booth—spanakopita, I hope. And there'll be two or three black restaurants serving soul food, several Thai. City Hall's handling that, and they got it all lined up. Mona Wilson is even going to bring her portable hot dog stand."

I laughed. "What could be more American than hot dogs? I bet Maggie and Jenny will want to work that stand. Still, I'm like Mike. Wish the mayor hadn't sprung this on the city so suddenly. There's not enough time for planning."

"José said Mike is happy that most of it will be indoors. Makes security easier. Though neither of our guys have experience with a huge citywide event like this. They're callin' in experts—city has folks they regularly use, guys that do the stock show, political conventions, stuff like that."

"I haven't seen any publicity yet," I said tentatively.

"You will, starting tomorrow. They're gonna hit it hard and heavy, newspaper, TV, flyers in businesses, online stuff. I volunteered us to sponsor a TV spot."

"You what? How many thousands of dollars will that cost?" What little promotional budget we had was slim and surely didn't cover television. I got up from my desk and went for more coffee.

Keisha grinned. "Calm down. They're public service announcements. I committed us to five hundred dollars."

I sat back down, relieved. "Okay." It was still a lot of money for a shoe-string realtor's office.

"I also told them you'd man the T-shirt booth. They're getting a local artist to design it, gonna order it in quantity."

I thought she was being kind of high-handed about this and gave her a skeptical look, but Keisha went right on.

"You'd rather be outside with the kiddie rides? That's what José and I will be doing."

T-shirts didn't sound so bad after all. Before I could even say that, the door to the office was flung open and Tom Whitehead stormed in. He marched right past Keisha without giving her a glance and came directly to my desk. He was trying so hard to look haughty and, well, superior, that I almost laughed. Didn't that young man have a smile or a bit of politeness in him?

"Ms. O'Connell, I will not be intimidated. And I will not live next door to nig—" He pretended to catch himself as he glanced at Keisha. "To black people. This is a white neighborhood."

Keisha couldn't resist. "Since when? I've lived here seven years, and nobody ever told me that. Now I own my own home." A definite dig at his tenant status.

He ignored her and ignored the chair I offered. "I prefer to stand. The only other thing I have to say is that my roommates and I will move out if that black policeman moves in next door." As an afterthought he added, "Shouldn't be blacks on the police force anyway."

Keisha raised her arm, with her stapler in her hand, taking aim at his head. I've no doubt that she'd have cold-cocked him if she threw it, and I was almost sorry for the small, negative shake of my head that made her drop her arm.

Pushed beyond the point of too much, I was on my feet. "Mr. Whitehead, you move out, and you'll be breaking your lease, which will cost you a pretty penny. I'd evict you if I could, but I have no grounds that will stand up in court. And you do something now, anything to get evicted, and I'll sue so hard and fast your head will spin. Grow up, sonny, and stop living in your own world of hate."

He drew his breath in quickly, and I really did think he turned a little pale. At any rate, he almost tripped over his own feet in his haste to turn and get out the door.

Keisha assumed a vaudeville-style black accent to throw a line at him as he left. "I sho nuff wouldn't want to live next door to no white trash."

He never turned nor acknowledged, but the slight twitch of his shoulders told me he heard all too clearly.

"You think we made an impression?" I asked, thinking that maybe, like the visit from José and Jason, we had intimidated him a bit.

"Naw," Keisha said. "You can't change nasty like that. He's probably going to be nasty all his life."

I retreated to my desk and sank dejectedly into the chair. We were through talking about the celebration, except when Keisha told—not asked, but told me to work out what I wanted said in a thirty-second ad about Spencer & O'Connell Real Estate. I knew the message would be about the diversity of our clients. Keisha would be prominent in the video.

Mike worked late that night, telling me on the phone they were still planning security for the celebration. It was a big issue for him, and I wondered if crime was running rampant in the city while he focused on the mayor's celebration which, by now, I resented more than a little bit. By the time he made it home for a late supper, though, I could almost laugh about Tom Whitehead. He was, I decided, a scared young man hiding behind a lot of bravado, and I told Mike as much.

He didn't laugh with me. "Kelly," he said seriously, "don't ever underestimate a scared man. They're the kind that can do the unexpected, the terrible. They act out of fear, and they shoot you in the back. Give me an honorable, brave man any day."

My thinking sobered.

Contract for Chaos

Chapter Twenty-One

I would love to report that things got better during the week, but they did not. Mike called one afternoon when the girls were doing homework and asked if I could meet him at a local wine pub on Magnolia not far from the house, so we could talk. Could the girls watch Gracie just for an hour? I sensed a heaviness in his tone and quickly agreed, without even consulting the girls. But they proved agreeable. Then I flew around, making grilled cheese sandwiches for all three, cutting a half into small bites for Gracie, slicing bananas, and putting out oranges.

Ran a brush through my hair, slapped on some powder, and I was out the door. Mike already sat in the darkened space, nursing a Scotch on the rocks—a rare drink for him. He apparently hadn't looked at the menu. He rose when I approached, kissed me on the cheek, and sat back down, all without a word. The one thing I really noticed was that Mike, usually so erect, sat hunched over, his shoulders down. I asked for a glass of wine and, hungry, grabbed the menu.

"Want to order the charcuteries?" I was trying too hard to be bright.

"Sure. You pick the meat and cheese. I don't care."

I studied him covertly while I picked from a rather complicated set of choices. He didn't raise his eyes, didn't look at me. The minute the waiter left, I put my hand on his arm and said, "Look at me."

He did, sort of blankly. Nothing near a smile. "What's wrong?"

"Routine inventory of the evidence room this morning. The bullet casing is gone."

It took me only a fraction of a second. "The casing from Jason Pickard's house? The one Henry found in the bushes?"

He nodded, and I pressed on. "How can it be?"

"It can be because someone stole it. Forget the sign-out, not even a name that sounds like anyone in the department. Regular guy wasn't on duty; his substitute let someone get away with it and now says he doesn't remember who signed it out. Kid will probably lose his job. Doesn't matter. Casing's gone, and I have no idea how to get it back. We probably can't."

"That means even if you find out who shot Keisha, you can't prove it?"

He shook his head. "It makes it a lot harder. That would have clinched things. Easily. Now it will be harder. But it means a lot more than that."

"What do you mean?"

"It means, as I've said all along, there's someone—or more—rotten in the department. I'd have suspected Al Johnson took it, but he's still suspended, and nobody's seen him around."

"Do you suspect anyone else?"

"Kelly, this is a big city, with a big police force, and I'm new at the center. Sure, I knew everyone in the Central Division, but I don't know the others. Since Jason's house is on the East Side, I'd suspect someone from there, but I don't know those guys. And how did some guy from the East Side walk into headquarters and get away with the casing?"

We sat in silence, without touching our food—which looked amazing—until the waiter came over to ask if anything was the matter. I thanked him, shook my head no, and reached for a corner of a slice of paté. Mike put a bit of meat and cheese on his plate and then toyed with it. He ordered another drink, while I nibbled at Manchego on toast with fig jam, then switched back to the paté and some cornichons. My kind of food and not what I got at home.

Mike talked some more, stressing the seriousness of having someone rotten in the department, how it would undermine morale, foul up some of their investigations, do all kinds of damage that couldn't be repaired easily or quickly. "Everyone will begin to distrust everyone else. It's like a plague that creeps into the entire department."

I remembered his earlier analogy. "Like the plague of racism has crept into our city."

"Yeah, and I'm not sure there's not an element of that in the department. I know Al Johnson is still hanging out with guys on coffee break."

"Mike, you've got lady officers. How do they fit into this?"

"So far they don't. I haven't heard of any problems. No women have come to me with complaints, and far as I know none are dissatisfied. Sometimes I think it would be a lot easier to have a force completely composed of women."

I let out such a whoop heads turned to stare at me, and Mike came as close as he would all evening to smiling.

But he sobered quickly. "One other thing. How about company for supper Sunday? I'm about ready to pull José from NPO duty. Poor guy's working double time—for me and doing the NPO patrols with Jason. I want to get them together informally to talk about things. Keisha would come, of course, and Jason's wife and two kids."

I counted on my fingers—ten people. "Sure. What do you want to serve? Might be cold and rainy, not good for grilling."

A slight smile flitted across his face. "I'll gamble, because grilling will give me a chance to talk to the guys alone. You and the girls can gab inside with Keisha and Carol."

So my mind went to steak for ten people— yikes! Baked potatoes, a vegetable casserole (Maggie had a spinach casserole she wanted to try), and salad. Em could bake a cake. Easy.

When we got home, although it was still early, Mike barely greeted the girls with an absent-minded hug for each, and then went to bed, where he nearly slept the clock around.

"What's the matter with Mike?" Em asked solicitously. "Is he sick?"

How do you explain exhaustion to a teenager? It never enters their vocabulary.

The next day I was hesitant to tell Keisha about the missing bullet casing. After all, it meant they might never find out who tried to kill her. Turned out my caution was unnecessary.

"José told me about it last night. It's okay. I'm at peace with it." She fingered her scar lightly.

To my surprise, Keisha had not changed her hairstyle to hide the scar. She still wore it short, spiky, and whatever color of the day suited her. Today it was sort of a light blue to match the long, swirly skirt and high-heeled sandals she wore.

"Different topic," she said. "My neighbor's cat had kittens. One of them is just adorable, and I think it has Em's name written all over it. She's talked to me about how much she wants a kitten. She says Clyde is Gracie's dog and won't play with anyone else except Mike."

It was true. Clyde came into our family to protect Gracie, and he was pretty much a one-person, devoted dog. And when Claire Guthrie lived in our guest house for a spell several years ago, she brought with her a fluffy cat named Emily. Em thought she and the cat had an affinity for each other beyond the similar names, and she had just simply adored that animal.

"I can't say yes or no until I talk to Mike. I wouldn't mind a kitten. Of course, we'd have to see how the kitten got along with Gracie—I don't want my baby to get cat scratch fever. And if Clyde doesn't like it, game's off. He stays."

"Sure," Keisha agreed. "You talk to Mike and let me know. If he agrees, I'll bring the kitten Sunday night. It's a female, which is easier, I think. You got to decide if it'll live indoors or out. I read somewhere the life expectancy of an outdoor cat is three years. Kept indoors, they can live into the mid-teens and beyond."

I thought about the choice. Somewhere I had picked up a distinct dislike for litter boxes, but Em would probably take on that chore. And outdoor cats—who knew what germs they'd bring in. If Em wanted the cat to sleep with her, as she undoubtedly would, it would have to be an indoor creature. A bridge to cross when it came up and hit me in the face.

That night at home I talked to the girls about Sunday's dinner party and the menu.

"Can I invite Dave? He hasn't been here in a while."

I didn't see why not. Exposure to more black citizens, especially a policeman, might be part of the ongoing education we were giving Dave. And Mike had developed a certain liking for Dave, as though he were a protégé.

Em happily agreed to bake a cake. "I think another chocolate one. Little kids always like chocolate."

"But no spinach casserole, Mom. Little kids—and big ones—don't always like spinach. How about that broccoli-rice casserole you make? It's huge, and then you wouldn't have to mess with potatoes."

I agreed that was a great idea. So our menu was set, and we could do some of it Saturday. I was never good at last-minute cooking.

* * * *

Keisha and José arrived early Sunday evening, while Maggie was still gone to get Dave. Keisha clutched her coat around her tightly. But once she was inside, with the door safely closed, she opened her coat to reveal a coal black kitten clutching her shirt front.

My heart sank. I'm not superstitious, really, I'm not, but a black cat? Isn't that like asking for trouble?

We had not told Em about the cat, thinking it would be a great surprise. When she saw it, she squealed with delight and nearly grabbed the kitten off Keisha. Keisha's gentle but steady hands slowed her down, and she carefully loosed the cat's grip on her shirt and handed her to Em with an admonishment to be gentle and speak softly.

As Em took the cat, she turned toward me, and I saw that it had a white mask on its face and a white patch on its chest, almost like a tuxedo cat. I couldn't hold back my sigh of relief.

"Her name is Button," Em announced with great satisfaction.

Gracie screeched and held out her hands, so Em took the cat over to her high chair and let her stroke it, which to my relief she did gently.

Button was the hit of the evening, though I watched carefully for any sign of trouble. Gracie managed to be gentle, and Clyde ignored Button, though the kitten spent much of the evening in Em's arms, a safe harbor for it. Keisha sent José back out to their car for the food, litter box, and toys she had brought. We were cat owners.

Dave's arrival brought a whole other surprise. The boy sported a shiner. About half of the left side of his face was purple, just turning to greenish-yellow. We all exclaimed, and he stood a little taller. No, it didn't hurt. Yes, it hurt at first. He wore it almost like a badge of honor.

Before we could question him, Maggie explained. "He unintentionally fouled a guy in the basketball game the other day, and the guy's buddies jumped Dave afterward."

"Did you fight back?" Em asked, staring in horror at his discolored face.

He smiled at her, a sort of big brotherly, patronizing smile. "Too many of them, Em. I figured four to one wasn't good odds. I just tried to protect myself."

"Tell them about the coach," Maggie urged. I wanted to tell her to hush and let Dave tell his own story, but I didn't.

He was trying to be humble, but it sure was hard. "Other team's coach came along. Pulled those guys off me and sent them to their locker room with orders to wait for him. Then he got ice for my face, made sure I wasn't hurt anywhere else. Also made sure I had a ride home. My dad came along just then."

"I think he was smart and brave," Maggie said.

"And lucky. Glad that coach came along, Dave."

"Yes, ma'am," he said fervently. "Me too. I was really glad to see him."

We might have then gone on with our evening, except Keisha asked the sixty-four-dollar question: "Dave, what color were the boys who attacked you?"

He looked surprised for a moment, and then a look came over him as if he wanted to say, "Oh, I get where you're going." Aloud, he said, "They were white, ma'am."

We all let out a sigh of relief, but the question had brought the whole racism issue back to the foreground once again.

I cannot tell you how successful Mike's talk with José and Jason was, though I would guess it went well. They were all three jovial at the dinner table, and neither racial troubles in Fort Worth nor the upcoming celebration were mentioned, though that theme was like the elephant in the room. The next day Mike pulled José from his NPO duties, and Jason made the rounds alone.

But that night, Button was still pretty much the focus of everything. She danced and played with a piece of yarn that Em dangled in front of her. She chased Clyde's tail when he wagged it. She pounced at nothing and jumped at her shadow, and she held us all captivated. It was good to be lighthearted.

Chapter Twenty-Two

We were two weeks away from the Celebration of Neighbors. The mayor had wanted to call it A Holiday from Hate but was dissuaded from that title, to my relief. There was pretty good hype about it in town. Newspaper ads, an occasional public service spot on TV, flyers in a lot of businesses and public places. And it was wild on the internet, a lot of buzz. I sensed that some people, like Keisha, were looking at this one big event as a panacea for all the city's woes. I knew better, and so did Mike.

Mike reported more than the usual racially tinged incidents came across his desk these days. He was particularly troubled by four reports of young men, dressed as neo-Nazis, who jumped black teens they encountered either singly or in pairs. So far no one was seriously hurt, but the police had been unable to identify the gang.

"Mike, I'm sure it's not Tom Whitehead and his bunch. They don't dress like what you describe—studded leather jackets, those ridiculous short haircuts—and they sure don't have swastika tattoos, at least not any place that I can see." I didn't add that the fourth member of that group would

275

never start such a fight. I still hadn't told Mike the whole story of Morty Berman.

"You have something against ridiculously short haircuts?" He rubbed his hand over his own buzz cut and then, pointing to his cheekbone, asked, "How about if I put a swastika right here? I could do it with a black Sharpie."

"Be serious," I told him.

"I am serious, Kelly. Serious about finding those guys. I think you're probably right. It's not Whitehead and his bunch of lightweights, but if there is such a gang—three or four guys, best I can tell—why haven't we seen them at protests? They sure as hell won't come to the mayor's big celebration." Mike had never quite gotten on board with the celebration, still resented the monkey wrench it threw into the running of the police force and thought the title the mayor wanted to give it was inane. "People are going to take a holiday from hate to eat kraut and sausage and listen to a black jazz band? Give me a break!"

"And then there's the other side," he said. "One of the biggest and oldest black churches downtown, a church we've always worked well with, is having a Black Lives Matter rally this weekend. Ezekiel and his mom are sort of star attractions. We'll have to provide protection and crowd control. See that things don't get out of hand on either side."

"That's what's wrong," I mused. "The city is divided into sides. We should be one side, all citizens of a truly great city. That's what the mayor hopes to accomplish."

"Good luck with that," he muttered. "The whole city's on edge."

"Did you ask Ezekiel's mom not to go to the rally?"

"I don't think I have that right." He sighed and walked away from me, ending the discussion.

Ezekiel was a bright spot in the gloomy picture. He was back at school, the center of attention for teachers and classmates alike. Keisha reported that he was getting an ever so slightly big head, and she attempted to take him down a peg or two. But he was healthy and full of good spirits. City agencies had helped his mom get a daytime job and find affordable day care for the preschoolers, and the family was on a list for affordable housing, so they could get out of the company of drug dealers and ladies of the night at that motel. The story was a picture-book illustration of what can be done to help people who are willing to help themselves too. I was a bit surprised that the mom would take part in that rally.

Joanie was not such a bright spot. Her work for the agency seemed to go well, but there was no progress, none, on finding out who shot Buck Conroy or why. As Mike said a hundred times, it just didn't fit. Buck annoyed a lot of people but not to the point of shooting him, especially not planning a sniper attack. And in all of Fort Worth, there probably weren't that many people who were marksman enough to have pulled it off.

"Once we get some clues, if ever, we should narrow the field pretty easily," Mike told me once. "Just find out who shoots really well and keeps in practice."

Joanie, meantime, was relentlessly impatient. She called Mike almost daily, and he was forced each time to tell her there was nothing new. Then she called me to explain how hard it was to move on with her life when there was this huge unanswered question. "I know you understand," she said once. "You went through it when Tim was murdered."

I didn't tell her it wasn't quite the same thing. Tim and I were long divorced, and he was a sharp thorn in my side, always threatening to steal the girls and take them to California. Besides, he was into some shady dealings with some unsavory people. I grieved for Tim and for the waste of what could have been a good life, but a part of me let out a sigh of relief when he died. Awful of me, and I felt guilty over it, but there it was.

Joanie and I met for lunch again one day, this time the restaurant in the Botanic Garden. In spring it was a lovely setting; in winter, with plants dormant and grass brown, it was a bit depressing. It fit the mood of the lunch.

"The kids cry for their dad every night," she said over a Cobb salad. "They can't understand why any mean man would want to kill him. I can't either, Kelly. He was a good man. I can't understand why Mike can't find out who did it."

She had said variations of this to me so many times that I was totally at a loss for words.

In saner moments, if Buck had been in Mike's place, she'd have understood in a flash. But she made it sound as though Mike personally were stalling the investigation, and of course, I bristled a bit about that till I got myself in hand.

It was, like all my recent encounters with Joanie, an exhausting lunch, and I went back to Keisha, Gracie, and the office dispirited and depressed.

All this was on my mind that night when sweet Em asked brightly, "Who's coming for Thanksgiving dinner?"

I hadn't given it a thought, hadn't looked at the calendar, and now my child brought home that the holiday was a little over a week away. After I got my breath back, I said, "Let's make lists. I think we'll just have family this year. Everything is so hectic. Yes, that's it. We'll invite Nana and Otto."

That didn't sit well with Em at all. She wanted Claire to see Button, and Maggie wanted Claire's daughters so there'd be someone "my age." I didn't point out that Claire's oldest, Megan, and her longtime boyfriend, Brandon, were both out of college and working, and the younger girl, Liz, was a sophomore in college.

Mike piped up with, "You can't have a holiday dinner without José and Keisha," and I realized he was right. I couldn't. Before long, the list included everyone—Anthony and his sons, now also almost grown, Mona Wilson and her Jenny. Who had I forgotten? Keisha's mom, that's who. We always included her.

We started on a menu. With that crowd, I'd make it potluck, but I'd do the turkey, dressing, and potatoes.

"I'll do a cake," Em volunteered. "I think a Bundt cake, this time."

"You've never made a Bundt cake," I said.

"I know. That's why I want to do it."

Maggie said she'd make an appetizer, though she'd have to go online to choose a recipe, and Mike bravely said he'd go to the liquor store. We were set—sort of. I began to make calls, lining up what guests would bring. By the end of the evening, we had fifteen guests joining us for the meal, and our tables would be laden with more food than we could possibly eat. My mother was suspicious that Em wanted to make the cake.

"I always bring a cake," she said. "At least, I better help Emily."

Em made a face.

* * * *

The next evening, Mike came in the worst funk I'd yet seen, and believe me, he'd been in a lot of funks since Buck was shot.

"Al Johnson resigned from the force today."

"Does that mean he won't be punished for beating Ezekiel? Other than that, aren't you relieved?"

Slumped at the kitchen table, while I stood at the stove stirring a pot of chili, he said, "There's so much more to it. He won't be punished by the department, but there's that civil suit Ezekiel's mom brought. I'm afraid she doesn't have the best legal counsel, like maybe a lawyer who's held out promises of a huge settlement in hoping to get a bundle himself—or herself. But the DA is reviewing the case and considering pressing assault charges. That's probably better, because Johnson can't claim I meddled in it. He'd probably do that if the internal affairs investigation comes down on him, which I expect it will any day now." He was thoughtful for a minute. "If it ever came to a jury trial, I'm sure Johnson would be convicted."

"But Ezekiel's okay now." I sat down beside him.

"Yeah, and, glad as I am, that weakens the case. But, Kelly, internal affairs is just finishing their investigation. No, they don't move fast. And if they found against Johnson, he resigned quick before we could take his pension and rank. I think someone tipped him off. Probably same guy that stole the bullet, one of those who listens to Abe's wild talk. Now he can say he resigned, won't have to admit he was booted in disgrace."

"Well, at least he's out of your hair." Honest, I was trying to be helpful.

"No, he's really not. If I know Al, he'll still be stirring up trouble, just now from the outside. And, worse, who tipped him off? How many in the department has he drawn into his circle of corruption? I've got to get to the bottom of this...or resign as chief. We can't operate with a mole in the department. One more thing for me to worry about."

"You don't want to do that, do you?"

"Not in disgrace. I guess I share that with Al. If I go out, I want to do it on my own. Not because I couldn't handle a problem. Or several problems. I wouldn't even think of quitting until this city settles down...and I'm not sure I would even then." After a moment, he muttered, "We really need that shell casing now. That, and we need to catch Al with a rifle in his hands."

Mike was quiet that night at supper, and the girls kept throwing sidelong glances at him, but his mood set that for the dinner table. We were all quiet, even Gracie. The girls had tests the next day, so I did the dishes, while Mike settled Gracie for bed, a chore he always enjoyed. It was a quiet evening at our house.

After we were in bed, each propped up with a book, Mike said softly, "I'm working on a theory."

"A theory?"

"Yeah. Too many things go together. You know how the department has periodic training checks, physical checkups, all that kind of stuff?" He didn't even wait for me to say yes, I knew. "Al Johnson consistently scores high on marksmanship. Without checking, I'd say he's one of the five best shooters we have, er, had. And he's the department malcontent, plus he's the racist."

My mouth fell open in horror. "You think Al Johnson shot Keisha?"

His answer was slow and deliberate. "I think it's a possibility. It gives me some place to start."

"But it doesn't explain Buck's death," I protested.

"It might. Al has long harbored unrealistic notions about his place in the department pecking order. He was outrageously ambitious and not getting any younger, yet Buck showed no signs of going anywhere."

"Mike, if even half of your wild theory is correct, we're dealing with a madman, and I'm terrified."

He took me in his arms and whispered, "Don't be. I won't let anything happen to you. And half the battle, even in dealing with a madman, is to identify the enemy."

Something struck me. I thought of Morty's special friend, Jim. How many other children did Al have? What about his wife? An entire family was about to be caught in a huge tragedy, and I grieved for them.

Mike just stroked my hair and whispered, "Shhh. I'm tired of talking about Al Johnson."

Much later, I lay awake, restless, trying to process it all in my mind and half angry at Mike, who slept peacefully beside me.

Next morning, Mike woke me early with a cup of coffee. "Kelly, this is important. Don't breathe a word of what I said last night to anyone."

"What will I tell the girls?"

"Nothing," he said flatly. "Absolutely nothing."

"But, I'm worried…."

"They'll be safe." Somehow, he could always reassure me. Well, almost always.

"Keisha?"

He shook his head. "It's important, Kelly. My life may depend on it."

He could have gone a year without saying those words that struck terror all the way through me. I just stared at him.

"Come on, get your game face on. The girls will be up any minute." He scooped up a still-sleepy Gracie and headed downstairs.

Numb with fear and confusion, I followed him.

I made it through breakfast but with little grace. I splashed hot coffee on myself, enough of a shock to make me cry out involuntarily, and I spilled Gracie's orange juice down her front, wet and cold enough to necessitate a change of clothes. If the older girls had been wary of Mike last night, they were now cautious about me.

I wasn't any better at the office, where I set a pattern for the coming days. My sense of humor deserted me. I jumped whenever my cell phone rang. I stared out the front door a lot, and I doodled on scrap paper, filling my wastebasket. Keisha was like the girls—she kept one watchful eye on me.

Finally, the third day after Mike had told me this theory, Keisha looked at me and said, "Mike will be all right."

"How do you know?" I asked.

"You know how," she replied cryptically. Her sixth sense, but my faith in that wasn't strong enough, despite all the times she rescued me.

At home I was cranky, burned almost everything I tried to cook, didn't listen carefully to the girls, even was irritated with Button.

Finally, Mike said late one night. "Kelly, you've got to get a grip. I would not have told you what was on my mind if I knew you'd respond this way. We share things, and I know you're wrapped up in what's going on in the department—and the city—right now. But you're not being fair to me, the girls—or to you."

All I could say was, "I am so scared."

He was gentle. "Don't be scared. Don't bring those bridges up here and burn them. We've got to get ready for Thanksgiving."

I think it was Thanksgiving, the thought of it, that galvanized me into action. That and a totally unexpected conversation with Keisha one morning in the office.

"Did you know I'm having an affair?" she asked.

I stared at her in astonishment. First, I didn't believe her, and second, why would she tell me if she were. Finally, I echoed, "An affair?"

"Kelly, I been trying to make you laugh for days, and if you don't laugh at this, I'll give up on you. Yes, an affair. With Mike." She waited for that to sink in, but when I was silent, she said, "José told me about it at breakfast this morning. First I knew about it."

Completely puzzled, I wondered where her mind was going.

"Mike and I are having an affair, in our spare time, of course." She slapped her knee and laughed heartily. "Can you figure that out?"

"What are you talking about?"

"Rumor's goin' around the police department. I'm sure Mike didn't tell you. Almost to a man—and a woman—the regulars laugh and ignore it, but some of the rookies don't know any better. Thing is, it's a rumor to discredit Mike by claiming he's not just having an affair, cheating on you, but with a black woman. My, my!" She slapped her knee again.

I laughed a little, but I didn't think it was funny. I couldn't tell her my first thought, which was "Al Johnson." He'd stoop to anything to discredit Mike, but at least this was better than killing him. Somehow, the thought that Al's mind turned to an affair reassured me that he wasn't planning to kill Mike. Twisted logic, if you will. But it worked for me.

"Mike and I actually had lunch together one day downtown. We'd been in one of those endless meetings with the mayor, it was noon, and we were both starving, so we dodged into that old-fashioned café on Throckmorton. Didn't either of us see anyone we knew, but someone must've seen us."

"Keisha, I think you should be complimented. If Mike were going to have an affair, I can't think of anyone more worthy than you."

She looked puzzled. "Thank you, I think."

And then I laughed aloud, the first time in a week. Keisha looked at me for a minute, and then she, too, was laughing.

And that's how Tom Whitehead's real landlord, the woman for whom we managed the property, found us when she arrived unexpectedly at the office. Fortunately, she was a longtime client and knew us well.

"What is the matter with you two?" she demanded, with a laugh in her eyes. "I want in on the joke too."

I shook my head. "Someday, Arlene, someday. But we can't tell you today. Trust me, it's good."

And Keisha was off into gales of laughter again.

Arlene Tuttle was a criminal defense lawyer, and I doubted there was much levity in her office. In her mid-fifties, she was successful, stylish, self-assured—all the things I always wished I was. She had come, though, to ask about the tenants in the Alston house, which was only one of several properties we managed for her.

"A friend who lives in Fairmount told me some disquieting things about the young men you've rented that house too. I was in the neighborhood—lunch at Lili's Bistro—and just thought I'd pop in and check."

I sobered quickly. "What have you heard?"

She took the chair by my desk, and I could see Keisha leaning across her own desk so as not to miss a word of the conversation.

"That they're Nazis," Arlene said bluntly. "I won't have such people on any property I own. I lost grandparents in the Holocaust, and I will never forget." There was no laughter in her now.

"I'm not sure they're even what you'd call neo-Nazi, Arlene. They're not skinheads. What they are is blue-collar workers, with long hair mostly, who are racist. You'd be right to dislike them if you met them—they probably don't like Jews, but they're mostly white supremacists." And there was Morty Berman flitting through my mind again. I wondered quickly if he and Arlene knew each other, possibly attended the same synagogue. Not impossible. Life was too full of coincidences these days.

"Let me tell you," Keisha muttered.

I went on. "Keisha's had some unpleasant encounters with the young man who seems to be their ringleader, and we're not convinced that they aren't responsible for some racially motivated vandalism. Anthony went there to make a repair and tells me they have swastikas and tiki torches—sort of ridiculous to me. Right now, there's a colleague of Mike's, a black man, who's looking at the house next door, and the tenant, or the spokesman for them, has threatened to move out if a black man moves in next door. I had a firm talk with him about their lease. I think he's all bark and no bite."

"I don't like it," she said. "I hate people like that."

I wished she hadn't said "hate," a word I taught the girls never to use in relation to a person. "I feel confident we have things under control. They're not ideal tenants, and we won't renew the lease, but for now it's okay. If it changes, I'll let you know. I promise we won't let them disgrace you."

"Oh, that's not it," she said. "I guess it's just my sense of justice and fair play coming out. I have a lot of hate stored up, revenge for my grandparents. On another note, what do you know about that festival next weekend?"

"Keisha can tell you all about it. If you have time for coffee, I'll make a fresh pot."

And so she stayed, and we had coffee and a visit, and proselytized for the mayor's big lovefest. An hour later when Arlene left, saying she was tardy for an appointment, I looked at Keisha.

"Funny how hate works, isn't it? Crops up everywhere."

"Can't let it win," she said.

That night I told Mike what Keisha had said and asked, "Were you going to tell me about this?"

He spread his hands, palms up, in a gesture of, oh, maybe, "I don't know." But what he actually said was, "I forgot."

Hands on my hips, I demanded, "Mike, how could you forget? That's big. Huge. Have you issued a denial? I mean, what have you done?"

Now he was grinning. "Nothing, and I don't plan to do anything, except maybe take Keisha to lunch again. Kelly, there's an old Dorothy Parker poem—I won't get the words right, but it says something to the effect that if people spread lies about you, don't bother to deny them. But if what they accuse you of is true, then you scream and holler and claim they're lying. I think if I protested, it would look like I was covering something up."

"I'm going to look that poem up on my computer. Dorothy Parker, huh?"

Chapter Twenty-Three

A protest darkened our Thanksgiving dinner. Oh, we had a jolly time at first—a happy hour with marinated shrimp and a cheeseball, plus plenty of wine and beer. Then the turkey, moist and succulent, old-fashioned green bean casserole (yep, mushroom soup and fried onions, both straight from the can), the northern-style dressing I grew up with, mashed potatoes, and enough gravy that we even had some left over. Seemed to me we usually ended up skimping on gravy, and I quietly and surreptitiously supplemented what I could make from the drippings with some prepared gravy from the store. Didn't even tell Mike.

At first, it was as though we'd all put hate and racism and all the troubles behind us. Because it had been such a busy, dare I say disastrous fall, we had lots to catch up on. Where kids were in school, how Mona's hot dog store was doing, whether Claire still liked her job at the small, independent bank. Because so many of us were involved in the Neighbors Celebration, now just two days away, there was lots of talk about that. Maggie was going to help Mona and Jenny with the hot dog stand, which was expected to do a land-office business,

293

and Em had volunteered to stay with me at the T-shirt booth. Keisha and José, as she had forecast, would be outside in the kiddie wonderland.

Mom and Otto were the only ones clueless. While Mom asked, "What celebration?" Otto scorned, "America was a white country once. It should stay that way."

Keisha was on top of him. "Listen, old man, you better keep that opinion to yourself in this house. I'm overlooking it now. In fact, I'll even get you another beer. But I don't want to hear another word like that come out of your mouth. You can apologize now."

The best he could manage was a lame, "Well, I didn't mean *you.* "

She got him another beer and soothed Mom, who kept repeating, "It's our generation. It's how we grew up."

"Now, Miss Cynthia, you know me and you are good friends, so you know the color of someone's skin doesn't matter. It's what's inside."

Mom ended up hugging Keisha, who winked at me over Miss Cynthia's head.

We were clearing the table and thinking about dessert—pumpkin pie, of course, and Italian cream cake that Mom couldn't resist making, and Em's chocolate Bundt cake which was moist, so good, and came out of the pan perfectly—but then Mike's phone rang.

There was an impromptu protest in the neighborhood. One street to be specific—the one block on Alston where Tom Whitehead lived and where by now Jason Pickard had offered a contract on the house next door. A small group of men marched up and down the street, chanting and carrying protest signs and flaming tiki torches. Why on earth had those torches become a white supremacy symbol? Weren't they associated with the tropics, where most people had brown skin? And why would those men be marching on the holiday?

I knew part of the answer to that last question. Jason had put down an offer on the house, and I was pretty sure it would be accepted. For the shape the house was in, it was much more generous than I would have suggested. But after a walk-through with Anthony, Jason came to us with the terms he wanted to offer. Keisha tried to dissuade him; I tried to dissuade him. All he said was, "You ladies don't understand how bad we want this house. Carol and me. And Henry's all excited about it too."

We had no choice except to refuse to handle the transaction, which I wouldn't do to Jason, or submit his offer the way he wanted. I was able to suggest a few safeguards that he might not know about, like having a home inspection.

"Anthony's already inspected it," he protested. "Believe me, he told me everything that's wrong with it."

"Anthony," I said, "is a man of many talents, but he's not a licensed home inspector. You need someone impartial, because there are some things the owner will be required to fix at his expense before the sale can proceed. Like dangerous electrical outlets, insufficient sewer pipes—hazardous things. In some cases, the homeowner may lower the price to compensate, but it's really better to have these things fixed before the deal closes—and before you move in."

Jason banged his fist on the desk. "That'll just slow things down. We want to get in there yesterday…and out of where we are. We've become a pariah to the neighbors. Even those who were our friends before are sort of distant now, 'cause they think there might be more trouble as long as we're in that house. I think that too."

I calmed him down and told him we'd move things along as fast as possible, but beyond presenting the contract, we'd heard nothing by the day before Thanksgiving. When Mike got a call about the demonstration, I was both indignant and puzzled. Whitehead and his geeks shouldn't have known anything about the contract, unless the owner talked to them. And since the owner lived out of town, I doubted that. Unless Whitehead tracked him down for some reason. I began to have a suspicion. Could that clueless racist want to buy that house himself? He didn't seem like a fixer-upper type at all.

Whatever the motive and however he found out about the pending sale didn't matter at that moment. What mattered was that about twenty men were marching, and the neighbors, peeking from behind closed curtains, didn't like it. They called the police.

Mike thought it was important for him to go to the scene in person, so off he and José went. Mike was back about an hour and a half later, with all of us still waiting. No one wanted to leave, but few were much interested in dessert—oh, the kids ate heartily, but for the adults the wait was a time of emotional hand-wringing. Angst hung heavily in the air.

Keisha was immediately alarmed. "Where's José?"

"He's bringing the Pickards for dessert. Had to lock up that house. They were there, with the owner's permission, having a Thanksgiving picnic in what will be their new house. I thought it was…well, cute isn't a word I use often, but it was cute. Kids were so excited. They had a card table spread with a colorful tablecloth, but they were eating off paper plates. Carol said she couldn't bring turkey and all the fixin's, so they got the colonel's fried chicken and an ice cream cake for dessert. By the time the evening was over, the ice cream had melted all over that table."

"Did they come outside?" Em asked, concern written on her face.

"I wouldn't let them," Mike said flatly. "They turned out the lights and watched out the window."

297

Keisha broke in. "Wait till Tom Whitehead learns they were eating fried chicken! Talk about stereotyping." She laughed aloud but sobered quickly to ask the question that was on my mind. "They still want that house?"

"They do," Mike said. "Jason said they're more determined than ever. When we finally got the street cleared of those young men, two or three neighbors knocked on the door to welcome the Pickards. They'll be fine. But those young men are like a cancer growing in this city."

Mike reported that the men were chanting, so police ticketed them for disturbing the peace and unlawful assembly. "Textbook case of what the books call disturbing the tranquility of a neighborhood," he said.

"They have signs?" Maggie asked.

"Oh, yeah. Signs that said, 'Make America White Again,' and 'No Black Neighbors.' That's what they were chanting. A couple of neighbors came out on their front porches and yelled at them to get out of the neighborhood. I don't suppose they realized the ringleader lived on their block."

"There were enough to call it an assembly?"

"Only takes three or more," he said wearily "Hope the Saturday celebration really is a holiday from hate, but I'm more worried now."

As José knocked on the door, Mike warned us all not to mention the protest but to be happy and in a holiday mood. We tried. Jason introduced himself all around, along with Carol, Henry, and little Ella. We fed them dessert, but everyone seemed sort of tongue-tied. With something that big having just happened, how could we not talk about it?

Finally, Jason put his dessert aside—pumpkin pie and Bundt cake—and asked, "Aren't you all going to talk about what just happened?"

And then conversation, questions, and opinions filled the room. It made my head spin, and I didn't see how a one-day celebration could fix what was wrong in our city. I was the one who began the maelstrom of talk, by asking, "Jason, are you sure you want that house after tonight?"

Carol clutched Jason's hand tightly, little Ella began to cry in her mom's lap, and Henry said frantically, "Daddy, we are going to live in that wonderful house, aren't we? I love it so much!"

Jason held up his hand, palm out, asking for quiet. He turned to his family, hugging Henry, stroking Ella's back, and staring into Carol's eyes. "Yes," he said quietly but firmly, "We are going to live in that house."

A chorus arose. Keisha jumped to her feet and almost yelled, "Jason Pickard, you don't got to prove nothin.' You've already proved what kind of good man you are. Let it lie."

José said, "I wouldn't do it if it were me. Wouldn't put my family through that."

Claire seconded his statement, and Anthony kept repeating how much work that house would be in the best of circumstances. Mom looked spellbound, if a bit confused, and Otto seemed scornful again, just nudging Mom to get him another beer. The only reason Gracie didn't cry was that Em was cuddling her and rocking. Maggie had, of course, disappeared to talk to Dave on the phone, probably hiding in her bedroom.

Mike sat back and watched all this. When the tumult died down, he said quietly, "I think you're doing the right thing, Jason." Then, turning to everyone else, "You didn't see what I saw tonight. The street, or at least part of it, came out to help Jason and Carol. They'll be behind him. You can't let one house of hate speak for the whole block." He shook his head. "I'm afraid that's what's been happening to our city, ever since the Hardin boy tried to rob that store."

Jason hung his head for a moment at the mention of the incident that had suddenly thrust him into unwanted fame. But then he raised his face and said, "Thanks, Mike. I need the encouragement. We all do." He looked at me. "Kelly, did you submit the bid on the house? I know you didn't agree with the terms I offered."

"No, I didn't. But it was your decision, and yes, I submitted it. I'll call in the morning, if you want."

"Please," he said.

Keisha and José stayed behind to help clean up after everyone else left, and she was still muttering under her breath about your punks and crazy people and foolishness. But José wrapped his long arms around her and said, "It ain't your decision, babe, so just hush."

She hushed.

* * * *

The next day was a holiday—but not for me, nor Mike. Keisha even kept the office open, mostly in case people had questions about the celebration. Before I could call the owner of what I thought of as Jason's house, he called me. I don't know what I expected but the shape of that house had not prepared me for a polite, well-spoken, deeply masculine voice.

"Ms. O'Connell? Asa Crandall here. I've had a busy morning on the phone and thought I better get back to you before anyone else from Alston calls me. Several of the neighbors are upset over what happened last night...."

I braced myself for the words, "I've decided not to sell to Jason Pickard" and began mentally planning how to break the news to Jason and his family.

Crandall went on. "They don't want those tenants speaking for them. Then Arlene Tuttle called me. Neighbors had called her too, protesting. They want her to evict those young men. That's up to the two of you whether or not and how you do it, but I want to help the Pickard family. I'm countering with a lower offer and a guarantee to do some of the neglected maintenance. I won't remodel for them, but I'll make up for my deferred maintenance."

I dropped the phone. Literally. Such an offer was unheard of us in real estate. For a second, I just sat stunned, though I could hear him saying, "Ms. O'Connell? Are you there, Ms. O'Connell?"

Keisha picked up the extension on her desk and said, "She'll be right back with you." Her voice and the stern look she gave me made me pick up the phone.

"Sorry," I said. "I felt like I was going to sneeze and didn't want to do it in your ear." A little white lie never hurt anyone. Then I proceeded very cautiously. "That's generous of you, Mr. Crandall, but are you sure? Such a move is highly unusual." Now, there's an understatement.

"Allow me to explain. This will salve my conscience a little. Not enough, but a little. I've ignored that house for years. A distant relative lived there, free of rent, because I felt the family obligation. I had no affection for this person and tried to put the whole thing out of my mind, in spite of my wife's nagging that I needed to do something about it, especially since the relative went to meet his Maker. I haven't been fair to the neighbors by leaving it in such condition."

He paused for breath, but before I could say anything else, he went on. "Besides, prejudice makes me angry. This young cop seems to have gone through a lot of unpleasantness. Let me help a little. I've talked with my lawyer, and he'll have the papers to your office by courier by ten this morning. If they look all right to you, I'll sign. Problem is I can't leave my property today—waiting for a vet. Got a sick horse."

Things were whirling in my mind. How did a sick horse get into this conversation? "Uh, where are you?" I asked.

"Just outside Springtown. Not quite an hour from town. Could you possibly…." His voice trailed off as though he knew he was asking a lot.

"Can you text me directions? I'll drive the contract out to you. Warning, I'll be accompanied by at least one toddler and probably a teen."

"Terrific. I'll give them a tour of the place. We've got a miniature donkey that loves kids."

And that's how Gracie, Em, and I spent an afternoon, or at least part of one, on a small Texas ranch. The girls got to pet the donkey, ride in the ranch's all-terrain vehicle for a tour to look at cows and horses, and have lemonade and cookies at a round oak table in a cozy, pine-paneled kitchen.

Asa Crandall in person was much like his voice—a good-looking man, probably in his sixties, standing tall and straight, with a cordial and polite manner and traces of a polished career before ranching. His wife reminded me of Ree Drummond, the pioneer woman of cooking shows. Her cookies were delicious, and her kitchen smelled of a roast for supper. If anything ever made me want to think about retiring to the country, these two people in their brick bungalow were it.

Before we drove away, Crandall said, "I've encouraged Jason to bring his family out for a day. You all come too."

I thought about Henry and how much he'd like those cows.

That night our whole house tingled with anticipation. The girls were so excited about the celebration that they laid their clothes out with the same care they devoted to the night before the first day of school each fall. With unusual foresight, I had put together a meatloaf that morning, so that when I got home all I had to do was bake it with some potatoes and cut up a salad. A healthy meal designed to supply energy was my goal, and I guess it worked with Mike and Maggie, but Em toyed with her food, too wound up to eat. Gracie alternately played with and ate crumbles of meatloaf.

"Mike, will anything happen tomorrow?" Maggie asked.

After chewing a mouthful, he said, "Sure. Music will happen, dance, lots of laughter, a few speeches...."

"That's not what I mean, and you know what." She was a bit put out with him.

"You mean a protest?" He turned serious. "It probably will. Will there be trouble? Not if I can help it." He looked at each of us. "I would not let you…." He looked at me and quickly changed his wording. "I would not encourage you to be there if I thought there was any danger. But my officers and I have worked long and hard to make this a safe and secure event."

"Dave's mom is unsure about letting him be there, and I really want him to be."

Mike grinned. "So that's the concern. Not fear for yourself."

A little defiantly, she said, "I'm not afraid."

Em edged a little closer to me, and I could see uncertainty in her eyes. I knew there was also an uncertainty that lingered behind my feigned excitement about the next day's festivities, and I knew even better that Mike was troubled, but I hadn't realized it affected the girls. I'd missed the signals somewhere along the line. Now, even Gracie was silent, her little eyes going from one to the other of us.

Reaching for Em's hand, I said, "We'll be together, and Mike will be sure nothing happens to us." I thought that was reassuring.

Startled, Em asked, "What could happen?"

Mike looked at me, willing me to be silent, I thought, before he said, "Not much with all the protection I'll have there. You girls relax and enjoy.

It's going to be fun. Watch out—I may join the Irish dancers. There's some green in my blood."

"Shandy isn't an Irish name," I protested and then, laughingly, added, "Do you mean shanty, as in poor Irish?"

He wadded up his napkin and threw it at me. "No, I mean there's a Riley in my ancestral tree."

"Well, obviously, I can out-Irish you, so maybe I'll be the one to dance."

Without a moment's hesitation, Maggie said, "You won't either one really dance, will you? How embarrassing. I'll tell Dave to stay home." But she was grinning.

Mike pushed his chair back, stood, and began clearing the table. "Let's get the dishes done. I have to call Dave's mom, and then I'm going to bed. Early call tomorrow morning."

Sure enough. He was out the door at five o'clock Saturday morning.

Chapter Twenty-Four

I tossed and turned and was wide awake once Mike left. It was less anticipation than an edge of fear that kept me awake. I lay still, trying to think positive thoughts, until Gracie woke me, early for her. Did she sense my tension? Even Clyde seemed a little edgy when I let him out to do his business, and he was almost immediately at the back door, begging to be let back in. I didn't know if it was my projecting anxiety onto him or simply the fact that it was a chilly morning. Winter had arrived.

The girls were up early too, and we had a hearty breakfast—eggs and bacon, sweet rolls from a refrigerated tube, bananas, and an orange. Mike called to warn us that that cold front that had come in during the night made the coliseum extra cold. He advised layers of clothes, adding that it would warm up as the day went on and the arena filled with people.

"At least, I hope it fills with people. What if we give a party and no one comes? Mayor's already wringing her hands. Get over here soon as you can, Kelly. Maybe you can reassure her."

I agreed but warned him we were a long way from ready. The change in the weather meant the girls ha to rethink their carefully planned wardrobes, and I hadn't even planned mine, so I'd have to start from scratch. Besides, Claire wasn't coming to get Gracie until ten.

Reluctantly, I had made what Mike called a step forward in his campaign to get me to be a little less obsessively protective of my baby. Originally, I intended to ask Claire to spend the day at our house, playing with Gracie, but Mike pointed out what an imposition it was to ask Claire, who worked nine to five during the week, to totally give up her Saturday. So Gracie would spend the day at Claire's house (where we had once lived), and Claire's youngest daughter was looking forward to playing with her and feeding her. Liz would be coming to the celebration for the matinee performance, but Gracie would be napping then. I asked Claire not to take her out of the house—not quite rid of all fears—and I had an enormous pile of Gracie's things by the front door. When he saw it earlier, Mike reminded me she was only going for the day, not a week.

About nine thirty, Mona and Jenny came by to pick up Maggie. Mona was driving the used pickup she'd bought to transport her portable hot dog stand which, far as I could tell, wasn't very portable. Plus, the truck was loaded down with the supplies she needed.

"I'm only going to offer four basic varieties of hot dogs," she told me over a quick cup of coffee. "Sauerkraut, with a nod to our German friends; a traditional one, of course, with ketchup and mustard and grated cheese. My new one I just developed is Asian. I call it Banh Mi, which is really Vietnamese for the bun. But it has mayo, lime juice, carrot, cilantro, and cucumber. And of course, a chili dog, for our Hispanic citizens."

I laughed. "If they know food history, they'll know chili originated in Texas, not Mexico."

She shrugged. "Everyone thinks it's Tex-Mex. That's good enough for me."

The girls left, chattering happily, and Em looked after them with a fleeting glance of longing. I supposed it was a bit dull to spend the day with your mom. "Em, you want to call a friend to join us at the T-shirt booth?"

She shook her head firmly. "No, I'm going to be your helper."

The T-shirts were packed in my car, cartons and cartons of them, so many I had visions of lugging them home. I had sent Maggie and Jenny off with shirts to pull over their sweatshirts, and Em and I did the same. The front of the shirt boasted stock faceless figures, like you see on the doors of public bathrooms. They were holding hands, but each was of a different color—a deep rich brown, a lighter tan, white, and a sort of muted off-white, the latter for Asian, I was sure. The basic shirts were either a bright blue or Kelly green and lettered with, "Fort Worth, where everyone is your neighbor and your friend."

309

By the time Claire came, we were dressed and ready to go, and Gracie was bundled in her outdoor clothes. Em carried Gracie's belongings to Claire's car, including the old Pack 'n Play that had been in the family since Maggie was born. But Clyde began whining and dancing around, until finally he went over to stand over Gracie where she was sitting on the floor playing with a doll.

"I do believe he'd growl if I approached her," Claire said and then, with a sigh, "You want to go too, Clyde?"

Honest, he wagged his tail.

"Are you sure you don't mind?" I asked.

"Yep, the cat will just have to hide," Claire said with a grin. "But you're gonna have a problem when this child starts preschool."

I did not want to think that far ahead.

Finally, Em and I got in the car and headed over to the coliseum. My cell phone rang and, thinking it was Mike, I answered it on speakerphone, something he's told me never to do. It wasn't Mike, and I immediately regretted the speakerphone.

"Ms. O'Connell? I'll be brief," came from a cultured voice I recognized but Em didn't. She looked alarmed.

"Jim and I are moving out while Tom and Robert are picketing the celebration. We simply can't stay here another night," Morty Berman said.

I clutched the phone tightly. "What happened?"

"Nothing yet, as far as I know, but they left the house in high anticipation this morning, said something big was going down."

Something big? As in someone big? My heart exploded, and I could hear the tension in my own voice. "Were they armed?"

"Only with posters," Morty said wryly. "Those boys are afraid of guns, I do believe. I could handle a rifle better than they could. Used to hunt."

I wasn't in the mood for levity, and Em was looking at me in great alarm. Before I could say anything, Morty went on, "I want you to tell your husband."

"I will," I muttered. *Oh, you bet I will.* "Thank you. Keep in touch." My hands were wet and slippery on the wheel, and I could hear my heart drumbeating in my ears. I was momentarily afraid to look at Em, but when I turned toward her I saw that sweet face white with terror. She was too scared to talk.

I pulled over first chance I got and took her in my arms, stroking her hair while she sobbed on my shoulder. "It will be all right, Em. Those men aren't armed, and Mike is prepared for them. He's been one step ahead of them all along, and he will be today." I wished I believed what I told her.

She pulled away until I saw a tearstained face. "Here," I said, digging into my purse for a wipe, "clean your face and put a smile on it."

Wordlessly she did as I said and then stared straight ahead for the remainder of the drive to the coliseum. Abandoning all Mike's cautions, I drove with one hand and punched in his number with the other, but the call went right to voice mail.

We parked in a special vendors' spot, right by Mona's truck, and began hauling cartons of T-shirts. In no time at all, we had a line of police officers helping us. Then Maggie wandered up, took one look at Em, and asked me, "What's wrong with her?"

Behind Em's back, I gave Maggie the "Shhh!" sign and said, "Nothing. She was upset over nothing."

Maggie did not believe me, but she let it go. I certainly wasn't going to alarm her too. In fact, the fewer people I told, as in none, the better. But I was desperate to tell Mike. My repeated calls went to voice mail.

Inside, we found that the mayor had ordered a booth constructed, not just the table provided for other vendors. A banner across the top said, "Celebration of Neighbors" and a sign below the table surface advised, "Holiday from Hate." Other signs, tacked on the posts that held up the banner, listed the sizes and costs of the shirts and acknowledged that all profits would go to a community center.

Unpacking the shirts went quickly, and Em seemed enough absorbed in laying them out neatly that she put her fear aside for the moment. We stashed the extra cartons under the table, well hidden by the skirt that circled it. By ten thirty, we were free to wander and inspect other booths.

At one end of the coliseum, folding chairs were arranged theater-style in front of a stage that was bigger than I expected, but I guess if there were to be dance demonstrations, a tiny stage wouldn't do it. There were two multiethnic performances scheduled, a matinee at two and an evening show at six. Both would, so I heard, be full of music and dancing, with speech-making limited to brief remarks by the mayor, who had been quoted as saying she wanted this day to be about fun, not preaching.

The other end of the giant coliseum held booths and tables, still in seeming disarray as people worked frantically to be set up by the eleven o'clock opening. Delicious smells wafted in the air, sometimes fighting with each other for dominance. But there were offerings other than food.

The local Greek Orthodox church had a display of jewelry, most of it with religious significance, like crosses on chains or embedded in cuff bracelets. There was no dolma or spanakopita—my favorite—or anything requiring refrigeration, but a generous display of Greek pastries, including baklava, was offered for sale.

The local Jewish deli had a sandwich counter offering corned beef, salami, and the like, but no kosher hot dogs, to avoid competing with Mona's Bun Appetit portable café. The two booths were next to each other, and I thought someone had done a good job of coordinating to avoid conflict.

Mona, Jenny, and Maggie were busily setting up their table in front of the cooking cart. Maggie, who's known for her neat script, was lettering the hot dog choices on a whiteboard, while Jenny arranged containers of disposable flatware.

"Maggie's already called Dave to see what time he's coming," Jenny said with a laugh, flipping her long, straight hair over her shoulder. "And I saw the cutest boy at the Greek church booth. I think I want some baklava for lunch."

I envied them their ignorance. They didn't know about the threat I did, and they were lighthearted. I remembered Mike's call to Dave's mother, assuring her that her son would be perfectly safe. Pray God it remained true.

Maggie looked up from her lettering. "Yuck. You can't eat that for lunch. It's way too sweet."

"We have hot dogs all the time," Jenny said. "I'm having something else. Not tacos. We get those a lot too."

"Mom and I are having fried chicken," Em said, and suddenly she was clutching my arm. Em was not bored, as I'd feared when she realized she was stuck with her mom all day. She was frightened.

One of the oldest CME churches offered dashiki shirts alongside fried chicken and cornbread—talk about playing into your stereotypes! But it smelled heavenly, and I had told Em that was where we might come for lunch.

The Clans of North Texas offered tins of Scottish shortbread, cans of haggis (I was not going there!), with tartan scarves, thistle pins, and various other small Scottish memorabilia such as bookmarks and key chains. On a separate table, there was a display of Scottish literature, including some Robert Burns books.

Not one but three taquerias had reserved space and were offering their wares, as were two Thai restaurants with portable kitchens that looked much like Mona's cart.

The display of food and souvenirs was truly international in flavor, and I thought it must be everything Mayor Goodwin hoped for. Dressed in western garb, as though she'd gotten mixed up and thought it was rodeo/stock show season, she greeted us with a smile and casual hug. She apparently had gone from the frantic worry Mike had described to a kind of tentative hopefulness.

"I think people will come, don't you? I just hope there's no trouble." There was a note of anxiety in her voice.

"How could there be?" I countered crossing my fingers behind my back, remembering my decision not to share Morty's warning with anyone but Mike. "You've done such a good job of planning"—a few extra compliments never hurt—"and I know Mike's tried to think of every possibility and be ready for it."

"I know, I know. We had too many suggestions to do this, do that, do whatever, and we had to choose what would work best. The main thing I really wanted was for everyone to be an equal participant. Why, one council member even suggested we open the Backstage Club and sell outrageously expensive tables there for businesses…and any individuals who wanted to pay the price."

I glanced up at the Backstage Club, perched high above the floor of the coliseum, level with the top row of gallery seats and almost in the rafters. Today, curtains were drawn across the glass windows that looked down on the floor, but during the rodeo those curtains were pulled back and window tables in the catered restaurant went to the highest bidder. You'd never know, looking at it as I was, that a certain kind of western-style luxury lay behind those closed curtains.

"That's exactly what I didn't want," Mayor Shirley Goodwin continued. "This was never meant to be a money-making event. In fact, we'll never break even and will have to put some city money into it. I'm prepared for that. But more than that, I didn't want certain people to be above the crowd, literally and figuratively. Can you imagine?"

I thought she was right and said so.

"It's going to be fun," she said, as if she could will it to happen.

Em was polite but anxious, shifting from one foot to the other in that way that teenagers have. Finally, she said, "Looks like people are arriving. We better get to our booth."

Gracefully done, Em. Mayor Goodwin gave my hand a squeeze as though confirming we were in this together, for better or worse, and turned to worry with someone else who had approached her. With relief, I followed Em to our booth.

We had just barely gotten there when Keisha burst on us. "We're havin' more fun," she said loudly. "We have kids out there on those rides since ten o'clock, and they're havin' a blast. Miss Emily, you're not too old. You need to come on out there and join the fun. That José of mine, he's so good with kids. They love him."

And she was gone before I could say much more. I turned to Em. "You want to go with Keisha for a bit?"

She shook her head. "Nope. I'm staying with you. And as for Jenny and Maggie, they'll probably meet some boys I don't know. I'll just stay here where it's easy and safe."

I looked at her long and hard but said nothing. My sweet Emily was still terrified but trying to hide it, and for some reason, the booth and my presence represented security to her. Morty's call had scared her, but we had probably laid the groundwork for her fearfulness with all the talk about racism and protests and what she'd seen at our house. And who knew? She might, like me, still be carrying the fear that overwhelmed us when the threat of kidnapping Gracie hung over our lives like a great cloud. I gave her a big hug.

My phone rang. Mike was finally returning my call. I hated to repeat Morty's words in front of Em, but there was no choice. I turned my back to her and spoke as fast and as softly as I could. To my dismay, he seemed to dismiss my warning about hearing something big was going down. "We've got them in our sights, Kelly, and as long as they aren't armed, we can handle whatever they come up with. Don't worry."

My gut told me he was wrong. Maybe if I'd given him a concrete source, he'd have taken it more seriously, but I didn't want to take the time for a long explanation. I repeated his words to Em, who was twisting a T-shirt in her hands, unconscious of the damage she was doing to it. I hugged her and said, "Mike says not to worry. He's got it all under control since they aren't armed." I changed the subject abruptly. "Let's get out those bags the mayor provided," I said, reaching for a carton of paper bags—not plastic, bless the mayor—to give shoppers for their shirts.

I didn't see Mike until late afternoon, and, believe me, it was a long day. I had expected to sell an occasional T-shirt, and sit and lounge with Em in between sales, watch the crowd, maybe even read a book. That's not what happened. We were both on our feet almost all day, bagging shirts, making change, smiling and chatting with people. Em refused to go alone to get us fried chicken for lunch, so I left her in the safety of the booth for two minutes but kept my eye on her every one of those minutes. Fried chicken was a poor choice—we struggled to eat it and yet keep our greasy fingers from soiling the shirts. Sure was good, though. But being busy was a blessing, because it kept Em's fears at bay.

The matinee was loud, colorful, and lots of fun, but again, like the rest of the day, I felt I was being bombarded with noise, color, a blur of sensations. It was exhilarating, but when the show was over, the day crowd began to drift out, and a certain blessed quiet settled over the arena. The noise level went from a shout to a murmur, and that's when I realized how tired I was. Or overstimulated. Or possibly grumpy. And still scared.

And that's also when Mike wandered up to our booth. "Got things under control, I think," he said, "so I have time to visit. How about a couple glasses of tea?"

"Just what Em and I need," I said. "Are the protestors still outside?"

"You're asking about Whitehead and his guys, aren't you? Nope. They were here this morning. We had some pushing and shoving between them and some high schoolers, but it didn't amount to anything. I finally took Whitehead aside and put the fear of the Lord in him, told him I'd slap him with every possible charge I could find in the books. They all disappeared shortly after that— cowards!"

I was afraid my sigh of relief was audible. If Tom Whitehead had left, the threat had not materialized. For the first time that day, I felt safe. More so, because Mike was standing right beside us. "Everything else okay?"

"Yeah. We've had traffic problems and lost kids, all the routine stuff when you have a crowd like this. But nothing big. I think we're gonna luck out on this one. Mayor's bursting her buttons she's so happy."

"Good." I turned to give him a quick hug, and, for some reason, glancing over his shoulder, my eyes went to the curtains on the Backstage Club. They were pulled back, just a bit, but enough that it was obvious, and I thought I saw a brief glint of light, as though it were bouncing off something metal.

"Mike...." My words were cut short by a pop, distant but clear. A gunshot.

Almost simultaneously, the walkie-talkie on Mike's shoulder crackled into action. Close as I was standing to him, I could hear only the mumbled sounds of a voice, not what was being said. Mike muttered something into the mic and then turned to me and said words that struck terror into me.

"Shooter. You and Em run for the concourse *now.*"

"Maggie. I've got to get Maggie." My heart was beating out of my chest, and my palms had turned wet with nervous sweat. Em was clinging to me, her eyes wide with fear.

"Go! Maggie will be fine. I can't stand here and argue with you." His tone was the harshest he'd ever used with me.

Disobeying his orders, I stopped for a moment to watch him run up the stairs, three at a time, that led from the floor of the coliseum straight up to the Backstage Club. I was sure I'd hear the whine of bullets at any minute, but Em tugged me away and forced me to the ramp, safely shielded by seats on either side.

Someone was speaking over a bullhorn. I stood quietly so I could make out the words.

"Shelter now. In the concourse. Everyone!" The words were repeated over and over, booming out over frightened shrieks and screams and the sounds of people running, pushing, shoving.

People began to stream by us, and Em tugged again. "We've got to move out of the way."

But I was frozen in place, listening for more shots, wanting desperately to peek around the corner at those stairs, wondering if I'd ever see Mike again. I began to scream Maggie's name, until Em put a hand over my mouth.

Calmly but firmly, she said, "Mom, we've got to move. We'll find Maggie in the concourse."

What we found was maybe a thousand people, milling about, some in hysteria, some shocked into silence. Officers guarded the exits, and much as some people wanted to bolt for their cars, they were not allowed to.

Pushing through the crowd, still screaming Maggie's name, I saw people sitting on the floor, some quietly weeping. Mothers clutched young children to them, and one teenager kept moaning, "We're all gonna die." She touched my heartstrings, and I stopped to comfort her, tell her we were not going to die. We had the best protection ever. As I straightened up, I found myself staring straight into Maggie's eyes.

I threw myself at her, before I even noticed that Dave, Jenny, and Mona were all clustered behind her. With Maggie in my arms and Em next to me, I knew what I'd told the young girl was true—we would all be all right.

But would Mike? I kept seeing the image of him charging up those stairs alone. It was too noisy now—I knew I wouldn't hear those distant gunshots if they did ring out through the coliseum.

After a long wait, we heard sirens. Ambulances, I thought, and worried over who they were for. The crowd was kept pinned in one section of the concourse, so we couldn't see what was happening, couldn't see if those sirens really did bring medics or more officers. I shuddered at the latter thought.

We were there probably an hour, when officers began to leave their doorway positions and move through the crowd, assuring us we were now safe and free either to leave or to return to the coliseum floor.

My girls had been strong throughout this, but now I took control again. "We'll go to the T-shirt booth," I said in a definitive tone. "Mike will find us there."

Mona said she and Jenny would return to her hot dog cart to prevent theft and vandalism, and Maggie said she'd go with them to help put things up.

If I thought Mike was going to magically appear at the booth, I was sadly mistaken. We waited. We watched a few brave souls wander into the coliseum. We heard the voice on the bullhorn assure us all was clear, and then we heard the mayor give a brief speech to the effect that a "situation" had been resolved, but the evening performance was canceled "out of respect." She never did say respect of what or who, but I felt my tension ease a little. If something had happened to Mike, I would have been notified before the mayor spoke.

"The coliseum will close at six o'clock. Until then, we urge you to patronize our vendors and celebrate our fine city of good neighbors."

When she came off that makeshift stage, I was waiting by the steps. Em, still too frightened to be left alone at the booth, had grabbed the cash box and was on my heels.

"What happened?" I asked bluntly. I wanted to demand, "What situation?" but I stayed within the boundaries of politeness.

"There's been a fatal shooting," she replied. "Mike is fine. He's been a brick, and I've left it up to him what to tell the media. At six, just take the T-shirts that are left and the cash home. We can settle up next week."

Before I could ask another thing, she walked briskly away and never looked back at me. Looking around, I realized that men with video cameras on their shoulders were roaming around the coliseum, randomly filming groups of people but obviously on the lookout for the "big story" they'd come to cover.

The curtains in the Backstage Club had been drawn tight again.

A little before six, Em and I carried the remaining shirts to the car. Em clutched the money box, while we went to collect Maggie. Mona was directing the girls in the final close-up and cleanup of the hot dog stand.

"Got a few left, but not a whole lot. Want me to drop Maggie off in a bit?"

"Sure. Why don't you all come, and we'll have hot dogs for dinner? I can scare up some chips and dip and maybe a can of baked beans or something."

Mona thought that sounded good, and that's what we did. We scooped up Gracie and Clyde from Claire's house, though she declined to join us for hot dogs, and we gathered around our dining table to rehash the day and its surprise ending. Keisha joined us, and, of course, she knew the inside scoop. José was quite as involved in the wrap-up as Mike was.

Contract for Chaos

Epilogue

Al Johnson died about eight o'clock that night at the county hospital. Larry Peterson shot him in the left shoulder, and he went into cardiac arrest, maybe from loss of blood, despite the best efforts of the ambulance med techs and surgeons at the hospital.

Keisha told us most of the story, and Mike filled in the details later. Larry saw the same thing I did—the curtains parted, the glint of light, and his instinct told him it was trouble. Having hawked Cokes and hot dogs at rodeos as a kid, he knew the coliseum inside and out, knew the hidden stairs to the Backstage Club, and was up there in a flash, walking softly in rubber-soled shoes. He found Al, sighting through that small gap at the curtain, aiming at the crowd on the coliseum floor.

Larry's first thought was of mass murder, that Al would sit up there and pick people off one by one. Desperate to prevent any death, let alone multiples, he issued one quick, "Drop it!" and, as Al swung the rifle in his direction, shot him with his service revolver. Al's rifle went flying, he moaned but never screamed, and went down on the floor. In rapid order, Larry called 911 and then Mike.

Al talked, muttered, rambled, revealed a twisted mind and sordid story before he died. He shot Buck Conroy because he wanted his job and had convinced himself that with Buck out of the way, the position of chief would be his.

He shot Keisha because he would have shot every black he could, and he regretted that he only creased her skull, wanted those listening to know that his aim was usually on target but a night animal in the bushes startled him at the wrong moment that night. The protest gave him perfect cover, although he'd really hoped to shoot Jason Pickard. When he saw that wasn't going to happen, he shot the first black person he saw.

"I guess I was in the wrong place at the right time," Keisha said ruefully.

He beat up Ezekiel because the kid was stealing. It didn't matter that he was only eleven and that his family was starving; it only mattered that he was stealing—and he was black.

Al did not have extra magazines of bullets, and the one on his rifle had only three bullets. One for Mike, one for me because he thought of me as "Shandy's damn nosy wife," and the last for himself. He did not intend to be wounded, as he was, but to end it all.

I shuddered when I heard this part of the story, not so much for myself, but of course for Mike, and, in a way, for Al with his twisted mind.

Everyone had left, and the girls were down for the night when Mike came home, weary beyond words. He had sat with Al's wife and daughters in the hospital and then seen them home with a police escort and two men on guard all night at their house.

"You never can tell who will be angered and what they'll do as this story leaks out," he said. "The official statement was that an investigation will follow, but it's going to come out that Al had resigned from the force just before being dismissed, and then, sooner or later, the whole ugly story will be public. I've done everything I can to plug leaks."

"What about Emma Johnson?"

"She's upset, first that Al resigned—she doesn't understand that—and now that he's dead. She kept pleading, 'There will be an investigation, won't there? I mean, Al's name will be cleared?' I had to tell her the truth, which felt like a cruel thing to do on the heels of death, but she had to know before she stirred up a bigger mess than we already had."

Thinking I had come close to losing my husband, I said, "What a blow it must be to lose your husband and then find out something awful about him."

No, he hadn't seen Al's son the whole time. Mike understood there was an estrangement there. I'd tell him as much as I knew later. Meantime, I said a quick and silent prayer that Morty could help Jim through this tragedy.

Now was not the time to tell Mike the whole story, but I had to explain my fright of the morning. "Tom Whitehead's roommate called me, wanted me to warn you that Tom said something big was going down. Now I understand it. Tom Whitehead is Al's nephew, and I bet Al's ego was just big enough, his hatred just intense enough, that he told Whitehead something big was going down. I'm surprised he didn't stick around to see what his uncle did."

Mike mumbled, "Forgot to tell you. He did sneak back in. He was in the concourse with everyone else, still carrying his sign—or dragging it on the floor. We arrested him. Maybe a second night in jail will help him think clearly." He rubbed his head. "He kept saying, 'It wasn't supposed to be this way.' I didn't understand it, but maybe now I do.

"Enough talk. I need sleep." He went into each of the older girls' rooms to plant a kiss on their foreheads and then, once upstairs, stood looking down at Gracie. "I hope we made Fort Worth a safer place for her tonight, just a bit." He turned toward me. "You know, I've been thinking about B. B. Paddock and his tarantula map of railroads in Fort Worth. Evil is just the same."

I knew before Mike got so busy—well, before he married the girls and me—he studied a lot of Fort Worth history, but I wasn't following him at all. "The same how?"

"Evil, hate, they spread from a core in the center, and they reach tentacles out until they touch everyone. That's what Al did to our city, even if he wasn't consciously doing it. He reached evil into far corners, hurting a good cop, a struggling mom and her children, Keisha, shoot! He could have ruined the entire police force, which would have crippled the city. Today was one small step toward recovery. We've got a long way to go."

"Mike, do you want this job permanently?"

"Yeah, Kelly, I do. I see so much to be done. I can't walk away. I told the mayor that tonight, and now I'm telling you. Tomorrow, the girls."

"They'll be proud," I said.

Mike wrapped his arms around me. I felt secure for the first time in weeks. My family and I would be safe. So would my city. I knew a lot lay ahead—another difficult funeral, the problem of Tom Whitehead, the healing of Jim Johnson and his family, and of our entire community. Mike would have to clean house in the department, and it wouldn't be an easy task to find that snitch. I would have to let go gradually of my obsession with Gracie, we were rushing into difficult years with the girls. But through it all, we had made new friends— my mind jumped to Jason Pickard and Morty Berman and Asa Crandall. I knew we would add them to our little circle. We'd watch over Joanie and McKenzie and Nicolas and over little Ezekiel and his family. Yeah, it takes a village, but I was blessed to be in the middle of a wonderful village. I slept long and hard that night.

The End

About Judy Alter

An award-winning novelist, Judy Alter is the author of seven previous books in the Kelly O'Connell Mysteries series: *Skeleton in a Dead Space, No Neighborhood for Old Women, Trouble in a Big Box, Danger Comes Home, Deception in Strange Places, Desperate for Death,* and a novella, *The Color of Fear.*

She also writes the Blue Plate Café Mysteries—*Murder at the Blue Plate Café, Murder at the Tremont House, Murder at Peacock Mansion,* and *Murder at the Bus Depot.* With *The Perfect Coed,* she introduced the Oak Grove Mysteries. The 2017 title, *Pigface and the Perfect Dog,* followed. In 2016, she returned to her Chicago roots to write the historical novel *The Gilded Cage,* which uses one unusual woman's life to examine social structure and labor relations in the late nineteenth century.

Judy's historical fiction, stories of women of the nineteenth-century American West, and her mysteries are available in print and ebook on

Amazon, B&N, and other platforms. Retired after twenty years as director of a small academic press, Judy is a single parent of four and grandparent of seven. She lives in Texas, sharing her cozy cottage with her Bordoodle, Sophie.

Follow Judy at her blog, "Judy's Stew," http://www.judys-stew.blogspot.com, or on Facebook, https://www.facebook.com/judy.alter and https://www.facebook.com/Judy-Alter-Author-366948676705857/, or on Twitter, where she is @JudyAlter.

www.ingramcontent.com/pod-product-compliance
Lightning Source LLC
Chambersburg PA
CBHW020246200626
46816CB00001BA/150